No Greater Love: Martyrs of Earth and Elsewhere

Edited by

Robert J. Krog

No Greater Love: Martyrs of Earth and Elsewhere
Edited by Robert J. Krog

Story copyrights owned by the respective authors
Cover design by Karen Otto

First Printing, March 2020

Hiraeth SF/F
P.O. Box 141
Colo, Iowa, 50056-0141 USA
e-mail: tyreealban@gmail.com

Visit www.hiraethsff.com for online science fiction, fantasy, horror, scifaiku, novels, magazines, anthologies, and collections. **Support the small, independent press... and your First Amendment rights.**

Acknowledgments

Thanks are due to my talented and patient contributors to this volume, to my wife and children for understanding the time I had to spend away from them even when home, to the publisher, Tyree Campbell, for taking on this project with me, and to Laura Givens, our cover artist who produces unusually good cover art.

A Little Help, Please

In the world of the small indie press we fight a never-ending battle for attention to our work, as writers and in publishing. Here's an example: big publishers [you know who they are] have gobs of $$$ that they can devote to advertising and marketing. Here at Alban Lake, our advertising budget consists of the deposits for whatever soda bottles and aluminum cans we can find alongside the highways. Anti-littering laws make our task even more difficult . . . ☺

That's where YOU come in. YOU are our best promoter. YOU are the one who can tell others about us. Just send 'em to our website, tell them about our store. That's all. Just that.

Of course, we don't mind if you talk us up. We're pretty good, you know. We have some award-winning and award-nominated writers and artists, plus other voices well-deserving to be heard [not everyone wins awards, right?] but our publications are read-worthy nevertheless.

That number once again is:
www.albanlakepublishing.com
Friend us on Facebook at Alban Lake Publishing
Follow us on Twitter at
@ albanlake and @albanlakepub

Contents

Preface

These are works of fiction. History is replete with examples of martyrdom, yet martyrs and martyrdom remain an obscure topic to many readers. Hence a book of fictitious martyrs, a kind of easier and more accessible introduction to the subject inspired by the real thing. A martyr is a person who gave up his life for a cause he considered greater than himself, be it God, country, political freedom, or what have you.

The Seven brothers in Maccabees who were cooked alive, Jesus himself crucified, St. Stephen stoned to death, eleven of the Twelve Apostles by various means, and numerous other individuals from that time on have earned themselves the title of martyr because they gave up their lives rather than compromise on what was true and just. The Roman martyrdom is a long, long list. Then too, nine of the signers of The Declaration of Independence died in battle during The American Revolution and five more were captured and executed by the British during the war. Martin Luther King Jr. gave himself over to danger time and time again, knowing each time he exposed himself in public he might be killed, and he was eventually shot to death. These are the kinds of people who were on my mind when I wrote up the guidelines for this anthology, and no doubt the contributors to this book had similar inspirations. Their stories are inspiring and well worth the reading, even if little more than the general circumstances of their sacrifices are known. It is good to know that there are causes so much greater than ourselves that innumerable men and women down the ages have sooner died than give them up. They died for their families, their friends, their countries, and they died for the glory of God rather than renounce Him.

This volume focuses on fictional martyrs who died in the Judaeo-Christian tradition or for another cause close to the heart of Western Civilization. This is not to denigrate other traditions, even ones openly hostile to Western Civilization, but simply to narrow the focus. Perhaps there will be another volume devoted to martyrs

1

of other traditions at some other time by an editor more knowledgeable in those traditions.

The tales of the Martyrs of the Catholic Church, from which the terms martyr and legend both come, were called "legenda." I briefly considered using that term for the title of this book, at the helpful suggestion of one of the contributors to this volume, but I soon rejected it due to the fact that I have included fictional martyrs from Christian denominations and secular causes as well as from the Catholic Church. Mr. Campbell, the publisher, and I came up with the more poetic "No Greater Love," referencing John 15:13, and we went with that and my original subtitle.

I hope, dear reader, that you enjoy these tales of sacrifice, that they inspire your imagination and actions. I hope too that you look up the true stories of the martyrs of past ages and find even greater inspiration in that source.

Robert J. Krog
12-16-2019

2

Perchance to Dream
H. David Blalock

St. Louis Cathedral stood in stately surveillance of Jackson Square, haughtily watching the throng of tourists, peddlers, workers and homeless that strolled, hawked, scurried and slept in the park. It was full summer in New Orleans, hot and sticky, with the sour-sweet smell of flowers, sweat, and exhaust filling the air.

Simon Telone sat on a bench facing the river walk and stared blankly at the passing traffic. He'd lived in New Orleans for nearly seven months, but not in the posh rooms of a Bourbon Street hotel or the quaint atmosphere of a shotgun house on St. Charles. His was a humble abode: a cardboard carton tucked between a maintenance shed and the fence that surrounded Jackson Square. It kept him fairly dry and gave him shelter from the wind, but it was a poor substitute for his home in the bayou.

He closed his eyes to the hubbub around him and remembered the quiet green of his shack, the frogs singing, the splash of a fish jumping, the cry of a loon. He could almost feel the oar in his hand as he paddled his johnboat down to check the traps. The weight of the club always felt good in his hand as he dispatched the nutria that gnashed its teeth at him from the jaws of the trap. Life was simple. Trapping and fishing, a little 'shine to warm you on the nights the wind blows chill from the water through the open front door.

"All right, buddy. Move along."

Telone opened his eyes to see the black uniformed policeman watching him suspiciously. During the tourist season, they were very nervous, not as bad as on Mardi Gras, but bad enough. He pushed himself up, shoved his hands into his pockets, and shuffled away with his head down. He knew the cop would watch at least until he turned the corner, so he didn't even look back. He watched the cracks in the sidewalk pass as he went.

The collision knocked the breath out of him. He staggered backward and would have fallen but for the hand that gripped his shoulder. Its strength startled him, and he winced under its pressure.

He looked up. In that moment, the image of the man steadying him was etched into his memory.

It began with the almond eyes, burning with a cold, black fire, eyes feral yet intelligent, luminescent with cunning ferocity. Then came the face, ageless and androgynous. Such a face could have belonged to any man or woman on earth, but the expression was kindled in a heart not human. The expression on that face, that mask, was intense examination, scrutiny of a kind he'd never experienced.

Beyond these impressions was the sense of power that embodied the intellect behind it. Timeless, defying definition of sex or race or even individual size, it was a background only for that visage that bored into his soul and explored all of him, instantly knew him. Good and evil, secret and public, done and imagined, Simon Telone was an open book to this study. Worse, he was no more than an idle, passing diversion.

Suddenly, a memory sprang up in him, and he was transported years into the past, back to the rice paddies, back to his boyhood.

The cool of the approaching dark spurred the men to wrap themselves more tightly in their coats. The sharp smell of rotting vegetation wafted from the jungle whose edge they hugged as they moved. The others might have grown accustomed to the smell from months in theater, but at his age of nineteen and having just been deployed, he'd had little time to adapt.

Out in the fields, he could see stooped figures making their way from one end of the rows to the other, old men, women, and children; no men of fighting age. They were either dead or gone to war. He wished there was something he could do to help those people. They hadn't asked for the war any more than he had. It didn't seem fair.

A small figure stopped to look in their direction. A little girl, maybe nine or ten years old. Would she survive?

4

The area around them darkened as the sun set, its browns and greens turning into grays and blacks as the light failed. The oily water of the rice paddy they waded hissed against the sides of their boots as they passed. Frogs kept up a constant barrage of sound, thousands of chitterings and croaks to accompany them. In the canopy overhead, birds fluttered from tree to tree, calling their challenges and responses.

Dark came quickly, more quickly than he had expected. Then, all sound suddenly stopped. The men paused, crouching to scan their surroundings, straining to hear any movement that might betray the enemy.

All was still.

Simon heard the squad leader say something under his breath to the man beside him, but a softer sound, a more rhythmic sound caught his attention. It was a soft swishing, a noise like that made by the wings of an owl, quiet and slow.

Something landed among the men, and Simon felt a horrid chill, as if he stood in front of the freezer in his father's butcher shop back home. Whatever hit the water in the paddy stirred up that rotting vegetation smell, and he choked back his rising bile.

"Grenade!"

He dove away from the sound as far as he could. There was a sound that shook him to his core then a deeper silence broken only by a high-pitched whine. He struggled to his feet, realizing with a sinking heart that his weapon was gone, lost in the dark.

Through the high-pitched whining, he began to hear an odd popping noise, and it took him several seconds to recognize it as gunfire. Again, he dove into the mud of the paddy. In between the firing, he could hear the moaning of someone in great pain, a pain of the soul as well as the body. He thought he could make out his father's voice framing a prayer, then again, all was silent.

After several moments, there was another explosion, and everything went dark.

Telone found himself standing on the sidewalk crying. The bitter taste of fear was sharp in his mouth, and he felt the warmth on his leg that explained the looks of disgust and hurried glances aside he got from passersby.

The man was gone, but something of the encounter remained, stirred to life by that ancient memory. Blindly, he staggered on, placing one foot in front of the other mechanically.

Telone next woke standing in line at a street mission. He looked around at the others in the queue, at their threadbare clothing, leathered skin, gnarled hands, and weathered faces. Though they might be freshly bathed at the local YMCA or convenient spigot, they looked dirty and unkempt. No amount of washing can give a man back his dignity and self-esteem. Without these, he is little more than an animal.

He stepped out of the line. It was as if he saw his surroundings for the first time. When had he come here? Why had he come here?

It was thirty years earlier, and America was still reeling from internal squabbles and external embarrassments. He had been only 19 when they sent him to Vietnam. He was much older when he returned after the fall of Saigon.

He had the nightmares for months after his discharge. They made him unfit to work and the shrinks explained it away as "post traumatic stress syndrome." That the nightmares had a name made them no less terrifying. Some nights the medication worked, and he slept heavily, dreamlessly. Other nights he spent screaming.

Life became less of a series of events and more a series of emotions. Moods followed moods in a chaotic array, patternless, undirected.

In the years that followed, he made abortive attempts to fit in to a society that refused to understand him. He worked odd jobs, moved constantly, always uncertain of his surroundings, of what might lurk behind a building or in one of the passing cars. The mindless routine of construction work and ditch digging sometimes gave him some peace, but that peace was always shattered in his dreams.

Then, there were the waking flashbacks. They were worse than the dreams. At least he could wake from the dreams. The flashbacks took on a life of their own and forced him to relive them without regard for his surroundings. More than once, he was arrested for breach of peace though he had no memory of what he had done.

Finally, his wandering carried him back to Louisiana. Perhaps he was trying to return to his bayou home, though after Hurricane Katrina it was not likely to still be there. Perhaps, he was back in New Orleans, because this was where he was ordered to report when he was drafted. Full circle.

He walked north past the cathedral, avoiding eye contact with the tourists who gave him a wide berth. A hot breeze hit him, and he smelled rotting vegetation from a restaurant skip somewhere nearby.

A large engine roared, and he saw a truck hurtling south down St. Peter toward him. The sound was so much like the deuce-and-a-half that took him from the airstrip to his bunker at Camp Evans. He could almost hear the other guys sitting in the back with him hollering insults at each other to cover their fear. It was a long way from Fort Polk.

He realized a flashback was comin,g but this one was different. Before, they were just as if he was back in 'Nam, either fighting or slogging through paddies, or hiding from the Cong. Not this time.

The street ahead of him became a mixture of pavement and mud, a complicated combination of the balconied buildings on either side and green overhanging branches of palm and black star protruding impossibly from the walls. The people along the sidewalk began changing, their walks becoming less certain, their manner more furtive. Did he catch a glimpse of olive drab on the figure that rounded the corner at Chartres?

The truck was still coming. Everything seemed to have slowed to a crawl. One of the pedestrians on the other side of the street paused... to look at him? Or to check something in his hand... He couldn't tell, the figure had blurred and become a little insubstantial. The child beside them looked directly at him and smiled. Her eyes were bright and her teeth oddly straight... They shouldn't be that white.

7

She began to cross the street, still smiling at him, her flowered dress melting into a tattered homespun, her bare feet leaving little prints in the mud.

He caught again that flash of olive drab, saw the weapon in the gook's hand, heard the truck, and knew. He'd seen this before. The Cong would shoot the little girl just as the truck came to a stop, stunning the driver long enough for him to be taken out. The troops in the truck would be sitting ducks for the ambush to follow.

Not thinking, he ran across the muddy track and grabbed the girl. He just had time to toss her to safety before the truck hit him, and the pain began, then slowly faded.

He vaguely knew he was dying. Not that it mattered. He'd saved the girl from the NVA soldier, and that was what was important. Soldiers knew the risks when they came and could fend for themselves. They had weapons and training to handle the combat to come, but not her. She was an innocent and didn't deserve to be a victim of their war, not even thirty years later.

Telone closed his eyes and sighed. It was good to be able to sleep

Seed
Ian DiFabio

Dr. Emily Zhou looks out of the friary window at the wet gravestones. The flood lights atop the mausoleum illuminate the summer rain falling down from the night sky. Across the mausoleum parking lot, she looks over at the fresh grave. It is a mass grave, the recently disturbed earth slick, muddy. For almost two centuries, the Franciscan Friars had lived here in the middle of St. Dionysius Cemetery. Far from being creepy, she imagines that living here in the well-kept cemetery would have been peaceful. She closes her eyes and tries to focus on the guards outside chatting and laughing, tries not to recall that she is the reason these friars came to their sudden end.

Looking around the cream washed room she's being held in, with its single bed, small chest, and desk, she wonders about all the friars that had occupied this tiny cell. Her gaze focuses on the corner next to the desk. Dr. Zhou knows she isn't alone. She's never actually seen a figure or heard a physical voice as Brother Patrick did, but the presence is no less tangible. She laughs sardonically, "And here I am knowing all about disorders of the brain. Maybe I *am* truly crazy." She continues staring at the corner, "What say you, my philosophical friend?"

She's answered with silence.

The guards outside stop their chatter as the government vehicle pulls up outside the former friary. Dr. Zhou groans. She watches the civil servant, "the kid" she calls him, because he looks like he's about seventeen, bounding purposefully out and almost skipping up to the friary door. She was interrogated by this kid when the study was leaked, the study that sealed the fate of the friars. The kid works for the WCOCC, The World Corporation of Citizen-Consumers, works for the North American territory which includes her home and university, in what used to be the State of Michigan in the former United States.

The cell door is knocked on primly, and, a second later, the young bureaucrat steps in. "Dr. Zhou, it is a pleasure to speak with you again." He offers his hand. She doesn't take it. The kid ignores this and continues, "I trust you're being well-cared for? I'm pleased we'll have a little more time to talk tonight, unlike our first meeting." The kid wears a fashionably dark suit in the new style, form fitting, a red V at the collar.

"I want to see my husband and kids," she begins. "I don't see why –"

"—We just want them to be safe, doctor. And we're concerned with your own safety."

"Safe from what?"

"I was hoping we could settle in first. Would you like a latte?"

"Like friends meeting for lunch? Are you really offering me a latte?" Dr. Zhou can't help laughing.

The kid shrugs. "I understand. Well then, yes, safe, doctor, safe from your mistaken and dangerous ideas. Ideas which are dangerous for society. Your ideas are not merely dangerous they're..." the kid looks at the ceiling struggling for the right word, "...unsound. The Corporation is worried about your mental state." The kid sits down on the desk across from Dr. Zhou who sits on the bed.

"Ideas? I go where my empirical findings take me. I know why you have brought me here to the friary. What I don't understand is why the Corporation is being so polite. Clearly, I am going to follow the friars."

"The monks, friars, whatever, were beyond rehabilitation," the kid said. "The Corporation was not unaware of this strange, old graveyard monastery. As they kept to themselves, we considered them relatively harmless for the time being. Involving themselves in your work, well, that changed things."

Brother Patrick is conjured before Dr. Zhou's mind. She tries to hold back the tears, the guilt crushing her. How? She continually torments herself. Who betrayed her? Who leaked the study results and her personal information? Had to be a colleague?

To her surprise, the kid looks genuinely concerned. He hands her a black handkerchief. "Don't think that way, doctor. Actually, you did them and society a favor. You relieved them and saved society from their delusion. But the Corporation believes *you* are not beyond reintegration."

"What you mean, you little bastard, is that I'm more *useful* to society."

"If you must put it so harshly—yes. You are a neuroscientist, and the study of the human brain is crucial for our future. Especially as we depend so much on AI. The Corporation needs experts like yourself who understand how the meat computers inside our skulls operate." The kid laughs at his description.

"Artificial Intelligence is a pipe dream. At least how you mean it. Consciousness is the point, and the focus of my work. Meat computer? Computers are not conscious. No matter how sophisticated AI programming has become, it is still a program, lacking what the human brain has: consciousness, thoughts, memories, feelings. Genuine consciousness, not a program to simulate it."

"And here it is. The problem, doctor. Why we're here tonight. Your so-called studies appear to suggest that human consciousness is immaterial, yet we know this is impossible. The brain creates the illusion of mind, the illusion that there is a—*you*. Are we to go backwards and start believing again in something as silly as a soul? Here in 2119?"

The kid pauses.

"As I told you last time," Dr. Zhou answers, head down, fatigued. "The study says nothing about God or the soul. I simply follow where the research leads. My faith doesn't guide my empirical findings. Science cannot say whether or not God exists. Scientists overstep their expertise when they make such pronouncements, when they go beyond the physical, observable world, beyond their competence. Stephen Hawking made that mistake a century ago. And, as the Corporation knows, my study was not intended for publication."

The kid takes off his watch and swipes his finger across it. Now expanding to become a tablet, he lays it on the bed in front of her. The tablet shows the statement she is to sign. "Doctor," the kid sighs, "you know the Corporation

11

cannot allow you to continue teaching and researching right now, not in your current condition. The fact that you and your colleagues are keeping research findings secret actually makes things worse. Laws are being broken. Whether it was your intention or not, you upset the average citizen-consumer, whose mission is to be just that, a good citizen-consumer, not to ponder the meaning of life."

"It's bitterly ironic," Dr. Zhou says, not sure if she's addressing the kid or herself. "My parents left their beloved China hoping to find religious freedom in the United States. They knew what was coming, but I'm glad they're not here now to see it."

Dr. Zhou's parents were Catholics who emigrated to what was still the U.S. in 2070. Religious persecution was going on in the West. But it was still the soft variety, though they could see it was slowly turning to the hard kind they fled from.

By 2095, The People's Republic of China was no more. Its old capital, Beijing, was now the headquarters of The World Corporation of Consumer-Citizens. That same year, the Pope was forced out of Rome, now the capital of the Corporation's Southern European Territory.

Religious practice outside the home was against corporate policy; with its repressive moral teachings, outdated objective truth claims, and focus on useless illusions beyond this life, beyond the concerns of the Corporation, religion was labeled an enemy of the people, a public danger. Labeled a mental pathology, religious belief, with all its violence and bigotry, had to be stamped out. Violently if need be. Neither did it help that the Corporation's largest critics were religious leaders.

The current Pope now resided undercover somewhere in Africa. Still not a part of the Corporation, the African continent was home to small Jewish, Hindu, and Buddhist communities, as well as the few small Muslim states that still challenged the Corporation. Africa was now the center of Catholic, Protestant, and Orthodox Christianity.

"Your parents came here, doctor, when the old United States was a fading power, and their former country the rising one. We were lucky. Just as fading Britain peacefully handed power over to the U.S. after the twentieth century's Second World War, America peacefully handed it over to its own successor, China.

"From the U.S., China learned that getting and spending is the goal of civilization, its driving force. While China taught the U.S. to abandon its Western emphasis on individuality, because the good of the larger group is what's important. What individuality remains is expressed in personal consumption, which benefits the group.

"That's what you and your friars failed to see. Filling citizen-consumer's heads with fantasies about a God and an afterlife leads to disappointment and frustration; it distracts them from producing and consuming, which is where the human animal's only true contentment and fulfillment lies. It distracts them from their loyalty to the larger group and its interests. And the corporate state, the WCOCC, is charged with the solemn duty of protecting those interests."

Exhausted and afraid, Dr. Zhou looks down at the tablet and thinks of her husband and daughters. Never has she wanted to see them, to hold them so desperately. It would be so easy, so easy to simply sign her name, just to sign the document declaring that her studies were mistaken, and that she was no longer a practicing Catholic. Does it *really* matter? The document is meaningless. She knows the truth. As the kid keeps insisting, she can go on privately believing whatever she wants. The signature doesn't come from her heart. She bends, almost reaching for the tablet while watching the kid's face light up.

But she's too much aware of the presence still in the corner of her monkish jail cell.

*　　*　　*

Feeling a need to reconnect with her lapsed faith, Dr. Zhou and her family had begun quietly attending the secret Masses at the friary chapel. When she approached Brother Patrick about the possibility of being involved in a brain scan study on the neurobiology of mystical experience, she knew it was risky for herself and the friars.

The problem of explaining human consciousness within a scientific framework, the mind/brain problem, was still unresolved in scientific and philosophical circles. Following many neuroscientists and philosophers of the mind from the last century, she and several colleagues had become convinced that human consciousness could not be reduced to the physical brain alone.

She studied neuroplasticity, the ability to physically change one's brain structure and patterns through cognitive behavioral therapy techniques. Showing that the mind can change the brain, which would be impossible if the physical brain alone created what humans experience as their perceptions and inner world, their mind.

There was psi phenomena, such as extrasensory perception and psychokinesis, the ability to move objects with the power of the mind. Some forms of this ability were noted in lab experiments.

And of course, there were near death experiences, particularly non-anecdotal scientific studies of people brought back from clinical death. She studied patients who had been revived after they had stopped breathing, their hearts had stopped, brain waves ceased; yet upon resuscitation, they were able to accurately recount word for word conversations relatives had in different areas of the hospital. Or patients who were born blind, and after coming back from clinical death, were able to give visual descriptions of people and surroundings.

Dr. Zhou was convinced that although the mind depended entirely on the brain's physical function during life, the mind was more than one's physical brain. That mind, or what she even went so far as to call spirit, needs the brain to connect with the physical world, but that the human brain doesn't generate mind any more than a radio generates music.

Scientists knew that The World Corporation of Consumer-Citizens held firmly to the materialist worldview, and that any theory that contradicted this view would be suppressed. So she and her colleagues published in secret, only for each other's eyes, keeping a record they hoped could one day be brought into the light. Someone leaked her study and private essays on the internet. The corporate controlled press took notice, and shortly after, the WCOCC was knocking at her lab.

Brother Patrick and his fellow friars sat under a Functional Magnetic Resonance Imaging Scan during

14

prayer. Dr. Zhou wanted to see what was going on in the human brain during prayer or meditation. While under the FMRI scan, the brothers were asked to pray or to recall a past spiritual experience.

By the end of the study, her findings suggested that religious and mystical experience involved the entire brain, from the inferior parietal lobule to the visual cortex to the left brain stem, involving emotion, cognition, memory, perception, and self-consciousness. Religious experience could not be tied to one section of the brain, or "God spot" within the temporal lobes that some neuroscientists of the twentieth century had assumed. The findings were modest, but they confirmed results found in similar studies from the last century. As this was only the first in a planned series of studies, she supposed it was a good start.

After Brother Patrick's final scan, he approached Dr. Zhou before leaving the lab. He touched her arm and said he needed to speak with her. His expression was concerned, serious, so she reluctantly stopped her work. He asked her to sit down. He explained again that he and his brothers were happy to be involved in her work, not only for its contribution to such an important area of knowledge, but they also hoped it might one day help to evangelize the culture. Yet, her hopes collapsed as he began speaking of an ongoing experience he was having while undergoing the scans. Like all study participants, she thought, hadn't he undergone a psychiatric evaluation?

"I have a degree in early Christian history," Brother Patrick began, "so I recognized the name when he introduced himself. Themistocles of Alexandria. A theologian and philosopher from the late second, early third century. He was one of those known for...well, he will tell you what you need to know. He tells me he doesn't fear for me and my brothers, that we're prepared. However, he says you will need assistance, and that he will help you, that aiding you is now his mission."

She nodded politely, inwardly groaning. Her months of long work probably ruined. How exactly would Brother Patrick's psychological issue affect the study? And this poor man she had so admired needed help, probably medication.

She went to bed early that night, too depressed to tell her husband or escape into her bedtime mystery novel. All that work, and now plans for the next study put on hold. The private funding would dry up.

She woke at three in the morning. She didn't know how, but she knew she must go downstairs to the living room. She sat down on the sofa in her bath robe. She didn't understand how, but she knew someone she could not see or hear sat across from her on the easy chair.

The voice sounded inside her head. "Hello, Emily. You know who I am. Brother Patrick needed to introduce me before tonight so you would know that you are not dreaming, hallucinating or imagining this, especially you with your logical, scientific mind."

She knew the speaker was smiling.

"Your area of study is fascinating. We Greeks never went very far with the physical sciences. For all our achievements in every other branch of philosophy, our natural philosophy remained primitive. It was medieval man who began to fully understand that one cannot stay in one's mind when studying the natural world. One must get their hands dirty. The natural philosopher must experiment.

"Now your modern world has made the opposite mistake." He chuckled. "Your civilization is incredibly advanced in the physical sciences and technology, but you have degenerated profoundly within the other philosophical disciplines.

"Though I stray from the matter at hand. Forgive me. Please allow me to tell you exactly who I am. Please allow me to tell you my story.

*   *   *

I was born in Athens. In the second half of the second century A.D. as your Gregorian calendar would later reckon it. My father named me Themistocles, after the hero of the naval battle of Salamis where centuries before, Greece was saved from Persian tyranny. My father, a wealthy wine merchant and lyric poet, was extremely proud of his Hellenic heritage and all that the Greek world had achieved. He hated the Romans. "The Greeks should

16

be ruling the world as they did under Alexander," he would say. "Not these savage Italian bumpkins."

I was a shy sensitive young man, and not so interested in politics. The meaning and point of existence occupied my thoughts. My father worshipped the traditional Homeric pantheon of Olympian gods, but my mother introduced me to what would come to be called the mystery cults. With the whiff of blood rites, the sexual allure, and shadowy danger, they were exciting for an adolescent boy. They offered release, meaning, and the promise of a future life beyond this dark world. But as I grew older, I became skeptical. I was drawn to philosophy. To me, both the Homeric gods and the mystery cults now seemed silly. The Stoic school of philosophy drew me because of its tough resignation and self-control. I hoped it would harden me, perhaps cure my natural melancholy and the emotional torment I suffered at the hands of the string of girls I had affairs with. At the same time I also felt the pull of Neo-Platonism's mysticism and its belief in an ideal world beyond our senses.

Like my future mentor, Clement, I sought out various teachers around the eastern Mediterranean before finally ending up in sophisticated, cosmopolitan Alexandria. The Egyptian city was the new Athens, the intellectual center of the Roman world. I fell in love with its great library, the museum, the gardens and palaces. There I hoped to find a teaching position in one of the city's many schools.

I was living with a beautiful Egyptian girl named Senmonthis. My family's wealth allowed us to live in the Beta district, or wealthy Greek quarter. Together we strolled through Alexandria's colonnaded streets which were laid out at right angles to take in the cooling summer breezes, the Etesian winds off the Mediterranean. We would attend the theatre, the games, and the festivals.

It was in Alexandria that I first encountered serious Christians. I really knew little about them. I had always been told that Christianity was a Jewish cult that worshipped a crucified rabbi and practiced an impossibly strict moral code. As a young Greek intellectual studying Plato and Aristotle, I sneered at it, especially the belief in physical resurrection. Plato tells us the body is the graveyard of the soul. Who would want to be physically resurrected?

Although not one herself, Senmonthis told me that many in her family were openly practicing Christians. Encountering these Christians, or Nazarenes as they were sometime called, I thought their beliefs ridiculous, but I was impressed with their lives. Some were wealthy, some poor. Class distinctions meant nothing to them. They cared about, and for, the sick and poor. They worked to provide medical help and education for slaves and orphans. I was shocked.

Whether it was out of admiration or bored curiosity, I don't know, but I managed to obtain some of their writings. I began to read what they called the Gospels, or good news, and a few of Paul's letters. At first I had difficulty persevering, because they were written in the vulgar koine Greek; far from Plato's polished Attic prose. Despite this, I was soon entranced. All night in my chamber I read, even Senmonthis's enticements could not get me to stop.

The words and deeds of this Rabbi Jesus affected me greatly. I found them both comforting and frightening at once; I could scarcely explain the effect this man was having on me. I could see that Paul was highly educated, but that he wrote in a way that would reach all, not just the sophisticated. He seemed determined to ensure truth reach everyone, not just the philosophers.

Plato and Aristotle had pointed to truth, but I could see that they had missed something: Love. If God exists, surely as the gospel said, this God must be pure love. Why else would God, the Uncaused Cause, create and sustain a good universe that had chosen darkness? Why else would God, the Unmoved Mover, sustain and redeem selfish, miserable human creatures? Only love explains it.

Quietly, I sought instruction and baptism. Soon after converting, I found, to my joy, that there was indeed a place for learning and philosophy in my new faith. I saw that human reason, though limited, is real and important. Faith goes beyond reason but doesn't contradict it. I found that reason, which Greek philosophy has given the Church, actually supports the faith. I partly learned this from my friend, the Christian thinker Clement, known to history as Clement of Alexandria.

Clement gave me a teaching position in his theological school. I spent my days teaching and spending much of my wealth on the city's sick and poor. I could not put Senmonthis aside, but we planned to marry, and I was trying to bring her into the Church.

About a year after my conversion, Church leaders had begun to warn their congregations that Alexandrian mobs were crying out against Christians because they refused to participate in the city's religious festivals. Fear of renewed persecution spread through our community. I heard stories of Christians being tortured and killed in the days of the emperors Nero, Domitian, and recently under Marcus Aurelius.

Soon dark rumors blowing down from Rome told that the new emperor, Septimus Severus, was cracking down on the Church. At that time, I was distracted and more concerned with Clements's writings. I found them thick, hard to penetrate, his ideas strange. Leaning away from Platonism, I was now more interested in Aristotle's thought. Studying Paul and the Hebrew Scriptures, I was convinced that Aristotle's cool realism was a better philosophical support for Christian teaching.

In 202, my speculations and disagreements with Clement were made suddenly insignificant. The emperor's orders reached Alexandria: converting to Christianity was forbidden; and all citizens had to participate in public religious ceremonies honoring the emperor as a god. Few if any believed in something as ridiculous as the Emperor's divinity, but it was considered an essential civic symbol. The Emperor wanted to be referred to as "lord and savior." Obviously, Christians could not do that. So now, converts that refused to offer sacrifice before the emperor's statue were in trouble.

Before Senmonthis and I could follow Clement and others out of the city, soldiers were at my door. My position in the community as a teacher must have made me conspicuous. Torn from my weeping Senmonthis, I was led to the city's western border near Rhakotis Hill. Praying desperately for strength, I was shoved into a small building a block or so away from the temple of the Greco-Egyptian god Serapis. This temple, the Serapium, was at the center of anti-Christian sentiment. Everyone knew of the beheaded bodies of Christians piled inside the temple's inner chamber. As the temple occupied the highest spot in the city, I could see and hear the mob outside it.

I was brought before an official serving under Quintus Maecius Laeus, the Roman prefect. The man looked bored, tired, as I and other Christians stood before him. Unlike the crowds before the Serapium, you could see he possessed no personal zeal for his task. He was merely following orders.

He smirked my way. "Well, one of the more illustrious followers of the cult." He waved me over to a small, separate chamber, perhaps wishing to avoid our being interrogated as a group, avoiding the strength some find in numbers.

The room was small, lit from above by a single Roman oculus which let in the powerful Alexandrian sun. It shone down on a chair placed between two marble sphinxes. To the right of the official's chair stood a bust of the emperor. I stood and waited for hours, not being allowed to sit. Finally the official entered. He sat down between the sphinxes and smiled.

"Dear Lord," I whispered to myself, "give me strength."

"So...you're one of the philosophers." He said the last word with amusement.

"I am a teacher," I answered in a shameful, cracked voice.

"No, I don't suppose I should call you *philosopher*, because if indeed you were one, you wouldn't have joined this pathetic cult." He shook his head. "Socrates too was executed, but *his* followers didn't claim that he came back from the grave to become a god. This oriental mysticism has clouded your Greek mind, Themistocles."

I don't know why it shocked me that he knew my name.

"Can you offer a defense?" Amusement still on his face.

After a minute or so of hesitation I answered, "I, I have found that Christ is actually the logos that the best Greek philosophers were unknowingly searching for. Aristotle intuited much of—"

"—Please," the official waved his hand. "Spare me, Christian thinker...if such a thing exists."

He paused.

"Let us speak plainly. Alexandria doesn't want to lose a mind like yours. It would be a waste. Your intellect has fallen under a spell." He glanced over at the emperor's bust.

My head was down as I looked at the floor, willing it to not be there.

"It's simple, Themistocles. I really couldn't care less about what you believe, and neither does the prefect or even the emperor. Not really. The emperor's edict forbids conversion, not those already members of the cult. Yet you, my friend, are not only a convert, but one who is also teaching and defending these perverted doctrines."

Again, he paused before continuing. "Listen," he leaned toward me. "Do your civic duty, Themistocles, and I can see to it that you're given a position teaching at the library. Teaching *true* philosophy. Don't tell me you don't want that. Am I correct? You can continue quietly believing in whatever crazy nonsense you like. You know Rome has always been very tolerant of religion—as long as belief doesn't stand in the way of patriotic duty. As long as one swears their allegiance to the emperor.

"Picture it, Themistocles, picture a position with the other scholars at the famous Alexandrian library, residing there among the beautiful lecture halls and shaded marble porticoes with your lovely native tart. You want to be back in her arms tonight, don't you? Didn't your resurrected rabbi say to 'render unto Caesar?'"

I looked up and spoke, "He meant our *true* civic duty, we must render unto God what is His due, to worship only Him, not Cae—"

"—Again, you're becoming tiresome, professor." He sighed. "I have little patience for tedious Greek theory, and even less for a Jewish rebel's opinions on politics and the gods."

I was shaking. *Dear God, give me the strength.*

"Do you hear that mob outside, Themistocles? Does your merciful god want you to be torn to pieces by them? Is that the sort of thing your god asks of his followers?

Because I wouldn't want to follow a god like that. I hear that your god is merciful, forgiving. Surely he can overlook something as harmless as throwing a bit of incense at your emperor's likeness. Don't you think? You're a reasonable man, Themistocles, aren't you? Why don't you listen to reason? Your crucified god said to 'render unto Caesar.' And *that*, my friend, is *exactly* what you are about to do!"

It felt as though I watched someone else kneel before the Emperor's image. As though I watched someone else place a handful of incense in the brazier before Caesar's bust. As though I watched someone else ignore the official's smirk as he handed him his libellus, the certificate officially guaranteeing he offered sacrifice. The document which would save my life, such as it was now. As though I watched someone else holding the libellus in front his face as he scurried home. As he hurried through the crowd that had spilled out of the temple of Serapis screaming for Christian blood.

Back to Senmonthis I hurried, the recent words of the Christian thinker Tertullian ringing in my head, "The blood of the martyrs is the seed of the Church." The words repeated themselves again and again, mocking me. My heart was broken, dead, but my mind still worked. It realized that the intellect is a significant aid, but not what ultimately brings us to Him. It's the heart. My faith isn't an abstraction, it is a relationship with a Person. I had forgotten that God is not an idea; He is love. He is fidelity. And I, I was another Judas. I betrayed Love itself.

My mind may have been converted, Emily, but my heart wasn't. It wasn't prepared, but...I believe your heart is.

*   *   *

Agents at her side, Dr. Zhou is led out of the friary. The rain now drips softly, as if the sky has sprung a slow leak. It feels good on her skin after the oppressive heat of the stuffy cell. Heading toward the mausoleum, she avoids looking at the grave. She tries not to think about Brother Patrick and the others. She smells the freshly turned earth and almost collapses as she pictures herself being added to the mound. Both agents are in front of her, yet she feels a strong gentle hand on her back. It steadies her.

Another, larger corporate vehicle is parked at the mausoleum's side. The rear doors open on what looks like the inside of an ambulance. She's taken inside and seated on a side bench; a stretcher separates her from the kid sitting next to what looks like a nurse on the opposite bench. A final push to frighten her. She admits it's working. She tries to calm her shaking body as she prepares for the kid's last attempt.

The doors shut. Fluorescent light illuminates the faces of the kid, the nurse, and the two agents sitting at the door. The heavy-set middle-aged woman stares vacantly at her. The kid drops his tablet in front of her on the stretcher. The situation is past courtesy. His friendly tone now gone. "Your husband and children are home right now, waiting for your return."

His face smears, is soon blotted out entirely from view as tears run down her cheeks. She can't even focus on the tablet which she is just about to sign. "Oh God, please forgive me," she whispers past caring if they hear. "I have to." Again she hesitates.

"Your family needs you, doctor." He almost yells. Do you think they'll remember you as a hero? Or will they think you horribly selfish? Isn't martyrdom really just false heroics? A grandiose selfishness? Think of your children. Think of the scientific discoveries you haven't yet made. The work you have yet to accomplish."

"*My* discoveries, or the discoveries the Corporation will *decide* I've made."

"We've covered this, Doctor Zhou. You have only to drop this mysticism and get back to true science...."

She isn't listening any longer. Emotionally and physically exhausted, she wipes her eyes, now staring down at the tablet, praying for just one more day, even one more hour. Does it have to be this very instant?

The voice, his voice, now speaks to her. As clearly as he did that night. *You are stronger, better than I, Emily. Paul said we must make up for what is lacking in Christ's sufferings for the sake of His Church. We must die with Him in order to rise with Him. I can tell you that you will be a greater help to your family on the other side. I promise you.*

The kid yells, "Are you listening to me, Doctor?"

Startled, Dr. Zhou looks up at him.

"No one will ever know this even took place here tonight." Now the kid speaks lower, gaining control of himself. "Martyrdom is even sillier, more meaningless when it's a secret."

She knows this is a lie. Her husband, her colleagues, everybody will know. Since her name and work are now well known, this will go throughout the WCOCC and beyond. Her death will only make her already published studies more famous. The Pope in Africa will be aware of her, if he isn't already.

She knows why the Corporation is so anxious to fix this problem. If she signs, renouncing her faith, saying her studies were flawed, other scientists are warned, their studies invalidated, and the Corporation is happy. She can continue to work on what the Corporation considers useful. Their ideal outcome. If she dies tonight, it may not be what the Corporation prefers, she may be considered a martyr, but they'll have sent an even more serious warning. The Corporation allowing her to live, secretly practicing her faith and even continuing her work, is not an option. She is too dangerous.

She looks directly at the kid. "You and I both know that isn't true. The Corporation is scared to death of me. They know my study, and similar studies, are right now being replicated by peers in other labs. It's too late. Whoever betrayed me did the world a service. Whatever happens tonight, the Corporation will call it a victory. But they know that victory is only short term, and they're afraid."

For once the kid is at a loss for words.

A minute later, he rallies, "Sign it! Go home tonight to your husband, doctor. Listen," he pleads now, leaning towards her, "the Corporation is even prepared to let me offer you freedom in the lab so long as they don't fund it, and if you allow them to see all of your findings. Again, damn it, you can privately believe whatever the hell you like!"

A warm hand touches her shoulder. *Belief is never private, Emily. You know that. I continued to believe privately, but in guilt and misery. We are physical creatures as well as spiritual. We worship Him and bear witness to Him with our spirits, yes ,but also with our bodies. He took on flesh and gave His physical body for us. You believe, not in an idea or a set of ethical principles, but in a Person.*

Of course you do not wish to die, Emily. Naturally. Every fiber of you resists this. The martyr doesn't desire death, the martyr desires God. He is Love itself; He will ultimately bring good from even the most terrible things. The martyr's blood is seed.

Dr. Zhou opens her eyes. "I..." She struggles through her breaking voice. "...I will not sign."

The kid sighs. He looks weary. World weary, she suddenly thinks. He rises slowly, moves to the door as the agents open it for him and says, "I sincerely hope you're right, doctor. That there is something waiting for you...after." The kid looks around. "Something after this...world, whatever this damn life is." The door closes. He's gone.

The agents help her to lie down on the stretcher as she hears, *I am with you, my friend, my sister. It will soon be over.* The nurse attaches a breathing mask to a tube. She moves towards her.

"God, dear God," she whispers. The nurse avoids making eye contact. She says in a cool, perfunctory tone, "This is pure nitrogen, Emily. Your body is not going to receive oxygen any longer. Nitrogen hypoxia is painless and acts quickly if you breathe deeply."

Said and done so efficiently, Dr. Zhou thinks. The agents needlessly have hold of her legs as the nurse gently places the mask over her face. She inhales deeply before exhaling her spoken prayer, "Hail Mary, full of grace...." She notices the expression on the nurse's face, as if she recognizes the strange, ancient words.

She feels again firm, gentle hands on her shoulders, softly squeezing. The voice is now audible as the startled nurse and agents look wide-eyed at something above and beyond her. The voice join's Dr. Zhou's as together they pray, *"Father, into your hands, I give my spirit."*

The Comfort of Lazarus
L. A. Story

The "episodes" always began with pleasure, but they always ended in pain.

Lazarus awoke with a headache, and waking was a lengthy process. He first tried to open his eyes but groaned when it felt like someone tried to cleave his skull in two with a blunt object. The pain nauseated him. He fought the urge to vomit, because he didn't know if he was capable of moving yet.

He raised heavy arms that did not feel like his own and pressed his hands to the sides of his head. Perversely, counter pressure seemed to help. He held his head together for fear it would explode.

A rooster crowed somewhere outside, announcing the birth of day. This was always the second thing he experienced after an episode.

"Do you know where you are? Do you know you've made it back home?" said a soft, feminine voice. Although she did not always know when he would regain consciousness, his wife, Honey, tried to be near when he woke. Currently, she was very close. He felt her warm breath against his left ear. She was beside him in the bed.

The rooster crowed a second time. The pain in his head abated by half, and he almost whimpered in his relief.

His wife was quiet as she waited for him. She was well-versed in this routine. God bless her. She was a good woman. She deserved it for putting up with the mess that was him for so many years.

The rooster crowed a third time, and the pain evaporated, but the memories of where he'd been still sat heavy on him. He fought the tears and sorrow, but he knew they'd come. They had to come. It was the only way he got through this.

Slowly, he opened his eyes.

The first blush of dawn softly pushed its way through the warped, leaded-glass window panes and the sheer, white curtains. Light slowly brightened in the bedroom where he woke from the dead.

He allowed his eyes to open, but experience had been a harsh instructor, and he knew not to make a sound until he got his bearings. He took deep breaths as he made a silent inventory of himself and his surroundings. Even if his vision hadn't confirmed it, he would have known by the musty scent that tickled his nose he was in the old farmhouse he shared with his wife and daughter.

He allowed his eyes to tentatively roam the closest aspects of the bedroom. The yellowed wallpaper might have been nice a long time ago. He'd inherited the house from his parents, and, between his work and his "episodes," there hadn't been time or money for renovations.

There was a small water stain in the corner of the ceiling above his head and to his right. His long, rangy body was stretched out atop the feather bed's thick ticking, and he was covered by a heavy, handmade quilt.

The silence had a presence all its own. The rooster crowed again, and he laughed. The sound of his own deep, rich laughter startled him. That fact set him off into another laughing fit.

"What's so funny, Lazarus?" asked his wife.

"I'm alive. Again. And, I am startled by my own sounds." His voice was even deeper than his laugh, a resonate bass.

He didn't move. His body was indescribably sore. There was a rustle next to him as Honey shifted her position so that her face suddenly appeared in his line of vision. The early morning light turned her skin luminous and ethereal. Her dark eyes were profoundly worried. "Was it as bad as last time?"

This time his laugh was a harsh bark.

"It's always bad," he said. He groaned as he turned his head toward her. "I'm getting too old for this crap, baby."

Honey blinked rapidly. She turned away from him. Her emotion poured forth in tears of her own. He slowly lifted his hand. He bit his lip in an effort not to groan in pain. He reached out and wiped her tears away.

She turned back to him and nuzzled her face into his palm, gently kissing his fingers. When she reached up and wiped at his face, and he realized he was crying, too. The initial tears led to sobs. He forced his aching body to move, and he turned onto his side and buried his face into the crook of her neck as he cried. He crushed her to him, and she wound her slender arms around him and whispered loving, calming, sweet things into his ear.

Outside, the rooster crowed again.

*   *   *

Sitting at their worn kitchen table a while later, Lazarus sipped carefully from his coffee mug as Honey made breakfast.

"What day is it?" he asked.

"Saturday." She said and then resumed humming as she fried bacon and eggs while checking on the biscuits she'd put in the oven earlier.

"So, Lily's home? No school today."

Honey chuckled. "Yeah, she'll probably be up soon, watching cartoons."

He nodded, carefully. "Good. I get to spend time with her, but it also gives me a day to recover before church tomorrow."

She paused in her task. He watched her shoulders tense and wished he could see her expression. "In your place, there are men who would say 'screw it' and never darken the doorstep of a church again, ever."

"That's hard to do when you're the preacher. Anyway, I am not one of those men," he whispered. It seemed appropriate. Quiet mornings felt holy. Reverence was required.

She turned around and gave him a gentle smile. "And, that's why He chose you for a job no one else could do."

He had nothing to say to that, so she turned back to preparing the food. He pressed his lips together. There were times, like now, when he was raw, tired, and broken and desperately wished for someone else to take over his lot. However, he did not voice the thought.

"So, when are you going to tell me when and where you were this time?" She turned her head slightly to speak over her shoulder.

"Not too far back this time," He rubbed his temples as he spoke, "around the 1990s I think ...in New York, so at least the surroundings were American and familiar this time. His name was Juan Correa. He was an undercover cop whose cover was blown. He was tortured for days before they killed him. He never gave up the other cops who were undercover with him. He never gave up the mission. He knew bringing down this drug ring would save so many lives." His breathing hitched for a moment as another crying bout threatened. He fought it back and continued, "It was unspeakable ... the things they did to him. I am going to look up his name online later. I was with him for several weeks before it happened."

She didn't have to be told what "it" was. They both knew "it" meant the death.

"Why do you do that?"

He lifted his coffee and took a sip. "Do what?"

"Why do you look it up? We already know it's real when you're ... pulled away." She waved her spatula around in swirling motions, like a magician. "We can't tell anyone else because it sounds so crazy, but we both know you were there. Why do you look it up?"

He stared down into the depths of his coffee mug as if it would deliver up the answer to that question.

"I know these experiences are real. I know the power is real ... I know this in here," he said as he pointed to his chest. "But here," he indicated his head, "it's harder. It's a compulsive thing. I have to make sure it really happened. It makes it real to me. It makes me feel closer to the people I Comfort. When I give Comfort, I am non-corporeal. When I find them online later, I am grounded in my humanity again."

He took another sip of coffee then cleared his throat. "I guess it's a form of closure for me. Full circle."

Honey filled plates and put them on the table. She prepared a plate for Lily and set it at Lily's favorite spot. She knew the smell of food would bring their daughter into the kitchen sooner or later.

"This closure is more real to you than that little box of proof you keep hidden in there?" She pointed with her chin to the area over his shoulder that led to their bedroom.

He knew she meant the small box that held the four "souvenirs" he'd managed to collect over the years. There was a small branch from an olive grove in Jerusalem; an antique, handmade linen handkerchief, and a small prayer book from Rome (Those two items were from different time periods. The handkerchief was not an antique when he grabbed it before being pulled back to his body.)Lastly, there was a circa 1940s silver locket from a woman in Minnesota (which he had grabbed during the actual 1940s).

Honey opened her mouth to ask another question, but Lazarus held up his hand. "Please, baby. No more questions for now. I can't take it. I have lived with years of unanswered questions. God doesn't see fit to reveal the reasons for what He has me to do. I am His Comforter. I know this. The rest ... I just have to take on faith."

His wife closed her mouth with a press of lips so firm that it seemed she was physically holding back against the relentless pressure of those unspoken questions.

He reached across the table and took her hand. They bowed their heads, and he gave a blessing for their food.

As their heads lifted, but before they could take their first bite, a young girl's voice echoed through the kitchen.

"Daaaadddddddyyyyyyyyy," Lily squealed as she launched her nine-year-old body at him. He caught her with a laugh. "Oh, Daddy, I hate it when you're like that! I'm so glad to see you're not dead, even though you looked dead! I get so scared that it will be real some day! You were gone FOUR DAYS this time! I missed you so much!"

Lazarus met Honey's eyes over the top of their daughter's head. There was a flicker of fear in his wife's eyes, but she hid it quickly. Four days? He hadn't realized. He knew it seemed he'd been with Juan for weeks, but time was a tricky thing when he was Called Away to Comfort.

He would speak with Honey about the implications of this later. Presently, he hugged his daughter to him and rested his cheek on top of her head. After a moment, he put her from him but kept his hands on her slender shoulders at arm's length. He locked eyes with her.

"Lily, you do understand that when I'm having an episode I am not really dead, yeah? I have a condition called catalepsy."

At least, that's the closest any doctor had come to diagnosing it. However, he and Honey knew it was so much more.

Lily nodded. Her brown eyes were huge in her face, and her bottom lip trembled. He hated that his child had to endure this. He knew there was one thing he could do to help her. One thing he was capable of in both states – both his corporeal and non-corporeal.

He could Comfort.

He didn't often do it in his physical state, but he knew when it was needed. When God Called Him to Comfort, he knew the reason for his power and the special ones who were in need of it. However, in his physical form, it seemed The Father allowed him some discretion to use the power for his own reasons.

There was a price to pay. In order to provide Comfort, he had to open himself up to send the Comfort power, but it was an exchange. In order to pour Comfort into someone in need, he had to receive the emotions that required his help. In Lily's case, it was a profound fear and helplessness. It filled his veins like an icy river and invaded every area of his body until it shot up his spine and pierced his brain. He shook with the power of the emotions his daughter nurtured within her. He pulled them out and then poured forth radiating warmth filled with love and strength that formed to make Comfort.

He knew when his offering took hold. He felt her little shoulders relax beneath his fingers. Her lip stopped quivering on the brink of tears, and a smile formed. Her eyes brightened and lost the troubled gleam. He closed the connection, and she sighed.

He hid his sudden heaviness of limb and the pounding of his heart as the fear tried to have its way with him.

"Go eat some breakfast, and we can go to town later. I'll take you and Mom out to dinner," he said, his voice was rough to his ears.

31

"Yay!" She hopped up and down and clapped before running around the table to settle down next to her mother and dig enthusiastically into her breakfast.

As he watched his daughter eat with gusto reserved for the young, he felt a soft hand brush over the back of his. He turned his gaze to find Honey staring at him. She silently mouthed "Thank you."

He nodded. Her expression was concerned. She knew the toll Comforting took from him. She was grateful that he helped Lily, but she had made him promise never to Comfort her. Honey was determined to bear his burden with him as much as she could.

God, he loved her.

He choked back his fear, and they enjoyed their breakfast as a family.

*   *   *

Lazarus' life routine fell into place, and time passed with a frightening swiftness. Routine was deceptive, and he knew it, but what else could he do? It was life, and it would go on as it should. He preached at Gethsemane MB Church, and his congregation sang, and he lifted them higher as he pushed the power of Jesus' saving love while assisting the deacons on the side to establish a security detail after a rash of church shootings in rural communities all across the state of Mississippi over the past year.

It was small churches–both black and white–that seemed to be the targets. It did not appear to be racially motivated, but even if the motivation for the deadly sprees appeared to be racial, he refused to preach hate and suspicion. Still, it was a fine line to tow–preaching love and caution simultaneously.

It had been a record six months without an episode. They celebrated Easter and Independence Day. In early September, they celebrated Lily's tenth birthday at the local pizza place, her favorite. Lazarus watched his daughter blow out her 10 candles as she officially entered the double-digit years, and a heaviness descended on him, a realization that stunned him. He grew quieter throughout the evening.

Once they were home, and Lily was happily down for the night, Honey asked him about his mood as they prepared for bed.

"Lily is now the same age I was when the episodes started," he said.

Honey, who had been applying moisturizer in the tiny master bathroom, stepped out into the room to gape at him.

"You don't think ... she's ... she's ..."

He gave her a small smile that may have ended up more like a grimace. "Like me?"

Honey nodded silently.

"I doubt it. I don't know of anyone in my family who has this ... this *thing*, but then I was raised by Auntie Mary and Uncle Luther. Mom and Pop died when I was eight," he said. "Still, no one has ever mentioned anything like what happens to me. I always got the impression it was unique."

He wasn't insulted when she breathed a soft sigh of relief. He walked over and pulled her into his arms. He was tempted to Comfort, but he knew she didn't want that.

He kissed her instead and tried to provide physical comfort that only a good husband could give.

*   *   *

The next Sunday, Lazarus felt the first stirrings of the distinctive pleasure that preceded an episode. It began toward the end of his Sunday morning sermon. Extremely inconvenient.

Had he really thought they had stopped? It had been over six months. He had never gone more than four months without an episode since they began when he was ten.

After church, he handed the car keys to Honey. "I think you need to drive us home, baby."

She froze. "How long?"

He shrugged. "You know how it goes. Maybe a couple more hours ... maybe a couple minutes. It's hard to know. I think I have at least the ride home."

As they drove, he rolled down the window and enjoyed the warm September breeze. He loved the look of the meadows of the farms nearby and the rolled hay neatly dotting the landscape. He realized some of the trees had a few leaves amongst the abundant green that were just beginning to turn colorful. Autumn was not that far away.

The pleasure was spreading more rapidly now, threading its way through his veins like morphine. That was what it was like–a pleasurable euphoria. He'd never had surgery, but from what people had described to him, the final phase was like going under general anesthesia. It began with a pleasurable warmth in his veins that morphed into a narcotic-like high, and then he slowly descended into a relaxed darkness.

He relaxed back against the car seat and realized his vision was going gray, and his body wouldn't obey his commands anymore. He could see they had reached their home. He'd been right about that, at least. "Honey, it's happening ... it's happening."

Across a growing distance, he heard Honey speaking into her cell phone. She was calling Deacon Davis to bring men to help carry Lazarus into the house.

Lily was crying in the back seat. "Daddy, don't forget to find your way back home ... please, Daddy."

"He's having one of his episodes ..." he heard Honey saying before the world went dark.

*   *   *

There was a period of nothing ... he knew something happened during this time, but he could never remember it; then there was a slow rise in sound, and the world brightened and came alive again.

Lazarus was suddenly dropped into a different reality. He was long seasoned to this and began to search the area around him. It was important to learn where and when he was was as soon as possible.

He was physically present, but people never saw him. No one could ever see him except the one he was sent to Comfort. They didn't walk through him like a ghost, either. Humanity just seemed to instinctively know he was there and walk around him. He saw lots of uniformed men around. A sprinkling of black among the grey uniforms spoke volumes, and he felt a chill go through him. He walked to the corner where he saw a street sign. It was

34

written in French. He didn't know how he knew it. He didn't question it. He just knew it was French and knew he could read and understand it.

He found a newspaper. It was the end of May, 1944. D-Day was just around the corner. From what he could gather, he was in a small city in coastal France. At least he had an idea of the where and when into which he had landed.

Now, he had to find the person he was meant to find. He never landed far away from the individual. He slowly walked up and down the sidewalk. He could feel the pull of that other mind. He was drawn further down the sidewalk until he came to a small café. Inside, he saw booths and a lovely, dark-haired woman speaking with a blond-haired man. Something clicked, and he knew she was the one. He was both relieved and saddened to know he'd found her. He was relieved because he knew his purpose. He was saddened because he knew this young woman's days were numbered, and the end wouldn't be pleasant or natural. It never was.

One thing he did know was that if he was sent to Comfort her when the time came, then she was extraordinary. She was worthy.

Lazarus trailed her everywhere for three days. He learned her name was Jacqueline Hebert. She owned a flower shop, and she spied for the Allied forces on the side. For her people, she desperately wanted freedom from Hitler's fist. She knew things others did not. She knew something of the atrocities that were being committed. The world had gone mad.

On day four, Jacqueline returned to the café where Lazarus first saw her. She met with the same man, and he passed her a piece of paper so subtly that Lazarus would have missed it if he hadn't been watching closely.

The man kissed Jacqueline's cheek, paid for their drinks, and left. She waited a while then also left.

She wandered just down the sidewalk and ducked into an alley. Lazarus followed her as close as he dared. It would not do for her to see him too soon. He peeked around the corner, and she was leaning against the wall. She wore a black beret and black sensible heels. Her legs were covered in what appeared to be silk stockings, and she wore a dark green, calf-length skirt with a white blouse and matching dark green jacket. A silver pin sparkled on the lapel of her jacket. It was a little flower, and she always wore it. Sometimes she would run her fingers over it if she appeared to feel nervous. It seemed to serve as a talisman of sorts for her.

Lazarus slunk back and looked outside the alley to see a man in French civilian clothes walking casually down the sidewalk. He didn't know how he knew, but this man was supposed to meet with her ,and she could get rid of the damning information and help the Allied cause.

The man abruptly changed his course, after a quick glance down the sidewalk past Lazaruswho looked behind him to see several German soldiers heading toward him. They turned down the alley and went straight to Jacqueline.

Someone had tipped them off. She had been betrayed.

They took her. Lazarus followed. The next three days were a nightmare. They stripped her, beat her, and tortured her in ways that made him sick.

She would not give up any information. When they broke her jaw and knocked out her front teeth with their fists, she did not give up the people she had been helping.

They shaved her head and put her in a thin shift. They took everything from her. Lazarus cried for her.

"Why, Lord, why?" he cried to Heaven when he was alone, having had to step away for a moment for the sake of his own sanity. No answers came.

Finally, they loaded her up in a crowded train car meant for livestock. She wound up at Auschwitz. The trip to the camp was brutal. She was thin, sick, and dirty when she arrived. They were divided into two groups – men, and women and children.

They stripped. The terror was palpable, the women feeling shame being forced to strip in front of the male guards. Lazarus wanted to hide his face from this degradation, but he couldn't. He had to bear it. If she had to bear it, so did he.

Finally, Jacqueline was herded with a big group of other women and children into a large shower chamber.

He already knew what it was, even if she did not. She was packed in tightly in a press of humanity. He made his way to her as the "showers" were turned on. It did not take long for the screaming to start.

He wanted to Comfort them all. They certainly deserved it. However, while these poor women and children were victims of birth or circumstance, Jacqueline had a choice. He'd heard the head officer make her a deal–her life in exchange for the information they wanted. She'd refused.

She gave her life for others and for what she knew was right.

He made it to her just as she began to panic in her struggle to breathe. She started as she looked at him. He understood. He was clothed, male, and black, quite a shock under the circumstances.

Her hoarse screams increased, and she tried to move away from him. He grabbed her shoulders, "Jacqueline!"

She froze. Her eyes were the color of caramel and framed by long, dark lashes. Doe eyes. He knew she would not hear him over the increasing screams of the others so he leaned forward and pressed his forehead to hers.

"Let me help you. I have been sent to Comfort you," he said.

She was wheezing and choking, and she grabbed onto his biceps. He opened himself and allowed her terror and pain to flow into him. He allowed himself to know who she was and feel her grief over the loss of her life and the loss of those she loved.

"You will see them again," he said. "I promise. You have fought the good fight. You have kept the faith. You have willingly sacrificed yourself to keep others from harm. You can rest now, Jacqueline. He knows your pain, and He's waiting to receive you. Your work was not in vain."

Tears flowed down her face. She grabbed one of his hands and pressed something into his palm. He gripped it into his fist without looking at it.

He allowed warmth and love to radiate toward her and through her.

"*Merci*," she whispered with a brilliant smile as the life slowly faded from her.

Once her life was gone, he felt his body falling as the world went black.

*   *   *

The headache was the first thing Lazarus felt upon waking. He groaned. The pain in his head never ceased to be stunningly excruciating. It was the only time in his life he ever felt pain so severe as to cause nausea. He fought the urge to throw up. He wasn't sure if he could move yet and didn't particularly care for death by choking on his own vomit.

There was a cool cloth on his forehead. He sighed at the tender touch.

Honey's voice spoke softly in his ear. "It's okay, baby. You're home now. It's alright."

The rooster crowed outside.

He slowly opened his eyes and stared up at the ceiling. Morning light had begun to brighten the room. He knew he had to do something about that water stain on the ceiling, but he was just so glad to see it.

"How long?" he asked, his voice was a hoarse whisper. It made him think of the gas chamber. He clenched his teeth against the onslaught of emotions.

She hesitated.

The rooster crowed again, and his pain abated by half. He could feel his own tears rolling back from his eyes and pooling in his ears.

"Tell me," he said.

"Six days," she said. There was a tremor in her voice. "It's Sunday morning."

He began to cry. "It was so bad, Honey. It was so bad."

He felt her curl up against his side, and she slid her arm around his waist and held him as he sobbed.

His tears had slowed by the time the rooster crowed the third time, and his headache disappeared.

He realized his arms were at his side, and his left fist was clenched. He remembered Jacqueline had put something in his hand. He slowly raised his arm, but couldn't get his fingers to unlock. He reached over with his right hand and pried his left fist open. A small object dropped onto the bed.

"What's this?" Honey asked. She reached down and picked it up. He turned his head. She held it up for him to see. It was a tiny flower lapel pin. He didn't know how she'd managed to keep it when the soldiers had taken everything from her, but she had. His tears began anew when he realized the flower was a lily – a little silver lily.

*   *   *

Lazarus was up and about in a few hours, but he was not in any shape to preach. Deacon Davis would present the sermon, but Lazarus was determined to show up for worship. He sat on the front row with his family. It felt good, clean. No martyrs here to Comfort. He understood this place. He couldn't seem to shake off the last episode. Heavy-heartedness hung onto him and wouldn't let go.

At some point, near the end of the service, several gunshots sounded from the vestibule.

"Daddy ..." Lily said. He looked down at her. She smiled a radiant smile. "I feel so happy ..." she fell over on the pew, unconscious.

Honey cried out and chaos ensued. Several things happened at once. He lifted his daughter and handed her to her mother. He began shouting for others to head toward the back of the sanctuary and through the doors. They had already made an exit plan in case of emergency. The doors burst open, and a masked man began shooting at the retreating church members. Lazarus took a hit in the arm as he stayed behind to rush people out. As the last person cleared the doorway, he came through and slammed the door behind him. He began to pull as many heavy items as he could to block the way and give the congregation time to get out and call the police. The shooter continued firing through the closed door. Lazarus could glimpse him through the holes blown through the wood.

When sirens sounded in the distance, Lazarus heard footsteps as the gunman ran out of the building.

He grinned triumphantly for a moment, but his smile faded when he realized his chest hurt. A crippling pain brought him to his knees, and he looked down to see his best white dress shirt was bloody. The red continued to spread across the shirt. He raised shaking hands–his right arm screamed in protest–and unbuttoned his shirt to find a hole in his chest.

"I'm shot," he said, simply.

"It's going to be okay, Daddy," said a young woman who had been standing in the corner unnoticed until now. She moved toward him, and he whimpered. She looked familiar.

"No ... no ... baby girl ... I didn't want this for you," he said.

He fell to his side and felt real mortal fear for the first time.

She knelt down next to him and took his hand. "It wasn't up to you, Daddy. He does what He believes is for the best."

"How are you a grown woman?" he asked.

She laughed. "You ask this *now*? Of all the things ..." She shrugged, but he saw unshed tears. "My first episode happened the day of the shooting, but it wasn't you I was sent to Comfort. Why where *you* sent into the past? Why does any of this happen the way it does? In my natural life, you have been gone for 12 long years, but I am sent to you now to Comfort you at the time of your death. Believe me, Daddy, I am as surprised as you are."

He smiled. He tried to smile, anyway. He wasn't sure if he managed it.

"You have fought the good fight and kept the faith. You have sacrificed your life so that others might live. He is waiting to welcome home. It's going to be all right now, Daddy. Go ahead and rest. You've earned it," she said. A gentle tremor shook her voice, and tears streamed down her face.

He felt the Comfort she sent him – the warmth and love threaded its way through him.

He closed his eyes to this world and opened them to a new one.

Dream Rebel
Teel James Glenn

I

"I want to see this man who is our 'ghost," Vladimir Azarov, of the Russian Confederation said. "You have the doctor with him?"

"Yes, Doctor Zalikov is with him," Lushencko spoke as the two walked down a silent corridor.

"She has been useful in the past," the General said. "This Bodrov was a trusted messenger and knows the location of the two choices for the meeting place."

The two stopped before a door marked "Dream Suite."

"So let us see what is in the head of this ghost, Bodrov," the General said, "before we end his life and turn him into a real ghost."

The two Secret Police in full battle dress in the room recognized the General and snapped to attention.

"The Doctor?" Luschencko asked.

"The second room, Comrade," one of the guards said.

"Only two guards?" the General asked as they went to the second door.

"The doctor requested a minimal presence for her freedom to work."

The inner door opened to a space where banks of monitors on one wall dominated the room. A dreampod in the center of the room was connected to the screens by a Medusa of cables.

Huddled over a monitor panel to the pod was a beautiful, blonde woman in a lab coat. Her rimmed glasses perched on a thin, aquiline nose. When the men entered, she looked up from the monitor with annoyance on her pretty face.

"I told you troopers I can't be disturb—" She stood abruptly. "General Azarov!"

The General smiled. "Please, be at ease. I am not here to make your job more difficult."

41

The woman took him at his word and went back to the monitor. "I'm glad somebody isn't. Your thugs at Police Central almost killed this man with their brutish interrogation techniques. We had most of our work just to stabilize him."

"Your tone, comrade doctor might almost be construed as obstructionist," Lushencko said sharply.

"No, Alexei," the General said. "She has a point; some of our own people can be, eh, enthusiastic." He smiled a politician's smile. "It is good to see you again, Doctor."

"And you, Comrade General," she said, her brittle manner softening. "I just hate to work with...uh...damaged goods. I want to give the best results."

"Of course," Azarov said in a conciliatory tone, "But we have only seven hours until the council meeting place must be determined, and, of the two choices, we must know which the rebels suspect."

"Why not switch to yet a third location, Comrade General?" Lushencko asked.

"It is not that simple," Azarov said. "We informed the council that one of the two would be chosen at the very last moment for security reasons. If we switch to a third, we will look weak." He looked at the pod.

"We must know if this man told the locations to the rebels," he said, "and if so which of them will the rebels strike at."

"Why would they not strike at both?' the doctor spoke up as she closed a medical chart.

"We know they possess a single, low-yield nuclear device," the General said. "And no delivery system. They could not possibly endanger both sites. Which is why we must know if he told them."

"What will you do, Doctor?" the General asked.

The woman worked as she spoke. "My methods are simple in concept. I use a psychoactive drug that allows for suggestions to the subject. His body will be flooded with nanites that allow us to induce certain sensations to make any suggestion of place or action 'feel' real."

"How will this help us find out if he divulged the information to the rebels?" Lushencko asked.

42

"If I had more time," the woman said with just a hint of chastisement, "I would present the subject with a series of choices in a created environment, paint a story from some fairy tale where the secret to freeing a princess, say, was hidden in some cave or castle room."

"A non-threatening environment," the official said.

"Exactly," the woman said. "It allows us to circumvent any anti-hypnosis training an agent might have, tricks them into revealing things."

"But in this case?"

"We can not afford long or subtle scenarios. After looking at the subject's background we find he has a rather juvenile taste in fiction- old period adventure stories and such—"

"It perhaps explains his idealistic nonsense with these rebels," Azarov said.

"Possibly," the woman continued, ",but it will allow us to insert him into scenarios where the urgency is extreme for him to make a choice."

"I must make a decision by dawn tomorrow," the General said.

"Seven hours?" the woman said.

"His life is not of importance, Doctor," Azarov said. "I must know which of the two sites is safe."

"Then we will proceed in two-hour increments," the scientist said. "So even if we must do the full three doses you will still know in time."

"Why three doses?" Lushencko asked.

"The drug, even in a healthy person builds up in toxicity. Three in less than a full day is fatal in a strong man. He might not make all three cycles."

"Why must it take more than one?" the General asked.

"It is possible his conditioning is not so deep, and we could break through in the first scenario—but I have learned not to get my hopes up. Still, we shall try."

"We will hope for you, doctor," the General said.

"But I will need something from you, Comrade General," Doctor Zalikov said. "I will need to know the names and physical characteristics of the two locations. I must program them in the scenarios."

The General looked at her for a long moment then nodded. "We shall all be together till the decision is made so, of course. There is a lakefront house on the Black Sea, and a mountain retreat in the Urals." He told her the names, and she programmed them in.

"Alright then," the doctor said. "We are ready to begin."

All turned to look at the figure lying mummy-like in the clear pod.

The object of their attention was an unremarkable man in his early thirties with the pale skin of his naked body now discolored with bruises from his first interrogation. His face was fine-boned with thin lips and a high forehead. He looked asleep.

"I will need you gentlemen to be quiet," the doctor said as she donned a headset. "I will have to maintain focus while in the illusion with Mister Bodrov."

"You will enter his...his dream?" Lushencko said.

"It will be the best way to steer the dream world."

"Proceed, Comrade Doctor," Azarov said. "And good luck."

She turned to her console and, with a sly smile, spoke into her microphone, "Help me, Gregor, my hero," she said in a plaintive tone. "I can't control it by myself..."

II

Gregor Bodrov felt dizzy for a moment and confused. He was in a strange place, with wires and metal struts all around him. He felt strange as well, somehow taller. He looked down at his hands to see that he was wearing a leather trench coat and leather gloves.

"I need help." A female voice caused him to turn with a start. There, crouching by the open panel that showed a number of wires and levers, was a beautiful blonde woman that was vaguely familiar.

"What?" Gregor asked.

"I can't control the lever, Herr Ghost," the woman said. She was wearing the remains of an evening gown, ripped to show her pale, flawless, white skin. "I need your help."

He started to move toward her then caught sight of himself in a reflective metal strut.

44

"I know that face," he said aloud. The image in the reflection was of a death's-head topped by a Fedora hat. He recognized his own eyes, pale blue, within the mask but the image was different.

"I've seen that face in an American Comic book," Gregor thought. "It is—"

"The Midnight Ghost is up there," Kapitan von Dunder, in full Gestapo uniform, screamed shrilly from below Gregor. "Get him!" The officer was at the stairway to the catwalk that led to the gasbags of the dirigible where Gregor and the woman were standing.

"They have control of the steering mechanism." The German pointed to the two figures high up in the spider web of support struts of the Zeppelin and added, "Kill that masked devil, and bring me that girl, now!"

Half a dozen leather-clad crew members scrambled up the struts holding knives and tools as improvised weapons for fear of the explosive discharge in the airship.

The trench-coated figure that was Gregor Bodrov was in a desperate situation. He and the woman that seemed so familiar were wedged in a tiny maintenance walkway between the enormous gasbags. He noticed now that he was bleeding badly from a stomach wound, the muddy crimson of his life seeping through his fingers as he pressed them against his abdomen.

"We have to steer this Zeppelin to safety," she said, drawing Gregor's attention back to her. She seemed to be wearing a white coat of some sort over her evening dress. "Look at the view screen."

The skull-masked Gregor did look to see a scene where there was a hospital in the center of a valley, to one side a lake, and on the other a steep mountain.

Beneath the mask, Gregor's eyes blazed with an inner pain.

"You have to tell me which way is safest," she cried. "The lake or the mountain!"

Before the wounded and confused Gregor could reply the first of the Nazi's from below charged up the gangway at him.

The first crewman slashed at the Midnight Ghost with a ten-inch blade. Gregor dodged with a growl of pain, lashing out with a wooden mallet-like tool used to tighten the cables. The mallet head crunched into the man's hand with a sickening sound. The man yelled and fell away from the ladder, striking several cables on the way down so that he bounced back and forth like a grizzly human pinball.

A second leather-clad assassin was upon the 'Ghost' brandishing a ceramic wrench. He slammed the wrench down at the masked intruder with all his body weight. The confined space defeated him however, when his wrench caught momentarily on a strut.

The Midnight Ghost lunged forward and smashed the mallet into the attacker's knee. When the German dropped with a yell of pain, the 'Ghost' struck again with a backhanded uppercut that pulped the man's face.

"You have to decide where to crash this ship, Ghost," the woman cried. He looked back at the screen, suddenly conscious that it was a modern Tri-V screen.

"That doesn't seem right," he thought. Pain from his gut and the vertigo made it hard for him to concentrate.

"We will destroy you, *Giest!*" Kapitan Von Dunder yelled.

The Midnight Ghost gave a strained laugh that echoed through the Caligarian chamber of the dirigible. "You may kill me," he called, "but you'll not dump this cargo of poison on innocents, Von Dunder." He coughed hard, spitting up blood.

"You've had so many near misses, Ghost," the blonde woman called, "this time your number is up. You have to tell me where to steer the ship to save lives."

He looked at the screen again, and it was clear that the airship was lumbering toward the hospital with alarming speed. The masked man grabbed the railing in front of him. "I have to decide," he said aloud. "I have to save the people."

The woman looked up at him with wide, pleading eyes. "The lake or the mountain? Which is the safe place to steer the ship?"

He stared at her. "Yes, Lake-mountain. One is safe." He tried to remember her face and something else, something he should know from another place but was dancing at the edge of his thoughts like a ghost.

46

"You have to decide," the woman said insistently. "The poison gas that the Nazis planned to rain on the hospital will kill everyone. You must decide what to do. Lake or mountain?

He felt his head spin. The blood pounded in his ears.

Crew members were barely four yards away and were sure that the cornered man would not dare risk discharging his gun near the gasbags.

The cornered man raised the gun to take deliberate aim at the nearest of the hydrogen-filled bags.

"No!" the woman screamed. "You have to decide!"

"No," he yelled. "This is the way!" He pulled the trigger twice.

The airship erupted in an apocalyptic ball of flame.

*　　*　　*

Doctor Alanna Zalikov jerked back at her console with a gasp. She blanched , drenched with sweat.

"Comrade Doctor?" General Azarov asked.

She looked up at him with unfocused eyes. It took her several seconds to register where she was.

"No, thank you, Comrade General," she said. "I am fine ...the shock of separation was just more than the usual."

He offered her a sip of his coffee, which she took gratefully.

"What went wrong?" Lushencko asked. He looked bored. The General looked at him with venom.

"You are not, as the Americans say, a people person, Alexei." Azarov said.

"Bodrov is a stronger mind and personality than most," the woman said. She took the coffee cup from the General and drank deeply from it. "How are his vitals, Dieter?"

The lab assistant consulted the readout. "He is steady, but weaker than he was, Doctor."

"Often the first fantasy does not get us the results we want," she said. "But he was beginning to tear the construct apart—that is an amazing amount of will power." She had admiration in her tone.

"You can find what we want?" Azarov asked.

"Yes," she said but not as firmly as before. "I will have to find a different way."

"But you can do it?"

"He reacted to the two cues—the lake and the mountain—so I know for certain that he does know which one of the locations is safe and since his code name with the rebels was, apparently, 'ghost,' it fit perfectly with our scenario."

"Do what you must," the General said.

"In a moment, Comrade," the woman said. "We should let the prisoner recover as much as possible, in isolation. Then my assistant will prepare the shot for him."

She took off her headset and stood. "I think we should retire together to the outer office."

III

Gregor Bodrov woke up in a cell whose floor was littered with hay. It was dark and dank with a small glow panel in the ceiling for light. The stonewalls dripped moisture. He was confused. The last thing he remembered was...

"The secret police," he whispered. The men in trench coats had kicked in his door and grabbed him. Then there were the beatings. So many beatings. 'Where are the rebels?' they asked. 'Who are the rebels?' Over and over.

There was so much pain.

He stumbled to his feet.

They think they can break me to betray the others, he thought, *but I will not break. Never!*

But even as he thought it, he felt the weakness of his body. It was known that they could keep a man alive for months in agony.

"But they don't have months," he thought with a grin. "The revolution will destroy the heads of the hydra all at once by—" He realized he didn't know how long he had been in custody. The bomb might have already gone off.

He rested against the steel door with his cheek on the cold metal.

Abruptly, the scrape of metal on metal startled him.

Her stumbled back. He was not sure what to expect, but it certainly was not the pretty woman who stepped through the door.

48

"Quickly, Gregor Bodrov," she said in a musical whisper. "The drugs I gave the general and the guards will wear off shortly, we must be away."

The prisoner stared at her dumbstruck for a long moment until she repeated, "Quickly." She threw a long coat over his shoulders. He was dressed in the stained prison-grey shirt and slacks and simple slippers.

"Who are you?" he asked. He felt dizzy and weak in the knees. She led him out of the cell into a dimly-lit, stone-walled corridor.

"Don't you remember me?" she whispered. When he didn't answer she added. "I met you once at an assembly of the Freedom Front, and have known of your work as the Ghost. I am Doctor Alanna Zalikov."

"Alanna?" he muttered. He searched his memory.

The two fugitives reached a staircase. "We have to try to attract no attention," she said. "We must get away before they know either one of us is gone."

Gregor nodded, and she led him up the stairs. "Keep heart," she whispered. "We are almost out; there are friends waiting for us near by."

"I'll try." His head swam, his thoughts confused, but when he looked into her eyes, he felt a surge of strength.

Just as they left the building, and the outer door of the prison closed behind them, an alarm sounded. A bullet-headed guard on the wall drew an automatic handgun and fired two quick shots from his hip. The first went wide to Gregor's right. The second was so close that it went through his coat.

Alanna produced a gun of her own and fired a shot that staggered the hulking guard who dropped to his knees and lost his pistol with the shock. She did not hesitate and fired a second shot that shattered the man's head.

Gregor was stunned by the sudden violence and suddenly felt himself frozen. Alanna grabbed his right forearm and pulled him forward.

The frigid Moscow night hit him in the face like a hard slap and took his breath away. There was no one out at the late hour except the two fugitives. The blonde woman stopped for a moment to press a small object against the wall of the KGB prison.

"Down!" she screamed at Gregor, at the same time pressing him against the building base. The night was suddenly, blindingly bright as the explosive destroyed the entrance.

She ignored the cold and the blood streaming from a small wound on her arm. She grabbed the stunned Gregor, and they stumbled to their feet to race away from the flaming building.

Two blocks away they came to an alley and turned down it. "This doorway. Come." She knocked, and the nondescript portal opened to admit them.

The space they had entered was a warehouse containing a large box truck with the motor running.

The man who admitted the two was a rough, country fellow with a bulbous red nose and rosy cheeks. "He looks like his brain is scrambled," he said in a hoarse voice.

"Quiet, Mischa," Alanna said. "Of course, Gregor is confused. Now, is everything ready?"

The gruff workman grunted, "Da!" and pointed to the truck. "We must go; they will begin a search."

She pulled Gregor toward the back of the truck. He was still stunned by the quickness of the events.

"When they brought you to me, to interrogate," she said, "I knew it was the only chance we would get to free you from them so I contacted the Freedom Front to set up this escape."

IV

"You tortured me?"

The two of them were in the back of the truck now with the interior lights casting a bluish tint to all. It was fitted out as a travel trailer and horse stall.

"No," she said defensively. "I do not torture. I allow the subject's mind to go through guided dreams."

"It is the same thing," he said with a sudden flare of anger. "You helped them."

"No," she said defensively, "I was able to obfuscate results, often completely fool them. Or at least deny them vital information. When their butchers had no luck with you, I convinced them I could help. I knew it was our only chance to get you away from them."

He said, "They will hunt you."

"But I did not know what else to do," she said. "They would have tried their methods again if I failed."

"But they will capture me again," Gregor said with his hopes falling again. "Better you had killed me."

Her reaction was harsh. "Do not say that, Gregor Bodrov! You are important to the movement. We only have to keep you hidden for a day then what you know will make no difference. As for me," she shrugged, "I can claim I was kidnapped."

"They are not stupid, they will never believe that."

"Am I so important that I can't make a sacrifice for the Motherland?" she said. "Now, be quiet, we must make sure they cannot find you." She pointed to the animal in the stall to their right.

It was the first time that Gregor looked at the creature, a Lusitano stallion at twelve hands. As he looked at it, he realized that it was a very realistic, artificial-skin horse costume!

"It is a cyber-integrated nano-suit," she said. "It was an outgrowth of camouflage developed for the military. You will climb within the suit, and it will 'come alive' so to speak. They will have no idea you are in it."

She handed him a vial of greenish liquid. "Here, drink this."

"What is it?" He looked at the drink with fear, sniffing it.

"It is a solution of nanites and will allow monitors throughout your body that will interface with the suit. It will make it appear to be a living, breathing animal."

She donned rough work clothes which helped to disguise her. Next she directed him to climb the wall of the stall to the back of the great pseudo-stallion where an entrance portal was cleverly concealed. He climbed into the cavity and slid his arms forward into the spaces in the upper fore-thighs of the horse. The 'ribs' of the horse sensed his body and wrapped themselves snugly around his torso as he slid his legs backward into shaped chambers in the upper hind legs.

As soon as he was securely in the cradle of the beast's belly the flap above him closed, and he craned his head forward to place it securely in a molded mask that perfectly encased it. His own sensations began to fade as the suit took over, and he began to 'feel' through the horse. His vision through the facial mask transferred to vision through the cameras in the horse's eyes. He began to hear through the ears.

"There," said the woman who with a dark wig on and her face smeared with dirt now looked so very different from when she had come to his cell. "We are both in our masks!"

The blonde doctor, now looking more like a collective worker from the country, brought a mirror to in front of Gregor. "Take a look, Comrade." She smiled to reassure him. "You will see that there is very little chance of anyone finding you in there."

The ears of the image twitched, the eyelids blinked, and in every way, it appeared to be a real, live animal. He tentatively moved his head to tilt to the side. The servo-motors in the horse suit reacted as if they were his own muscles, and the long triangular head of the 'beast' tilted to match it exactly.

"Now, relax, tovarish," she said with a gentle smile. "We have all the papers and a clear path out of the city, east toward Zukovskij and then south on the Novoyanskoe Shosse toward the Ukraine. They will not expect that." She reflexively patted him on the long muzzle. "So be at ease, relax, and sleep while we drive you to freedom."

V

Gregor Bodrov dreamed: he was at the conference of the Freedom Front at an out-of-the-way house in St. Petersburg. Across a table Gregor saw the thin, blonde form of a younger Alanna Zalikov.

The girl smiled at him, and he smiled back. She started to speak to him but the words were jumbled, and then there was a loud roar and a blinding light.

Gregor was jarred awake when the rear gate of the

truck was opened, and daylight flooded into the dark space. His blood ran cold as he saw two armed soldiers hop up onto the truck bed.

"But Comrade soldiers," the voice of Alanna called from outside, "he is a very high-strung animal."

The soldiers ignored her with their weapons pointed menacingly ahead of them.

"Be careful, you fools!" Alanna cried. "That is a very valuable horse that belongs to General Azarov!"

This stopped the two soldiers who looked at each other with a new understanding of their position.

"We have orders to search each vehicle for the traitor Bodrov," one of the men said. "The General will understand."

Gregor expressed his frustration with a stamp of his pseudo-hoof and a whinny of annoyance. The two soldiers jumped in surprise then laughed at their own skittishness.

"Yes, we have searched all we can," one soldier said. "Have a good day, Comrade." The two of them hopped off the truck.

"We are almost home free, Gregor," the blonde doctor said with a laugh at the soldiers' haste. "Keep courage!" She gave him a smile, and, despite the strange circumstances, he felt reassured.

The truck rumbled along for what seemed an endless time for Gregor, with nothing but wonder if the plan to assassinate the repressive council that would signal the start of the revolution had happened yet.

Then the vehicle braked to a halt, and the door was thrown open, and a concerned Alanna came running into the back to the truck.

"We must go, Gregor," she said as she pulled him from the stall and began to take tack gear from the wall. "There are more roadblocks ahead, and the papers on this truck will not get us through any really close scrutiny. We will have to go cross-country."

She approached him with a bit.

Walking on his new all-fours was not as strange as he would have thought. The way his arms and legs set into the framework of the horse form allowed him to move them as if he were dog paddling in a pool. The movement was translated to the faux-animal limbs as a natural-appearing, equine gait.

The countryside around the truck consisted of rolling hills and, though hardened by the first frosts of winter, was not yet snow covered. It was easy going for the newly four-footed Gregor.

"Mischa will drive the truck on a false trail back toward the city. You and I will ride off into the sunset like an American cowboy!" Alanna laughed.

The woman continued to talk to him as they progressed, speaking in a calming voice, rambling about her life and her childhood.

"So I never found the right man," she lamented after a time, "because with my leading a double life, fighting for the revolution and working 'for' the government there was never anyone I could trust enough."

They topped a small rise that presented a gentle valley leading to a large body of water and a range of tall hills. Just as they topped the ridge, she dismounted when her cell phone rang.

"Yes, Mischa, what is wrong?" she said with concern.

Gregor stopped and looked back at her. Her face darkened with the news.

"But how could they know about—" she began then stopped with a gasp. "No, not Ivan and Giela? Yes, yes, we will move quickly."

She hung up and then leaned in to hug Gregor's neck. "They have taken two of my contacts in the Front. I fear they will talk about us. They already know I had planned this escape for you. We must move quickly to safety," she continued. "But I don't know which will get us to the cabin the fastest." Her tone was at the edge of hysteria and Gregor wished he had hands to console her.

"I...I just don't know which way to go," she repeated. "You'll have to choose the safest way," she said. "It's up to you."

The disguised rebel snorted and galloped off down toward the lake and safety at full speed!

*   *   *

"So it is the mountain retreat where they have planted

the bomb!" General Azarov said with glee.

Doctor Zalikov took off the headset and slumped back in her chair, exhausted. "Yes, General," she said. "He chose the lake without hesitation so I can say with absolute certainty that it is the safe destination for your council."

"And you still have two hours before your deadline," Lushencko said.

"I am glad I did not have to use another dose," the doctor said. "He would not have survived."

"It makes no matter," the General said. "He is of no more use now." He turned to head out of the room then stopped. "Well done, Doctor, the party will not forget your good work. I must ask you not to leave this secure area until after the deadline has passed, however, just to be sure the word does not leak out."

"Of course, Comrade General," the Doctor said. "But—"

"But?" he asked.

"I would appreciate something to drink—not coffee. Something strong, Cuban Rum perhaps?" She gave her superior a weary smile.

Azarov laughed. "I will have Comrade Lushencko here send a bottle of his best down. You love the decadent American ways like I, eh?"

"Only some of them," she said meaningfully, casting a cold glance at Lushenchko. "But thank you."

The two men left, and her lab assistant set about shutting down the equipment. The Doctor walked over to the capsule where the still form of Gregor Bodrov rested. She put a hand on the cool plasteel of the surface and then leaned in to touch her forehead to it.

"We did it, Gregor," she whispered to the former lover and fellow rebel. "They believed I had broken you. They will be at the lake house in three hours, and, in four, the revolution will have begun."

In the capsule, the silent form of the rebel twitched, and his lips moved into what might have been the ghost of a smile...

Damascus
Tyree Campbell

The interior of the shed was dank and musty, like an abandoned cellar, but above ground. Not even the smell of the ocean, less than a kilometer away, could affect the air inside. Brine wafted right on by toward the fishing village the humans had established a decade of Earth years ago...or eight point nine years here on Sindios, as the human settlers had named the new world. The piscine stench of the Sind, confined to the steel chair, which in turn was bolted to the floor, only worsened the air in the room.

For the umpteenth time, Ladousz adjusted his nose filters. Why these confrontations had to be held inside a closed room and not outside in the sun was beyond him. *We have nothing to hide*, he thought. *Not here. This is* our world now. But such was the decree of the Chalmer, all praise to His Guidance. And he had to admit the room was better than watching the Sind desiccate in the hot sun. But only just.

"Do you," he asked again, wearily, "claim to believe in God, lamar?"

Lamar was not the name of the prisoner, but a term for the alien form on Sindios, and a pejorative. His true name—he was unquestionably male—was not easily pronounced, and only a few humans on the planet even bothered to try to learn the language. The Sinds, however, picked up English quite readily. Ladousz sneered that they did not speak it, but merely parroted it. Still, the Sinds' concept of God was troubling. Like every other form of life, they could not possess souls. Why then would they bother with a useless religion that was bordering on extinction?

"Yes," answered the lamar. A coughing fit wracked him.

"Throw some more water on him," ordered Ladousz. "Don't let him dry out."

"Thank you," said the lamar. "Most Christian of you."

Ladousz half-rose from his stuffed chair. "*Damn* you! Don't *ever* say anything like that to me!"

Donya Savage laid a gentle hand on his shoulder, nudging him back down onto the chair. Her configuration was reminiscent of a woman composed of spare parts, slender down to the waist, and much broader below. Short, mouse-brown hair capped a round face that bore a perpetual mask of disapproval, much like a spinster aunt, which she was. "The lamar does not know what it is saying," she soothed. "Pay it no mind."

"I know exactly what I am saying," returned the lamar. "Did you think we would not study your history, to know what sort of neighbors you would make?"

Ladousz snorted, and dragged a hand over his scalp, slick now with sweat brought on by the heat in the closed room. "You can't even read."

"You have audio books. Even so, yes, we can read in many of your languages." Yellow eyes narrowed at him. "How is it that you do not know this?"

He controlled himself with a will toward patience. "Look, all we want from you and your kind is to do your work, and to show proper respect to the Chalmer, our magnificent and magnanimous Protector. That's all. Speaking to your overseers and task-masters about this impossible God that you proclaim only causes you suffering. Do you like it when we withdraw the hoses while you work, so that you cannot keep yourselves wet? Is this what you want?"

The lamar's shrug involved his entire body, from his great sagittate head down to the smallest sucker. "Have our labors displeased you in some way?" he asked. "Do we not properly erect your homes and places of work and gathering? Do we not see to the care of your younglings while you yourselves go about your routines? Do we not tend your yards and clean your homes? In return, we ask only the courtesy of allowing us to keep ourselves wet when we are on land. Surely, this is what Jesus would have done."

A hard look from Ladousz alerted the man behind the lamar, who carried an electric cattle prod. He jabbed this against the sagittate head, and laughed while the lamar spasmed at first then slumped unconscious in the chair, prevented by his bonds from spilling onto the dirt floor.

Scowling at the inert prisoner, Ladousz rose, jerked his head in a signal to Savage, and stepped out into the cleansing sunlight.

"You're getting soft," she said, as they headed back to the village. The sea breeze blew wisps of hair over her eyes. She ignored them. "'Just do your work' and acknowledge the supremacy of the Chalmer, may his Empire endure forever? Is that what it comes down to?"

"Technique," Ladousz answered, his voice gruff and hoarse after the two-hour interrogation. "A plea for sanity. We're all sane, right? We have our duties; we all have our places. By the Chalmer's Bracelet, we certainly know ours. Some of the lamars still do not know theirs."

"But their numbers are growing," Savage countered.

"They reproduce like ribbiks, true enough. Each female launches a million larvae. Most of them get eaten, and a good job, too. Otherwise, those Christians would swallow us up by sheer numbers." He paused for a long and tired sigh. "Where do they get these outrageous ideas?"

"From something that is hidden from us, perhaps?" Savage suggested. "Perhaps they have a secret society to foment disharmony."

A note of derision crept into his tone. "Do you think they're organized? They can't even arrive at their jobs on time. They have to hold some kind of meeting first." He sighed again. "Well, the Chalmer, all honor and glory to His name, is said to be developing a policy to control their numbers and to diminish the waywardness they encourage in some of our young people."

She brightened. "Tell me!"

"Money."

She soured. The lack of comprehension made her face slack. It was an expression he had not seen before on her; it changed her looks from median to ugly. He put a pace of distance between them.

"Money," she repeated. It was more accusation than question. "We already have money."

"But don't you see?" he went on, almost pleading now. "We are a small settlement; we have primarily a barter economy. You do this, we do that. A jar of jam for a loaf of bread. In the case of the Sinds, they work for us in exchange for water and occasional other benefits, such as heads from the fish we catch and smoke. What if, instead of those benefits, we paid them money, with which they would have to purchase sprays of water or heads of fish? As long as we control the coastal waters, they will have to come to us for food."

"The fish are abundant," she argued.

"We already operate smokers and canneries," he countered. "We produce enough to satisfy our own needs. If we take more fish, and produce more tins, we diminish the Sinds' food supplies and produce more than enough ourselves to trade with other settlements on other worlds, worlds which perhaps are not gifted with proteins from the seas."

"I still don't—"

"What we control, Donya," he said gently, "we can enforce."

"So you're saying to them, 'If you want food, you must stop your preaching this Jesus nonsense.'"

Ladousz beamed. "Now you've got it."

"I suppose. Imagine a god creating a son and having him slaughtered to save nonexistent souls." She shook her head, and then brightened. "On the other hand, we still enjoy the use of our cattle prods."

He grinned without mirth. "I wouldn't rule them out just yet."

*   *   *

In the evening, on his way home, Ladousz decided to make a stop at the interrogation shed to check on the progress regarding the lamar. Glancing past the shed, he skidded to a stop on the grass and just did catch himself from tumbling. On the hill between the shed and the ocean, under the hot afternoon sun, stood a great wooden star. It had been assembled with rough lumber from the mill, seven points for the star, and one as a center pole to be driven into the ground. It stood facing away from the ocean, and against the sun.

Onto the star—and this is what turned his stomach—the lamar had been attached. At first Ladousz supposed he had been tied there, but as he crawled and then tottered closer, he saw that three of the lamar's ten tentacles had been hacked off, and the other seven affixed by iron spikes to the points of the star. Black ink and blood that was blue due to its copper content still trickled from the corpse into puddles around the base of the star.

He staggered closer. Above the sagittate head, someone had posted a notice of sorts. It read, simply, "Follow Your Leader."

The entire scene proved too much for him. He fell to his knees, fighting down his gorge. After a huge breath, he screamed, "But I didn't mean *this!*"

Long minutes later—perhaps an hour of them, perhaps three—he regained his feet. The sun had almost hidden itself behind the distant trees. He caught a whiff of something fried, like poultry, but not. Shoes squeaked in the grass behind him. He turned to find Donya Savage moving within range. In her hand she carried a paper bag. Oily stains darkened its sides. She extended the bag to him.

"Want some?" she asked.

He did not feel like eating. "No. What is it?"

"Calamari."

Though he felt the urge, Ladousz did not kill her outright. Instead, he turned back to the star. "To hell with Caesar," he said. A moment passed before he realized he had not said, "Chalmer." He had no idea where the word had come from. But he shrugged; he knew he had just sentenced himself to death.

He wondered whether the Sind's Jesus would take him in.

The Alpha Tau Challenge
T. Santitoro

Father Emilio Alverez eyed his new, little congregation with determination. He was the fourth missionary to be sent to teach the natives of Alpha Tau. The three previous priests had disappeared without a trace. Supposedly, they'd gone native. At least, that's what Father Alverez had been told by the locals. Of course, his knowledge of the native language and customs left a lot to be desired.

Emilio Alverez was a young Terran, only thirty stan'ars old, with unruly, dark hair, a slight frame, and dancing eyes. He'd attended Saint Gerard's Theological Academy on Io, in the Home System, where he'd graduated cum laude, and had begun his missionary work in this sector of the United Galaxy almost immediately.

After serving for almost eight stan'ars elsewhere in the quadrant, he'd arrived on Alpha Tau a mere standard week earlier, with only his implanted catechism chip, a crucifix the size of his palm, his cassock, a month's worth of under garments, and a few toiletries.

He had only been traveling and ministering in this quadrant for less than a standard decade now, bringing the new-age Christianity—with all its intrinsic rituals and customs—to the alien populations, and this trip was his first time on Alpha Tau.

The smell of rain hung heavy in the humid air, and dark storm clouds scudded across the planetoid's grey sky, between the brilliant yellow leaves of the huge, white-barked plants that passed as trees. Despite the alien flora, the other-worldly smells, and the uncharacteristic heat, Emilio was enthusiastic about his present mission. He had successfully ministered to infidels on Alpha Gamma following their civil war, had preached The Word of God to the zealots of Croy, and had served a brief stint as chaplain on an extra-galactic transport, but nothing had made him feel as needed as he did now.

He stood before his parishioners, a few little, grey people with large, oval, black eyes, who gazed back with what appeared to be intense interest. They seemed somehow eager. That's how he viewed their shuffling, bright eyed, muttering countenances.

He'd discovered just how much the natives had learned about the Lord, from the reports that had been lazar-zipped to the Archbishop by the three former parish priests. Apparently, they'd made great headway in their ministry, before they had mysteriously disappeared into the planet's jungle wilderness, first one priest, and then the others. The celebration of Mass had been encouraged by the Unified Galactic Christian Church, and, according to the reports, the indigenous population had readily embraced it, so the strange disappearances had been totally unexpected and unexplained. If the spread of Christianity had been going so well, why had the former men of the cloth disappeared?

Even as he stood before them now, Emilio remembered earnestly reading the communiqués regarding the welcome of the natives, the warmth of their initial treatment of the original parish priest, and the alacrity with which the population had accepted the Good News of the Christian Faith. The mystery of what had later happened to the three missing members of the clergy was, indeed, puzzling.

Father Alverez was still relatively young and passionate about his Faith, but in his almost eight stan'ars of preaching, he had never yet made First Contact with any indigenous population, and this mission was no exception. The Archbishop had only seen fit to assign the anxious Emilio to the already established missions, and this was the first time he had been relegated to replace priests that had gone missing, a fact that'd had the young scholar and clergyman more than a little worried at first.

When he'd arrived on Alpha Tau eight standard days ago, his galactic shuttle-taxi setting down in a clearing in the middle of a riot of overgrown jungle, he had looked out from the relative safety of its armored interior. But Father Alverez had not seen the indigenous yellow plant life, or the roiling brown waters of the river that snaked between mountains covered in the uncontained growth, or the white-hot double stars that served as suns. Instead, he'd perceived the humble, packed-mud huts and the short, poorly-clothed villagers with their charcoal-colored skin and shiny, dark eyes, their bellies swollen from malnutrition.

And he'd known that this was his task: to redeem these natives, to bring them into the fold of The Church. To bring God to these unfortunates, living in the squalor of an alien world.

Once his shuttle had ascended out of sight, however, he was alone in the village, the only off-worlder on the planetoid, and wondered for the nth time, if his language skills would be up to the challenge.

His first words to the villagers had been completely misunderstood.

He'd stepped from the cool interior of the departing shuttle and, breaking into an immediate sweat in the steamy atmosphere, had asked the native assigned to assist him, where he could find some water.

The small alien had rattled off a barrage of sentences spoken so quickly that they sounded like gibberish to the priest, and had then led him to the edge of bordering jungle, indicating a frail-looking latrine, shakily constructed of white-barked logs.

Emilio had blushed at the error in translation, running a finger around his collar. "Nem, nem!" he'd spoken in the native tongue, shaking his head, and then he'd made a drinking motion.

The little grey man's all-black eyes widened with understanding, and he had hurried to rectify the situation. He'd scurried into the surrounding vegetation, and had come back moments later, carrying a strange gourd filled with dirty water from the river.

Emilio had shrugged, knowing he'd have to adapt to the local water source sooner or later. He'd taken the proffered drink and downed it greedily, glad to relieve the dryness in his parched mouth. In only seconds, he'd regretted the action, as his stomach was suddenly gripped with horrendous cramps, and he had been forced to use the latrine after all.

Since then, Father Alvarez had been most careful with all things native, both in language and in customs.

The little mud hut designated as the village Church was slightly larger than the other structures surrounding it, and had smelled of incense and burnt candles, which had given Father Alvarez an odd feeling of familiarity, given its remoteness from his home world. The interior was cooler than the sunsbaked courtyard outside had been, but even the four square, open windows did nothing to dispel the dim heat within. He'd made his way to the front of the church, appalled at the lack of pews. The "altar" was a block of some local hardwood, with a white cloth draped over it, and topped by a dyplasite chalice and one lone candle. There was no sacristy, no statues of the saints, or stations of the cross, no crucifix--other than the small one he carried on his person--or bible. There was little to work with, here, among villagers who needed his tending so badly.

As he stood in the midst of the indigent surroundings, Emilio's heart bled for the simple villagers, and their lack of not only religious icons, but the cardinal trappings of civilization. Perhaps, when he was better settled, he might be able to convince the Archbishop to take up a collection for this neglected, little church and its congregation.

Surely the need to feed these people was tantamount. How were they supposed to learn about the Lord, when their most basic, bodily needs were left untended? Maybe that's where the previous priests had failed. Perhaps they had gone native in an attempt to understand the culture of these indigenous people, and their needs.

A movement startled him out of his reverie, and he noted the entrance of the alien designated as his assistant. The small, grey native moved into the church carrying a broom-like object, and proceeded to sweep the dirt floor, in preparation for the impending Mass. Choking dust slowly rose into the stifling air, churning into clouds that roiled in the meager shafts of sunslight slanting through the four, square windows.

Emilio coughed, rushing toward his helper, waving his arms empathically. "Nem! Nem!" he said urgently. It

64

simply would not do, to suffocate the entire congregation before serving his very first Mass.

Even now, church members were beginning to arrive, their grey complexioned faces and large, black eyes looking somehow expectant, as they piled into the hot, little hut for Sunday service, and immediately began coughing.

He grabbed the broom-like tool out of the little assistant's hands, motioning toward the small mob of newcomers, indicating to him that he take a place in the crowd, and wondering if the previous priests had had such trouble with their help. Had Jesus had to deal with such ineptness from His followers? He doubted it, but then again, the Lord had been in possession of extreme, Godly patience.

Father Alvarez placed the sweeper into a corner of the hut, lit the candle on the altar, then wiped grimy hands on his cassock, as the dust settled, and scanned the dim, candle-lit area. Already over two dozen natives had entered the church, gathering into small, chattering groups that spoke an alien language he could barely comprehend.

How was he supposed to preach sermons and say Mass, when the language barrier was so obvious? He knew that the apostles were supposed to have spoken in tongues, but these beings were aliens, not just people from differing tribes, and serious doubts began to arise within him, like the choking dust had done only a short moment earlier.

Emilio drew in a deep breath, fought the urge to cough, and exhaled, trying to gather his nerve. If God required him to preach, preach he would, and perhaps the Holy Spirit would settle upon them all, uniting them in a common language. But the idea all at once seemed ludicrous to him. If the Holy Spirit could really unite this parish of natives with their off-world cleric, what had happened to the three previous priests? He shook his head, dispelling that thought, then motioned his parishioners to join hands, glanced briefly at the thatched ceiling, and told himself to calm down. He didn't want to let the natives see his sudden weakness. This was definitely not the time to start having doubts!

He cleared his throat, gave his attention to the gathered natives, and began to speak. He labored on, in a broken mixture of his own language and the native tongue, reciting the Mass, giving a brief homily and the required sermon, soon converging on the all-important sacrifice of Our Lord, Communion. He took the dyplasite chalice, and raised it, blessing it, and set it down gently, part of his mind returning to the missing priests. He struggled to pull his wandering attention back to the ritual he was enacting, attempting to focus on the Lord's Holy Sacrifice. He tenderly removed the Host from its place, and stared at the shaking hands holding It, still amazed--after almost eight standard years--at the miracle he was about to perform.

So, he stood now, before the small congregation of perhaps 30 people, the pivotal part of the ceremony about to be performed. He paused, raising the Host above their heads—not hard to do, they being of such short stature—concentrating on the miracle he was about to reenact for them. Then he spoke THE WORDS:

"Take this, all of you, and eat it, for this is my Body, which will be given up for you."

How was he to know that his misunderstood invitation would be taken so literally?

Canaan
Robert J. Krog

As the red sun set, the wind blew in off the ocean, across the island and over the town of Canaan, whistling through the steeple of St. Brendan's Church. It blew through the open windows of the rectory, giving the pastor some relief after the summer warmth of the day. Father Smith, kneeling in prayer before bedtime, was disturbed by the clanging of Constable Resden going by in the street outside. "...If I should die before I wake," he had just said, and as the clanging came near and loud outside his window, he muttered distractedly, "Blast that mechanical monstrosity in its overzealous sense of duty!"

As the sounds grew louder yet, overwhelming his words and the pleasant sigh of the wind, he sighed too, crossed himself again, waited until the clatter lessened, and began over with an apology. He proceeded into his regular prayers, wondering if it were right to ask a blessing on the mechanical thing that protected the town to a fault and feeling rather repelled by the notion. He asked simply for blessing on the town and its inhabitants instead, as was his custom.

Outside and down the street a bit, the iron hulk that was Constable Resden, apelike and huge, walked on its hind legs and knuckles, soles and fists striking the cobblestones with annoying clatter. It paused at an intersection, its insectoid head turning this way and that, then twisting three hundred and sixty degrees as it searched the side streets for malefactors.

When Father Smith was ending his nightly devotions and crossing himself, a knock came on the door. He rose and went to it, not without regret. It had been a long day. He opened the wicket and peered out on an unwelcome sight for his tired eyes. Two excommunicates; Harold Flatly and his lover, Earl Stubbs, stood outside, their faces distressed and hunted. He wanted to shut the wicket and go away.

He didn't.

"Please, Father, help us," begged Harold.

He wanted to say, "Have you come to confess your sins and return to the Church?" Instead he asked, "With what do you need help, my sons?"

"Constable Resden's found us out. Hide us, please."

Resignedly, he opened the door to the two men, knowing that Resden would not rest until he had found them and carried out whatever sentence his programming dictated, which, given the puritanical nature of the town, would be severe, citing Leviticus 20: 13 among other verses. They entered hurriedly, looking over their shoulders.

He said to them, "Come in, my sons, but be sure that in my house, your behavior respects my hospitality." He eyed them sternly. Both men were of a rebellious streak.

"Thank you, Father," said Harold, but Earl flared up immediately. "Or what?"

"I only ask-" began Father Smith, but he was cut off by Earl's angry remark. "We have to repent, or you'll hand us over to Resden like a damned Judas. Is that what you mean?"

"No," said Father Smith. "That's a ridiculous comparison." His temper was quickly rising.

"Please," said Harold. "Please."

"I told you it was a bad idea to come to this self-righteous hypocrite."

"I am not throwing you out, Earl," said Father Smith, "but you are free to leave at any time if that is your opinion. I will ask you again to-"

"Come on, love, let's hide elsewhere," said Earl. "A sewer'd be better."

"Damnit—forgive me, Father—sweetie, we've no other place to go. No one'll take us." Harold spoke severely, angrily even, to Earl. Earl swallowed his next words and turned his back on them instead.

"Gentlemen, if I will be permitted to speak in my own house."

"Yes, Father. Please, what are your conditions?"

Father Smith hesitated, thinking, wishing. He offered a quick, silent prayer then said, "There are no conditions on

68

your lives, gentlemen. So long as you are in danger, here you may hide. I ask that you respect the rules of this house and behave as Christian gentlemen inside my walls. You will not lie with one another nor treat each other as paramours here, if you please."

"Or you'll put us out on the street," accused Earl.

Father Smith sighed.

"Thank you," said Harold.

About to speak, Father Smith paused. He heard the clanging of the constable's great, iron soles and knuckles growing louder on the cobblestones. They were approaching. "Silence!" he warned.

Harold's eyes widened. Earl's hand went to his mouth to cover his gasp.

"Quickly," he hissed at them, "into the back room and thence to the closet. You know the monstrosity has better ears than men, and perhaps a better nose as well. They say he can see through one wall, maybe two, so hide as far back as you can go."

The two men took each other's hands and fled to the back of the rectory to find the closet in question. It was the one in Father Smith's bedroom. He watched them go and, after they were gone, groaned at the thought of them in his bedroom at all. *It is silly, yet it irks me. Still, they are hiding for their lives, not sodomizing one another.*

The clanging in the street grew clamorous then stopped at his door. There was a surprisingly polite knock upon it. He went to it. *What shall I say if it asks if they are here?* He opened the wicket and looked into one red eye of the constable. Its great, iron, insectoid head looked in, focusing only one eye through the wicket, for it was too close for both.

"Good evening to you, Mr. Smith," it said, sounding, as it always did, hollow, and refusing, as the Protestant town in general did, to recognize his Catholic title. "I am following the scent of the recently-discovered sexual perverts, Earl Stubbs and Harold Flatly. Have-"

Quickly, Father Smith cut it off, "I was not aware of any recently-discovered perverts, Constable." *If it asks me directly, I must do as the Hebrew midwives did when questioned by Pharaoh about the killing of the male children. It must be as if innocent children were in my closet.*

"There have been," stated Resden. "The good citizens are refusing them housing. They have been cast out by their landlord to be turned over to me because they were found sodomizing."

"If you please, Constable," he said, "watch your language—you are just outside of a church."

"You are correct, Mr. Smith. The perverts have passed down this street."

"That's interesting, but I'm very tired. Unless I'm in danger from them, I would like to go to sleep now, thank you."

"It is not believed that anyone is danger from them," stated Resden.

"Thank you for the warning then, and good night to you," he said. He shut the wicket.

There was a loud whirring of the monstrosity's internal gears for a moment. He waited, listening. It did not knock again but clanged away. He sighed and said his "Glory Be," and went back toward his bedroom to reassure the frightened men. They met him in the hallway.

"Thank you, Father," said Harold, and this time Earl had no criticism.

"You are welcome." They stood an awkward moment before he collected himself to remember his manners. "Have you eaten?"

"No, Father," said Harold, "not since yesterday. We've been in hiding."

"I didn't know. Come to the kitchen. I'll find you something."

"The least you could do since it's all your fault," muttered Earl.

"Mine?" inquired Father Smith, remaining calm.

"If you hadn't seen to our excommunication, no one would have suspected."

"You suppose it would have been somehow better for you to have continued to receive communion in a state of mortal sin? I did not broadcast your sins to anyone, I simply denied you communion as I am required. For my part, your sin remained a secret between ourselves and

70

God himself. I have no desire to see you put to death. Our Lord would not cast the first stone at the adulterous woman, and I shall not cast any at you, though the law of this town would have it so."

"He's right, you know," said Harold.

Earl had nothing to say.

The kitchen was cozy enough, and the larder was decently stocked. Father Smith found half a round of cheese and some crackers to serve, as well as a handful of strawberries picked earlier from the garden. "Water, tea, or coffee?" he asked. "I think we should save the beer for later, when you're better replenished."

"Water," said Harold.

"Tea," muttered Earl.

He lit the gas range, put on a pot for tea, and poured water from a pitcher into a cup for Harold. The two men sat down to their meal and were quiet for a time except for the sounds of their eating. He took a seat himself and sat back to think. His parish was small and poor. None of his families were people of money and means, but mostly Irish and Italian immigrants, poor folk, laborers. The wealth in the town belonged to the descendants of Englishman and some Dutch. *How am I to keep these two from the gears of justice as this place delivers it? They do not much temper it with mercy here.* He looked at them, remembering how he had baptized them as infants, heard their first confessions, and put the host on the tongue of each at his first communion. How had they ended up as sodomites? He shook his head and looked out the window at the sky above his garden. The moon was a sliver above the apple tree, and the constellation Cygnus was visible beneath its lower branches. The air was cooling after a long, warm, summer day. Distantly, he heard the clanging of Resden somewhere in the town. Earl and Harold started.

"Be at ease," he told them. "It's likely near Market Street, by the sound of it.

They relaxed and returned to their food, clearly needing it. He returned to his thoughts, but came up with no solution. They should leave the town, but how to get them out? The bridge to the mainland would surely be watched by human constables, and none of his

71

parishioners owned a boat, so far as he knew. He abandoned thought on it for a time and concentrated instead on immediate matters. He said to them, "One of you may have the spare bedroom. The other, I am afraid, must take the couch, or if that proves too uncomfortable, a mat on the floor of the main room."

Earl sneered. Harold said, "Thank you."

They kept eating. Shortly, he rose and added tea leaves to the water. Out in the night, on the far side of town, a dog barked suddenly and ferociously, followed at once by furious clanging. They paused to listen. The noise almost certainly portended the imminent capture of a malefactor by Constable Resden. A firearm blasted loudly two, three, four times over the raucous barking of many dogs and the noise of Resden's appendages on the cobblestones. There was a sudden, piercing, protracted scream. Through the window, Father Smith could see the glow of flames and knew that that there would be no trial. Resden had taken recourse to the flamethrower his designer and builder had placed in his beetle-like mouth. The screaming ended after a few moments as the criminal's lungs gave out.

Behind him, Father Smith could hear one of the men gagging. "That was this side of Market Street, I guess," said Harold, "Must be in the Irish quarter."

"Yes, I suppose so," said Father Smith.

"There, there, love," said Harold to Earl. "It's over."

"Poor bastard," said Earl, thickly. "It was probably Sean O'Malley. That sounded like his rifle."

"He should have given up," said Harold. "There's no way a gun of that caliber would stop Resden. Its armor is too thick. It'd take a cannon."

"And yet, Resden used the flamethrower anyway," said Father Smith, "because the law allows a policeman to use deadly force when a weapon is in play by the criminal." He lowered his head and prayed, "Eternal rest grant to him, o Lord, and may perpetual light shine upon him, whomever he may be."

"Relieved that he wasn't caught?" asked Earl, regaining his composure.

"No," said Father Smith, turning, perplexed and annoyed.

"If he hadn't been burned up, and it was Sean, then he might have told the police that you buy his beer, which is prohibited, after all. You could've ended up in the stocks and been run out of town after."

"Nevertheless," said Father Smith.

Earl smirked as he continued eating. Father Smith, annoyed but tired, chose not to pursue the accusation. They ate in silence for a time. He poured tea into cups and set them on the table, forgetting that Harold had not asked for any. Harold looked at his, shrugged, and drank it. Shortly, all weary, they retired to their separate beds.

In the night, the clanging, four-limbed tread of Resden paced by on several occasions. Father Smith awoke each time and sat up, wary. Twice, it stopped outside the rectory. Once, he thought he heard Earl gasp from the spare bedroom. The mechanical constable clanged away though, gears clicking, knuckles and soles slamming onto the cobblestones, into the night, disturbing the rest of all in the houses it passed. "I feel so very protected and comfortable," muttered Father Smith, unable to easily fall back to sleep. He rose, went to the kitchen, and poured himself a cup of tepid tea. It did not, of course, help him to sleep.

What am I to do with these two sinners? He thought. The answer was plain before him. *Pray for them, hide them, and not give them up to the law, what else? But how to get them to safety off the island?* He sat up pondering that question for another hour before returning to his bed. As he slipped off to sleep again, the clanging steps of the vigilant constable sounded distantly from some other quarter of Canaan, and he wondered, *How much, O Lord, must I sacrifice for these perverts? Is there a point at which, for the sake of my parish, I may hand them over?* He stared out his window at the glory of the night sky, and did not later remember falling asleep.

It was late when he awoke. He rose quickly, washed, and made his way across the yard to the church for morning mass under the disapproving eyes of Mrs. Sanford, his protestant neighbor. Entering, he saw that the milk wagon was passing by, having just dropped off a jug and some eggs on his doorstep. He didn't have time to take it into the house, but rushed into the sanctuary to change. He had just three parishioners, for it was a weekday. He slipped into his vestments and said mass as speedily as ritual allowed. He was done an hour after dawn, still weary from the restless night, and still needing to answer the call of nature. He said good day to those present, returned across the yard, and went to the outhouse in one corner of his garden. After, he went through the house to the front door to pick up the morning paper and the milk delivery. Harold and Earl were asleep, so far as he could tell, and he did not wish to wake them. He tiptoed past Harold, asleep on the couch, and into the entry hall. He rubbed his face and opened the door.

Constable Resden was sitting on its iron haunches on his porch, its body facing the street but its manipled head turned so that one eye was facing the rectory door. Father Smith went rigid in the doorway, his blood running cold.

In its great, hollow voice, Resden asked, "How are you this morning, Mr. Smith?"

His mouth had gone dry, and he had to swallow hard before answering. "I'm fine, Constable." He found that he was stuttering. "You're sitting on my paper. If you don't mind, I'd like to pick it up." *Remember the Hebrew midwives.*

The hulking thing rose with a clanking of gears. He bent and picked up his paper. He turned, realized he was forgetting his milk and eggs, turned back, smiled at the constable's red eye, and picked them up.

"I have been unable to locate the fugitive perverts, Mr. Smith, but their scent is heaviest on this street. I believe they may have been here on this doorstep, last night."

He waved past the constable at his neighbor, John Jones, trying to smile. John waved back, not smiling, but concerned. "Really?" Father Smith asked not looking at Resden.

"Yes," it said.

"I suppose it's a good thing I lock my doors then," he said, turned and went in, shutting and locking the door

74

behind him. Remembering the constable's reputation for being able to see through a door or a wall, he forced himself to walk calmly to the kitchen. He found Harold and Earl in there. He paused in the doorway and looked at them, thinking.

"We had a visitor, did we?" asked Earl quietly, making it an accusation.

"Constable Resden," murmured Father Smith, nodding.

"Thought you were about to give us up, I did, what with the long pause."

"No," he said, shortly. He walked into the room, setting the jug on the table. He pulled out the oatmeal and one egg each. He was out of sausage. In a bit, they were all eating. "I have a few blackberries in the garden. I think I'll make a pie this morning, before I check the alms box and visit sick parishioners. You'd like a pie?"

"Yeah," said Harold.

"You're going to leave us?" asked Earl.

"I must, if I'm to avoid arousing suspicions. I suggest while I am away, you don't go near windows, and, if you hear the constable, stay well into the interior of the house with more than two walls between you and his mechanical eyes."

"You seem worried about us," said Earl.

He could not answer that easily. He merely nodded and went out into the garden with a bucket. He had barely enough ripe berries to make a small pie, and it didn't take long to pick them, but he stayed out in the garden anyway. He sniffed his roses and herbs. He found his clippers and removed old blooms. He told himself that it was to enjoy the morning, but he also knew he simply didn't want to go back in and be with his guests. *And are you, in your lack of charity, somehow not a sinner, too?* he asked himself after a bit. With a sigh, he returned.

"I made a pie crust yesterday afternoon," he told them upon entering, deciding not to see that they had been sitting very close and holding hands, "I'll make the filling now." He turned on the oven and lit it with a match.

"Fancy," said Earl sneering.

"A gift from the parish," said Father Smith. "It enables me to do a lot more cooking than I need for myself. Consequently, I cook for every parish event and make meals for the sick and hungry as much as I can." He gave Earl a pointed look.

"I'll write to the pope," said Earl.

Later, comfortably full between breakfast and dessert, Father Smith crossed the yard between the rectory and his little church, waving cheerily at frowning Mrs. Sanford, who did not wave. He saw that Resden was in the street, on its haunches beside a gas lamp, its red eyes roving. People gave it a wide berth as they went about their business. He shuddered.

The alms box had little in it, and he took it all, counting out the pennies, nickels, and dimes. Someone had put a shiny, new dollar in as well. It wasn't much, but he added a little of his own to eke it out. It would be enough to give a little to each of the poorer members. He sighed. *I should be able to get another meal out of the garden this week and next,* he thought, *probably. More squash will be ripe in a day or two, tomatoes also, and there are some small peppers.* He added a few more coins, and was satisfied then.

On exiting the church, he saw that the mayor, James Cromwell, who was also reverend of one of the protestant congregations, was in the street, standing by Resden. The two were talking. Cromwell was very animated, but he was not speaking loudly. Father Smith made a point of walking right by them, giving a cheery hello when the mayor looked. He couldn't make out what they were discussing, though. He didn't look back, but somehow, he knew, or thought he knew, that one of Resden's red eyes watched him. Before he turned the corner, John Jones fell in beside him.

"Good morning, Mr. Smith," he said. "It's almsgiving day?"

"It is," he replied, "and good morning to you."

"Here, let me add a little to it. I don't like to limit my charity. You Romanists need it too." John extended his hand and gave him six quarters.

"Thank you. This'll go far. Some of my parishioners are in great need on a regular basis."

They turned a corner. John leaned in close and kept pace, saying in a whisper, "Neighbor, it would be best if you stayed out of the affair. I saw them on your porch last night after the constable came by. You'll only get hurt. Cromwell won't tolerate any perverts. I know you've a soft heart, but even you heathen Catholics must admit the fate of Sodomites. Think of Lot's wife, Mr. Smith. Think of Leviticus, chapters eighteen and twenty-"

He cut him off, "Yes, John, but think of John, chapter eight, verses one through eleven."

"Well, yes, but are they repentant?"

"I don't recall that our Lord asked if she were repentant, John."

"But, surely, Mr. Smith, since they are perverts. Leviticus, chapter twenty."

"I am aware of the nature of their sin, but I don't recall our guiltless Lord hurling any stones.

"I don't think we can compare an adulterer and a pervert," John whispered fiercely.

"They are part of my flock, John. Think of Luke, chapter fifteen, verses one through seven."

"Perverts," he repeated.

"Yes, perverts, but wayward sheep and your brothers in Christ, nevertheless, whom we must protect."

"Those two?"

"Even them."

John stopped and put a hand on Father Smith's shoulder, stopping him as well. "I see your point, neighbor. I do. Still, it may be you or them, or you as well as them. I don't want to see you get hurt. You're good man, Romanist notwithstanding. I beg you to turn them over and preserve yourself. Think of the rest of your flock."

He paused, looking into John's concerned eyes, touched despite the fact that he had been called a heathen. How he wanted to turn them over and be done with them. He was not comfortable with them in his house. Then, he thought too of Resden's eyes following him. He thought of the flame thrower and the agonized screams of the night before. He wondered if he would soon discover that he must preside over another funeral. Had it been Sean O'Malley killed in the night? Surely someone would have brought news of it already. He was moved to fear, horror, and pity all at once.

"Please," repeated John.

"Neighbor, how blessed I am to have you," he said slowly. "I must do as the Lord commands."

"The Lord commands us to put them to death."

"Does he? Why didn't he stone the woman himself?"

"She repented."

"Did she? It doesn't say that. He said to her, 'Go and sin no more.' It doesn't say that she repented."

"You're impossible."

"I am obstinate for the sake of the Word," he said, smiling. "Thank you for the warning and the alms. You're a good man."

John looked him over anxiously, turned, and walked quickly away.

Father Smith smiled after him and continued down the street. His first stop was in the Irish ghetto. There was a man bedridden with fever who had not worked for some time. He had a family.

The round of almsgiving went on for several hours, and Father Smith was watched by a constable the whole time. He invited the young man to join him, but he was a protestant and kept his distance. Father Smith kept a smile and a cheery wave for him anyway. When the almsgiving rounds were over, he was ready for his lunch. He exited the Italian section and headed back to St. Brendan's. The alms had been given out according to need. He had anointed two newly sick women and one man, and had celebrated and prayed in thanksgiving with a family whose father was up on his feet again. It had been a good morning. Sean O'Malley had not been burned alive. Some drunk sailor, fresh off a boat, had been the unfortunate victim of Constable Resden's zeal.

He prayed for the man as he walked down the busy street. Carts rolled noisily past. People shouted across at one another. The mayor's motorcar rattled by on the next street, backfiring. He shook his head. A pastor and a mayor and a business owner, Mayor Cromwell was a renaissance man of sorts. Constable Resden had been invented and manufactured in his workshop. If only the Mayor had the sensitivity of an artist, Canaan might have been spared some of the puritanical fervor that possessed it. No dancing or gambling was allowed in Canaan. Though all other music was not strictly prohibited, the only songs that were actually sung were hymns. Unmarried persons of the opposite sex could not be alone together, even in public, without a chaperone. Women had to cover their bodies from neck to ankle and cover their hair as well. Unlike the Puritans of colonial days, those in Canaan had even banned the drinking of alcohol. The sole exception to that prohibition was that Father Smith was allowed to offer the sacramental wine during the liturgy of the Eucharist in mass, but only on Sundays.

His reverie was broken by a nearer, louder noise. With its usual clanking and clattering, Constable Resden walked off a side street and stopped in front of him.

"Mr. Smith," it said, its hollow voice booming.

People nearby stopped what they were doing in startlement.

"I... yes," he responded, his heart hammering against his ribs, "Good day to you again, Constable." He avoided its eyes.

"You have been among your parishioners?"

"Yes, I have."

"Have you seen the perverts, Harold Flatly and Earl Stubbs?"

"They were not around," he said. "Would you really expect them to be?" *I'm shaking. I'm actually shaking. Damn this thing.*

"They are somewhere, around," it insisted. "They have not left town. They would have been seen. The bridge and port have been under surveillance.

It leaned in close to him, focusing one red eye on his. Its beetle mandibles clicked together. They were sharp, and they were large enough to go around a man's head. Nearby, everyone who had stopped was hurrying away.

"Very good then. On with your search, I suppose. Good day. I must say an Angelus. It's about noon."

"It is twelve fifteen," said Resden.

"Well, then, I am late. Good day." He edged around the monstrosity and hurried on up the street. This time, he felt he could not refrain from turning and glancing back. He was right. It was watching him. He was relieved shortly to turn a corner and be out of its sight.

When he was nearly back to the church, he changed his mind, and instead went to find Cromwell. It seemed the motorcar had been headed to the meeting hall. He went that way. Perhaps there was a way to convince him to be lenient, to banish in lieu of executing.

The motorcar was there, and Cromwell was on the steps talking with several prominent men of the town. Father Smith approached and waited. After a minute, when they had yet to acknowledge him, he interrupted. "Excuse me, sirs, I must have a word with the mayor when he has a moment."

Cromwell turned to him slowly and looked down, "I'll be done shortly, Smith," he said, and he turned his back on him. Father Smith sat down on the steps and waited, silently praying his angelus. It was another quarter of an hour before Cromwell paid heed again to him. Laughing and saying goodbye at last to the men with whom he had been speaking, the mayor turned and said, "And what may a good Christian do for a Papist today?"

He was used to it, and did not attempt to correct it, but the implication that he was not a good Christian always rankled. He said instead, "Constable Resden has informed me that two wayward members of my flock are wanted men."

"Yes, the Sodomites, Flatly and Stubbs."

"Yes, them."

The Mayor leaned toward him, looming, "Do you know where they are?"

He had an answer ready and spoke without pausing, "Resden is convinced they are still in the town."

"You have not seen them?"

"They were not around when I was distributing alms this morning."

"Very well. I suppose you are fully aware that aiding and abetting them in any way may open you up to the penalty that awaits them?"

"I quite understand," he responded, hoping that he was not showing his anxiety over that very point.

The mayor regarded him sternly then said, "I suppose you have a petition to make?"

"I do concerning their case. If I understand correctly the law of the town-"

The Mayor cut him off, "The Good Book is the law of the town, so you should understand it correctly, Smith. Refresh yourself with Leviticus 18: 22 and 20: 13, if you are unsure." He nodded and turned to go. Somewhere, not far off, the clanging of Resden's limbs on the cobblestones sounded.

"Wait, Cromwell," he said, trying not to be impatient but fearing as he spoke that he sounded so. "Think of other verses besides those. Think of the Gospel of John, chapter eight, verses one through eleven. Think of the Parable of the Prodigal Son in Luke, chapter fifteen. Surely there is room in the teachings of Our Lord for mercy. Do you not distinguish between natural law and cultural law as found in the Old Testament?"

Several steps above by then, Cromwell turned and proclaimed, "Amen, I say to you, until Heaven and Earth pass away, not the smallest letter or the smallest part of a letter will pass from the law.' Matthew 5:18."

From where he stood below, Father Smith replied, "'Let the one who is without sin be the first to throw the stone at her.' John 8: 6. 'Go now and sin no more.' John 8: 11. Surely we must emulate the Lord."

"Are you suggesting that I am a sinner?" asked Cromwell.

"All men are sinners."

"Perhaps that is true of Papists, but here in Canaan, at the High and Holy Tabernacle of the Lord Jesus, we are saved and sinless, and we shall do as the Good Book requires and cast the first stone."

Astounded, Father Smith stared at the man. He stared back down at Father Smith, smiling broadly.

At last, Father Smith asked him, "Is there no way, if they are found, the men could not be sentenced less harshly? Could they not be cast out of the land, as Cain was cast out in Genesis chapter four? The punishment is death for the same crime in Leviticus 24: 17, but Cain was not executed. "

Cromwell regarded him a moment and said, "I'll think on it, but don't be too hopeful. Is there anything else?"

"Thank you. I suppose that's all I came to ask."

"Then go in peace, and pray hard about joining us for true worship on Sunday." The man seemed to think he was being magnanimous.

"I'll be saying mass on Sunday."

"Of course. You Papists are so obstinate in your heresy."

He merely nodded and started to turned away toward St. Brendan's.

"You know, Smith," said the Mayor, as an afterthought, "They probably won't make it to trial. Most don't. The good constable will likely be forced to defend itself."

He stopped mid-turn and looked up again, saying, "Your machine is out of control."

"I don't see that it is out of control," said the Mayor from where he stood at the top of the steps, "but I do see that the criminal element is all but eliminated. Don't you Papists approve of that?"

"We approved of changed hearts, not of corpses."

"They haven't all been killed, mainly just those who resisted arrest."

"And perhaps some were killed with the proper use of force, but surely not all. The constable is largely impervious to harm now and has been for some time."

"The law is the law. He is allowed to use deadly force to defend against deadly force."

"How is it deadly if he is not in danger?"

"Bullets might go astray," said Cromwell with a shrug, "Good day, Smith. Don't be surprised if they end up burned to a crisp. It's the fate of Sodomites anyway, if not in this life, then in the next." He turned and walked into the meeting hall.

Father Smith made his way down the steps and started yet again in surprise. There, across the street, watching him with red eyes was Constable Resden. He was already sweating from the warmth of the day, and he was glad, for he would surely have broken out in one from the presence of the constable. He crossed the street, trying to ignore the hulking machine. As if in answer to his thoughts, Resden said to him as he passed, quoting what he recognized as coming from Deuteronomy chapter thirteen, "Do not look with pity upon him, to spare him or shield him, but kill him. You shall stone him to death because he sought to lead you astray." Its voice boomed hollowly out from its iron body, and a spurt of fire shot a few inches out beyond its mandibles. He hurried away from it, shivers running up and down his spine, and his throat tightening.

Someone on the street laughed. He heard a voice call after him, "Your time is coming, Romanist, and it's about time too."

Someone else shouted, "You can run, but you can't hide."

He picked up the pace, turning a corner as soon as he came to one. The laughter of men followed him. He ran. He did not stop until he was back in the rectory, with the door shut and locked behind him. He was breathing hard, and he was shaking. *Oh, Lord, I am not ready to die. I want to say mass, work in my garden, take care of the spiritual and physical needs of my flock, and retire to a monastery to end my days in prayer and contemplation. Please take this cross from me.*

He realized as he finished the plea that he had sunk to his knees on the floor, still facing the door, with his hands pressed against the wood. He remained in that posture until Harold and Earl came in and found him.

"Having a bad day?" asked Earl in a sneering voice, but Harold came over and helped him up.

"What's happened, Father?" he asked.

"I can't say for sure, but I've had a fright," said Father Smith, rising unsteadily.

"Come to the kitchen and have a drink of water. We'd have fixed lunch, but that would've required the stove being lit and given away that the rectory wasn't empty."

"I'm sorry. Now that I'm here, we can light it."

The house was warm, for all the windows facing the street or neighbors were closed and curtained and only the ones opening on the back garden were open. Still, he found some meat wrapped in parchment that a parishioner had left on the back step, so he lit the oven and proceeded to make a soup. He picked a few vegetables from the garden and found some crackers in the pantry to complete the meal. They worked on the meal in nervous silence. He was glad, for the quiet gave him time to become calm and to think. It was only after they were done that Earl spoke up.

"You told us to burn in Hell, Father. Why are you helping us?"

He looked at them, remembering well how harsh he had been with them, nearly half a year before.

"I warned you of the danger, my sons, but I never wished for you to burn in Hell. I did not say for you to go there; I warned you."

"No, you told us we were going to burn. Don't deny it!"

"I said that you'd burn if you didn't repent. That's the fate of all unrepentant sinners. You're no different. Our injunction is to hate the sin; love the sinner. You know that."

"Well," said Earl, "It makes no difference to me. I don't believe in religion anymore."

"My son, think on what you're saying. Repent. Do you want you and Harold to go to Hell because you find this sin pleasurable now? Make your confession, and sin no more. I'm here, ready to hear you and absolve you."

"Oh, I've thought about it," he responded, sneering yet again, "and I plan to go right on sinning, as you call it, because I like it. There's my confession."

Father Smith regarded him sadly, then looked away out the window. There was quiet before Harold said, as if to fill the silence and somehow make up for his lover's attitude, "Thanks for the meal, Father."

"You're welcome," he said. He was still thinking hard about what to do. He had nothing. The bridge and the waterways were watched. The men could not stay indefinitely in his house without being discovered. He

84

could not turn them over to be killed. The only hope he could see lay in the possibility that the mayor might commute the sentence to banishment.

"We must consider how to help you escape Canaan," he said to them.

"We've been thinking about that too," said Harold.

Earl snorted dismissively.

"If we can't come up with a plan, our only hope is that mayor will be lenient in your sentence."

"It's not the mayor, but the judge," said Harold.

He shook his head, "You know as well as I do that everyone will do as the mayor says, regardless of the supposed powers of their offices, either from their fervor or from their fear. Resden answers to him."

"Well, I don't plan on throwing myself on his mercy," said Earl, "There're easier ways to die."

"We have to find a way to sneak out," said Harold.

"We'd be seen," said Earl.

"We have to try. No one'll help us except Father, and he can't exactly hide us in his pockets and carry us out. We'd need a cart or something. If we had one, we could hide in the back under something."

"I only have the handcart in the garden," said Father Smith.

"You could borrow one," suggested Harold.

"I'm being watched. If I left town, they'd search the cart."

"Then we're your permanent house guests, Father," laughed Earl.

"You don't have to be. I talked to the mayor today."

Earl sputtered.

"Be calm, boy. I didn't give you away. I have done for you as Rahab the Harlot did for Joshua's spies in Jericho and hidden you. I tried to convince him to banish you from the island rather than execute you. He said he would consider it. But for it to work, you'd have to surrender yourselves."

"Well, I'm not considering it, even if he says he is," said Earl, "and I think it's funny that you're playing the harlot for us."

Father Smith rolled his eyes and shook his head, "And I think it's funny that you should be compared to Joshua's spies, but I wasn't going so far with the comparison."

Harold broke in, "No, Father, I don't think it'll work to give ourselves up. Maybe if we can find no other way, and if the Mayor decides on it definitely, but not until then."

"What about disguises?" suggested Earl.

He looked the two men over and said, "I wouldn't know where to begin. I wish, like Rahab, that I had a house built into the city wall so I could lower you down out of a window, but I don't."

"Well, if we can't borrow a cart, or sneak out on foot, maybe we could sneak onto a cart without the driver knowing it," suggested Harold. "Maybe we could slip onto the milk wagon."

"It's too small," said Father Smith, "but the coal wagon might do, or the hay."

"But most of those come into town full and leave empty," said Earl.

Just then, a sudden clanging sounded not far off, and they knew that Resden was near.

"Quiet!" hissed Father Smith.

They froze in their seats, listening hard. The noise stopped just outside the rectory again. They waited, but the noise did not resume. At length, he rose and went the front door to peer out. He paused at the wicket and decided not to open it. What if Resden were there looking in with one great, red eye again? He shuddered and went to a window instead, peaking out through the curtains and shutters. The mechanical monster was there, sitting on its haunches right at his front door, one eye looking straight at the wicket, the other at the window. He jerked back, flicking the curtains closed. *It knows,* he thought, *somehow, it knows.*

He returned to the kitchen and sat with his index fingers to his lips. They watched, gulping, as he pointed toward the front of the rectory. He whispered, "He's right at the front door."

"It won't be long now," said Earl, also whispering, "before he breaks the door and the wall down and comes in after us."

"Stop it, love," said Harold. He turned to Father Smith. "The hay wagon comes in full and leaves empty, and so does the milk wagon, but the coal wagon comes in every Tuesday, laden with coal, drops it all off and leaves again full up with scrap metal and such. We just have to catch it on the way out, slip on and hide under something."

Earl's eyes lit up. "You get gas through the pipes, Father," he said, "but don't some of your neighbor's use coal?"

"But you need to catch it leaving and partly full, my son," he said, urgently putting a reminding finger to his lips.

"Oh, right." Earl lowered his voice again.

"We'll have to watch and wait, love," said Harold, "Someone in the neighborhood will be getting rid of some old scrap, and we'll crawl under it when no one is looking."

"Cozy," said Earl, smiling.

He watched them give each other sly, intimate smiles and shuddered. *What can I do for them? I might save their bodies, but what about their souls? Am I to risk my body for theirs, only to help them to damnation? Have I done enough? They know my mind and the truth of the church, and they reject it. Why did I let them into my house? Why do I not kick them out now? I cannot; Resden would burn them alive on my doorstep. Cromwell is wrong on so many points, but he is right about the path they are on. It leads to fire one way or another. They must get on the right path.*

He glanced toward the front door, though he could not see it for the intervening walls and shuddered for fear rather than disgust. Resden was surely still on his doorstop, watching, listening, smelling for Harold and Earl somehow through its iron receptors.

He looked at his guests again, suddenly, and realized that they had been on the verge of kissing in front of him. They turned their faces aside. Earl looked at him with a smirk. Harold had the decency to look embarrassed, quickly got up, and refilled his cup with water. Father Smith pretended not to have seen, but he rose and paced up and down, trying to focus on when and how they might escape, but letting his thoughts dwell again and again on the disturbing thought that they had probably been kissing each other or worse while he was away. Had they been committing perversions like concupiscent and unsupervised youths, sodomizing each other in his house in defiance of his hospitality and their own God-given nature? He began to fume inwardly. *Any idiot can look at the bodies of two men and know that they do not fit together! What is wrong with them?*

Across the little kitchen, standing by the sink, Harold cleared his throat. Father Smith broke off his train of thought and looked again at his guests. *And yet,* he thought, *they are still two men, flaws notwithstanding, made in the image of God, God's children, wayward though they be, facing a temptation I do not know. I should pity rather than scorn them. They are sheep that I must shepherd as best I can. The rest is up to them.*

"My neighbor, John," he said quietly, for the answer had come to him in that moment, sudden and unbidden, "has been tearing down and rebuilding a shed. When the coal wagon comes through tomorrow, empty, it will almost certainly stop in the alley out back and load up the rubbish there. You have but to wait for that, climb over the garden wall when no one is about, and get into the wagon under something. The wagon'll leave town, and you'll be able to escape. The apple tree should provide enough cover when you go over the wall, and it'll be easier to climb."

They both looked at him hard, considering his words, perhaps weighing them against the anger that he could not entirely hide, wondering if it was a good plan or simply a way to be rid of them. *It is as good a plan as we are likely to conceive,* he thought.

Slowly, Harold nodded his head. Earl's brow was furrowed, but he said nothing.

"You'll have to screw up the nerve to do it is all. I can see no way out that does not involve risk," he told them.

He left them then and went across to the church. He knelt in the first pew and prayed, *I am deeply afraid Lord, and offended on your behalf, I think, but lacking also in your love. I ask you for the grace to carry out your work selflessly.* He crossed himself and began the formal prayer, soon finding comfort in the repetition of sure, good words that took him out of himself.

He was at prayer rather longer than usual, adding a few Rosaries. The light was slanting in long beams through the stained-glass windows on the west side of the sanctuary when he rose. He hadn't realized that there were several people in the back waiting on him. They were parishioners waiting on the sacrament of reconciliation. He found a smile and went to the confessional to hear them one after the other.

The shadows were long, and the sky in the west was aglow with reds when he crossed to the rectory. Something else red was glowing in the shadows across the street when glanced that way. Resden was there, silent, waiting. A thin line of smoke rose from its mouth and snaked into the fading blue above the roofline. He thought he heard its voice but could not make out the words. He merely nodded toward it and continued across the grass.

"Mr. Smith," a voice shouted at him from the other side of the church behind him. He turned. Mrs. Sanford was standing with her fists on her aproned hips. He couldn't make out her expression in the deepening gloom of dusk, but her voice told him all he needed to know.

"Good evening, neighbor," he said, heading her way.

"Don't 'good evening' me, Smith," she shouted, "you damned papist. It's a crying shame that you're allowed to call yourself a Christian, what with sodomites in your congregation and those wicked extra books in your Bible. What's wrong with Catholics that they end up that way?"

"Catholics are as human and fallible as any other believers," he offered, reasonably.

"It's disgusting. You should have turned them out and handed them over to the law."

"Their actions excommunicated them, Mrs. Sanford. I have not mediated the sacraments for them since I discovered their sin and unrepentance. I am, however, not obliged to hand them over to their deaths." He kept a smile on his face though he saw her frown and the spittle that escaped her lips as she spoke to him. A shiver ran up his spine. A glance over his shoulder told him that one of Resden's eyes had tracked him and were watching.

"Ha!" she scoffed.

"Mrs. Sanford, are we not obliged to seek out the lost sheep and try to bring them home?"

"I don't know which passage you refer to, but it's probably only in the Papist Bible. My Bible doesn't mean filthy Sodomite when it talks about lost sheep. Sodom got the fire and brimstone, didn't it? You'd know that if you were properly educated." She spat at his feet and laughed.

He swept the hat of his head and nodded politely, saying, "Good evening and God bless, Mrs. Sanford."

"You don't get to bless me," she said, spitting again before turning her back on him.

He walked back in front of the church crossing himself before the doors, trying to ignore the deep, red glare coming from the shadows across the street. The west was a blaze of rosy fire. He concentrated on that instead. As he opened the door, he heard again the whirring, clanking murmur from deep in Resden's bowels. This time, he thought he made out the words. "Fire and brimstone." He stood with the door half opened and was ashamed of his quavering voice as he asked it, "What did you say?"

Resden rose, hulking and apelike, its hands on the pavement before it. "Fire and brimstone for Sodom and Gomorrah," it intoned hollowly. A little gout of flame shot out between its mandibles.

He entered and shut the door, suddenly breathing hard. "It knows," he muttered, crossing himself then locking it. "Somehow, it knows."

He put his hat on its peg and went to the kitchen. Passing through the living room, he saw that Harold was already asleep. The kitchen was empty, and he heard snores from Earl in the other room. He went to the pantry for food, stared into it for several minutes, realized he could not eat, and retired to his evening prayers and bed soon after. He lay awake staring into the sky outside his window. The stars swung slowly by in their glory. He drifted off from time to time, but all in the house were awakened more than once by the clanging fists and feet of Resden on the cobblestones in the night.

When morning came, Father Smith was barely rested. He rose and went through his morning rituals then crossed to the church to say mass. Against his own better judgement, he looked out into the street where Resden had been the evening before. It was there again, one red eye tracking him as he entered the church. He dressed in his vestments and went to the altar a stuttering mess, barely able to remember the rite. Several of his parishioners asked him if he were well. Several others asked him if he knew what had happened to Harold and Earl, wanting to know if the rumors were true. He told them to pray for the men. No one argued, but they warned him to be careful because the constable was watching in case the men tried to go to him for help.

"Better for Harold and Earl if Resden sees me rather than them, I should think," he told them cheerfully.

Last of all was Earl's mother. She came to him careworn and distressed. "What am I to do, Father," she whispered, "I know the rumors are true, I know it. He's never told me, but I know my boy's a pervert."

He patted her hand. "God forgives all, so long as there is repentance. Pray for your son, Maude. Pray for him and for Harold."

He spent a little more time comforting her, though he gave no indication that he knew anything about their whereabouts. She went away tearful, anyway, and he crossed back to the rectory the back way so as to see as little of the constable as possible. He still had to go to the door for the milk delivery though, and Resden was there on his doorstep again when he looked out through the wicket.

"The trail is still strong here," stated the constable when he finally worked up the nerve and opened the door. "Have Harold Flatly and Earl Stubbs been here, Mr. Smith?"

He looked at the mechanical monster blankly for a moment then said, "I... I haven't seen them at my door since last you asked, Constable. Pardon me; you're sitting on my paper."

It rose in a loud creaking and a whirring of gears. He took his paper, the milk, and a loaf of bread some kind parishioner had left for him.

They were up, sitting in the kitchen when he entered. He tried to give a cheery, "Good morning," but it came out a squeak. To his surprise, Earl said, "It does that to me too, Father. I'm scared to death of it. If we had no way out, I'd hang myself to avoid it."

Turning quickly, Father Smith found himself hissing at him, "Say no such thing. Better to suffer wrong than to do it. For the sake of your soul, Earl..."

"Do we have souls?" Earl scoffed. "I've never touched one, have you?"

"Yes," he answered, fervently, leaning in across the table to speak close to him. "Yes, we have souls. You know it, if you think about it. We have thought. That is how we are like God. He is the author of Reason. That is the image of him, the ability to choose between the path of righteousness and the path of unrighteousness. Don't you know that in your heart of hearts? Isn't the law written on our hearts and tongues as Moses said it was?"

Taken aback, Earl leaned away from him frowning and said, "I've never touched one, Father, sorry. My heart just pumps blood. That's all I know for sure about it."

"Then look to your doubts. Look to them and think on them. You know that your body and your lover's are uncomplementary to one another. You know that your seed is meant for a woman's body, that it has a purpose you deny in your physical relationship with a man. Think on it. We take part in and continue God's creation of us through our union with a woman, and that is holy when it is done in the bounds of matrimony. What you and Harold do is a waste, a perversion."

"I can't change what I am," he said, rising from his chair. Harold, leaning against a counter, regarded them both with a pitying expression but said nothing.

"But, you can. That's what differentiates us from beasts. We can control our impulses. Reason guides instinct. In school, you were taught the classics by Sister Ruth. Remember Plato. You quoted him as a boy."

"Well I don't remember it anymore!" Earl shouted. He was breathing heavily. Sweat was beading up on his skin. Father Smith straightened and relaxed his shoulders consciously.

"For Christ's sake, don't shout," said Harold urgently.

"Just think about it when you are calmer, my son," said Father Smith.

"I'm not your son." He turned and walked from the room.

"For Christ's sake?" asked Father Smith, looking significantly at Harold.

Harold smiled and said, "Old habits of expression die hard."

"Die is a word on which you should dwell, my son. Do you want to die in this state of sin?"

"I don't believe in sin anymore, Father. I think we make our own meaning in a meaningless world."

Father Smith shook his head, "What sophistry."

Harold shrugged and left the room too. Father Smith sank into a chair and put his face in his hands. *I don't know what to say or how to say it, Lord.*

They waited in uncomfortable silence, exchanging only what words aroused no conversation.

"Please pass the butter."

"Of course, my son."

"Excuse me."

"Thank you."

It was a tense morning moving slowly into a tense afternoon.

Father Smith spent a lot of time in the back garden, keeping an ear out for the coal wagon to arrive next door at John's house, aware the whole time that he had heard no sound of Resden leaving his post out front across the street. On the other side of the church, he could see Mrs. Sandford working in her back garden too. She seemed to be in the middle of quite a project. He worried and waited.

The sound of the wagon finally arriving in the middle of the afternoon startled him. He glanced around, saw that Mrs. Sanford was still in her garden at work and walked back into the kitchen.

Harold and Earl had gathered their things and were standing anxiously by the door.

"Was that it, Father?" Harold asked.

"Yes, but wait until I've distracted Mrs. Sanford across the way. Keep an eye out and go when I have her looking away."

"Right," said Harold.

He turned and went back out, crossing the garden. He wanted to refrain from looking out into the street but did so anyway. Resden was there, and a red eye, dimmed by the sunshine, was glaring across the street at him. He crossed the church yard and walked up to Mrs. Sanford's gate where he knocked politely. She turned and started in surprise.

"Neighbor," he observed, "your garden's always in bloom. How do you do it?"

"What?" she asked.

"Your lovely garden, neighbor. How do you do it?"

She stared at him a moment, perplexed. Letting himself in, he walked over and extended his hand. "It's a beautiful day, isn't it?"

"It is. God is good," she said, frowning at him. They shook. She took her hand away as quickly as she could.

"All the time, indeed," he responded. He drew her attention to a bed of flowers behind her and asked, "Are those morning glories?"

She turned as well. "No. Don't Papists know anything? Morning glories climb. These are Asters."

Now men, he thought, *now while she is distracted. Into the apple tree and over the wall as you are able.*

He did not look behind him but asked, "Oh, I thought they were morning glories because they're blue. So, these are Asters, you say?"

"I say it because they are."

"And those lilies," he began, pointing again because she was turning to look at him.

"Yeah. What about 'em?"

"When should I thin mine?"

"Thin 'em?"

"Yes. How do I know when they're growing too thickly?"

94

"Eh. Instinct I guess. They just look too thick. See here, they need to be so far apart or they choke."

While she was distracted, he glanced back and saw Harold and Earl disappearing into the lower branches of the apple tree.

"I see," he said to her. "I was wondering what the distance should be. You've explained it marvelously. Thank you."

"Okay," she said, turning and staring at him. They stood thus awkwardly a moment, and then he said, "Well, I must be attending to something. Thank you for your time." He nodded and left, closing her gate behind him.

"Get saved, sinner," she shot after him.

He trotted back across the church grounds to his back garden and passed under the tree, pausing as if to examine it. He looked up. Harold was just slipping over the wall. Earl was not visible.

"Thank you," Harold whispered as he dropped out of sight.

"Godspeed," he whispered in return.

He waited in a terrible state for a minute or two, listening for a sound that would tell him anything about their fate. Before his mind's eye, he saw them again as boys making their first communions, kneeling at the rail, receiving he Eucharist on their tongues. He crossed himself and prayed fervently. Minutes passed. He heard no sound that might indicate they had been discovered. Done with his prayers, he wondered what to do. Not knowing what else he could, he turned to go into the house. A movement caught his eye. Mrs. Sanford was standing at her gate, hands on her hips, staring at him. He waved cheerily and went into the house. *Surely she has not seen anything to arouse suspicions?*

He went about opening his windows to air the place out. From one, again, he saw her there, standing, staring. *What is she doing? Please tell me she's not at last using the intelligence God gave her, not for such a purpose, please Lord.*

He waved again, then stepped back into the shadowed interior and looked out at her, considering. She stood in the sunlight, surely blinded to his presence. Then suddenly something moved her to action.

"I saw the Sodomites," she shouted running toward the street. She disappeared behind the church., but he could hear her voice. "They were in the Papist's apple tree in his garden. He's hiding them,"

Help them, Lord! He prayed and rushed to the door. He exited into the street as she appeared from behind the church. Resden leapt from where it had stationed itself and clattered to meet Mrs. Sanford. Breathlessly, she pointed at the rectory garden. "There, constable, in the tree!" Resden whirled around, clattering and then dashed thundering that way. Desperately and without thought, for he hadn't enough time to think of what to say, Father Smith threw himself in Resden's path. The mechanical monstrosity did not swerve. One, great, red eye came close. A gout of fire licked about its mandibles. Father Smith gulped. His upraised hands stung on the impact. Resden's chest plate struck his head. Pain shot through him. He tumbled in the street as the iron mass paced over him swiftly. All went black.

When he came to, he was still in the street, and he felt numb. John Jones was kneeling beside him and leaning over him.

"No, don't move," John said.

He immediately tried to sit up anyway. John put his hands on him and held him down. "I was in the last war, neighbor, and I saw men injured as you are. If you move, you could make it worse."

He stared, confused. He didn't hurt much. Only his head was in pain.

John said, "I'd say you've broken your back. Can you feel this?"

"Feel what?" he asked.

"Your back's broken." John shook his head.

It didn't make sense. He lay there in the hot street, aware of the onlookers, hearing Mrs. Sanford talking nonstop to those around her about how the Sodomites had been hiding with him all along. The clanging steps of Resden were coming back his way.

"What did it find?" he asked John. How weak his voice was.

John glanced up then bent low and whispered, "Nothing, I think. I saw them climb into the wagon, but I said nothing. The driver doesn't know they're there. You've helped them, but look what it's cost you! I warned you."

"Thank you, Lord," he murmured, shutting his eyes.

There was quiet except for the sound of Resden coming close.

"No. Don't move him," said John, "I think you already broke his back."

"I am making an arrest," said Resden, its hollow voice booming over the noise of the crowd.

"But you could kill him!"

"By the law, he must be taken to the jail," stated Resden.

Father Smith felt the constable's great, steel paws slip under him. He felt something snap inside him. He opened his eyes and saw one great, red eye looking into his as his lungs and heart stopped. "Where are the perverts?" it asked him.

He could not have responded had he been so inclined. In his last thoughts, he offered another Glory Be.

The Church of Five Saints
Koji A. Dae

A lanky lad, Lorenzo had always seemed the type to blow away if too strong a wind struck him—which we had plenty of on Heika. Powerful dust storms made women shield their eyes with thick shawls and men stumble on the streets. Yet Lorenzo, whose scruffy beard was the most substantial part of him, walked in a straight line to the Church of Five Saints every Sunday morning.

In those days, myself and Father Jesper maintained the church. I still hosted morning mass, even though Lorenzo was the only member of the congregation. I kept the curtains drawn to one side and waited for the etched metal doors to slide open and Lorenzo's slim shadow to appear. Fear gripped me in the moments before six o'clock. Would this be the week he gave up? But it never was. He entered the sanctuary and took a spot near the center, kneeling and crossing himself before sliding into the pew.

If anyone else had been there to see his dedication, they would have considered him pious, but no one would have labeled him extreme. Certainly no one made claims of insanity as they do now.

Most days, he left the church as soon as the mass concluded. He didn't seem to be in a rush, simply strolled from the sanctuary, through the heavy doors, and down the black stone steps. He wove his way through the first tourists of the day, buffeted by them rather than the wind.

About a year ago, he paused at the door, milky light streaming through the crack he had made. "Father, why do you cater to the tourists?"

I glanced at the tapestries rolled over cold, red stones and nodded at the empty sanctuary. "Who would you rather I focus my attention on?"

Lorenzo's nod was slow and heavy, as if he inhaled my words and acquiesced to my meaning on the exhale. I expected him to argue, but he cloaked himself in his usual silence and lost himself in the gathering crowd. They were already stalling in front of the massive facade, taking pictures with their smarts from every angle, trying to get a glimpse of the church that hadn't yet been posted to the nets. It was a fool's task. Every inch of the crimson and black building had been snapped up and delivered years ago.

After that, he asked me a question every week, always a single question, and always one that bristled the stubbly hair beneath my collar and made me clench my teeth.

"Father, how much do you make from the tourists?" As if their money were dirty, because it didn't pass through a tithing plate.

"Enough to keep this church in good repair, as a testament to our Lord." My answer was true. The building—one of the first built on Heika—was one of the few with neither sand nor sun damage. It towered over the low buildings of the surrounding city, a testament to something. I just wasn't sure if it was still proclaiming the greatness of God. Visitors thought of it as a relic of Earth, not home to the living God.

With each question, he opened the door a little wider and raised his voice a little louder.

"Do you think they know God?"

"Maybe. In these times, many people worship in their own ways." But he knew the truth as well as I did—most people in the outer reaches of the galaxy thought God was only in charge of Earth, not the new planets.

As if a fount had sprung, I found myself thirsting for his questions. Anyone to test my knowledge and, more importantly, share my faith. When he was quiet, I lingered longer than necessary, waiting for this week's inquiry as silently as he waited for the communion wafer to touch his tongue.

After two months of these questions, I invited him to the rectory for a cup of tea. His steely blue eyes held me, and his head tilted to the side as if he didn't quite understand my invitation.

"It's no trouble," I assured him. "It would be nice to chat with a true believer."

He shrugged in a noncommittal way and stood in front of me. I took it as a yes and led him around the side of the church to the base of the bell tower where I lived with Father Jesper. Father Jesper was at the ticket office, selling admission to tourists from around the solar system and arranging private tours with our new tour operator, so he would not intrude. Not that I minded his company, but I wanted Lorenzo to myself, just for a morning.

He stayed close behind me, almost as if he were afraid of the gathering tourists despite the way his six-foot frame towered above them. When the door closed shut behind us, he gulped, as if he had been holding his breath.

"Not much for crowds?" I asked as I hit the button on the kettle.

He took in the bare room—a table with a bench on either side, a wall of cabinets, a small sink. It was a humble kitchen with none of the church's external grandeur.

"I work in the mines. There are crowds there." His voice had an even softer timbre than the one he kept in the sanctuary, and I had to lean close to make out his words. "But these people, these crowds, are different. They move without looking where they're going, without seeing anything or anyone."

The water in the kettle bubbled, and the button popped. I got two mugs down from the cupboard and put in tea bags. "You're perceptive Lorenzo."

"Your standards are low, Father Martin."

I bit the inside of my cheek and turned away. But I soon realized it wasn't meant as an insult, just another observation. He thought I was comparing him to the hundreds of people who tramped through the church every day, taking pictures on their smarts and talking too loudly in sacred spaces. He was right. Who else did I have to compare him to?

"If I may, how were you introduced to the faith?" I handed him a mug. He wrapped his slender, cracked fingers around it and pulled it close to the edge of the table.

"My mother." His always far-away gaze grew even more distant, and I remembered the way he came to church

100

early once a month to light a candle. He shook his head and took a sip of tea. "Are there stairs to the top of the bell tower?"

"Would you like to see?" A picturesque view of the city was the least I could offer him after opening such a raw wound. "The stairs are steep and narrow, but if you work in the mines, you should manage just fine."

We abandoned our tea, and I led him through the back room to a manual door. It took some prying to open—the bells were automated, and no tours went up the ten floors to the top of the square tower. The walls were so grimy I left slick trails where my fingers brushed against them as we wound our way up.

Lorenzo said nothing, but his breath reached my ears, amplified by my blood rushing in my ears.

Another manual door waited for us at the top of the tower, and I pried it open. It was a clear day. We could see the edges of the city and the first caverns of the mines in the distance. Below us, hundreds of tourists milled about, snapping photos and buying trinkets.

"They look like ants," he noted with the twitch of a half-smile.

"Do you know why the towers are built so high?" I propped my elbows on the stone ledge and let my chin rest in my hands.

"So people would know the greatness of God?" Lorenzo mimicked my posture.

"Sure. That's one reason. And probably why the Five Saints made a law that no building could be erected higher than the tower. Not that such a law was needed. This height is insane on a planet like Heika. But I think there is a different reason. When a person looks up, when they raise their head, they feel hope and happiness. That is the gift these towers give God's children."

He leaned further over the railing, and I fought the urge to pull him back from the edge. "But they don't look up. They angle their phones and look only to the screens."

I clapped my hand on his muscular shoulder. "And they are miserable. But me and you, Lorenzo, we know to look up."

He gave a weak, watery smile. I wasn't practiced in delivering individual counsel, so I couldn't be sure if my message of hope had hit home or not. But his shoulders seemed a little less slumped as he bid me farewell after reaching the bottom of the stairs.

The next week, he was late to mass. I waited for him, but the door refused to slide open to reveal his lean frame. Eventually I came out into the sanctuary and stood in the silence of solitude, wondering if I had overstepped my boundaries and frightened the poor boy away.

I opened the door to see if I might glimpse him hurrying up the steps, but the most unusual sight greeted me. A group of several people was clustered together near the steps. This, in itself, was not unusual, but they were looking up, pointing. Their smarts were down at their sides, forgotten.

"Call security," someone suggested. Their smarts still hung at their sides.

"Is he going to jump?" a woman's voice quivered above the din.

My gaze followed their fingers, up the sloping side of the church, over to the bell tower.

An unmistakably human form hung suspended from the uppermost edge of the tower. I squinted and could make out a contraption of ropes holding a bare-chested man around his middle, not just any man, Lorenzo.

"Have you called security yet?" a voice whispered from behind me.

I whirled to find Father Jesper at my sleeve. "No, not yet. I know him. Let me talk to him. I'm sure this is a misunderstanding."

Father Jesper's eyes flitted over the crowd. "Be careful. This could kill tourism if things go wrong."

Kill tourism? It could kill a lot more than tourism. I gritted my teeth but nodded. "I'll be discreet."

Adrenaline coursed through my veins and pushed me up the steps. I no longer felt stooped as I flew up the smooth stone surface. I forced myself to slow down and take a deep breath before opening the door to the balcony.

"Lorenzo," I called softly.

His feet were braced against the wall, and the ropes that held his chest were tied to a central pillar of the bell tower. His hand gripped an end of the rope so tightly his knuckles turned white. His gaze remained fixed on the crowd gathering below.

"Lorenzo, what are you doing?"

"Don't come closer, Father. If I pull this rope, I will fall." His voice held the same low, unemotional mumble he asked his Sunday questions in.

"I won't come close. But Lorenzo, tell me why you're doing this."

He licked his lips, already dry and cracking from the constant breeze. The wind picked up enough to stir a fine layer of the red dust around the crowd below. "They're looking up."

The dust almost concealed the crowd below, but he was right. The people were craning their necks back to see Lorenzo suspended from the bell tower.

"I suppose they are." A smile cracked my dry lips. "Now, you've made your point. You can come down."

He shook his head, and his entire torso swayed with the movement. I jumped towards him, but stopped myself before touching him. "Not yet. Now, I'll be another news story. Another picture to swipe through on their smarts. Not a lasting change."

"But Lorenzo, it's not your job to make a lasting change. That kind of change has to come from within. Not forced by a vulgar display."

He looked over at me. The wind swirled so hard I could barely see his face, and he had to shout to me. "It might not be my job, but if you and I are the last believers, who will remind them that God belongs on Heika as much as He does on Earth?"

Who indeed?

My smart buzzed in my pocket. "Lorenzo, I'm going to step inside. Don't do anything. Just wait."

Father Jesper's pinched face appeared bright on the screen in the dim, muffled silence of the bell tower. "You've got to get him down. A storm's coming in."

"I know. It's already bad up here. But he isn't budging."

"Then we have to call security."

Security showed up ten minutes later. Four guards in the standard gray suits of Heika. They gathered in the bell tower and spoke in hushed whispers, asking me various questions about Lorenzo's situation and motivation.

"Maybe you should talk to friends. Family. They might have a better idea than me. I've barely spoken to him," I said.

They had already completed a facial scan from below, though, and Lorenzo had no friends or family, only the church, and me.

One security officer pulled his visor down and stepped outside into the roaring wind. He came back a minute later, dusting dirt from his shoulders and shaking his head. "He seems secure, despite the storm. But we'll have to wait it out. I don't want to risk him pulling that rope."

We waited. Even after the storm passed, and we could edge out to talk with Lorenzo, all we could do was wait. Whenever one of us got too close, he would grip the rope tight and threaten to pull it.

Father Jesper called me from below. He held his smart up so I could see the crowd that had gathered. Hundreds of people, tourists and locals in the black mine suits, gaped up at Lorenzo strung up above them. "You need to come down, Father Martin."

"I'm needed here," I whispered.

"There are people asking for mass. It has been years since I have celebrated mass. Surely, you are better equipped."

"Mass? Now?"

He shrugged. "They are worried. Or inspired. Or something."

I went down and held a short liturgy of the word. The congregation was small compared to the crowd gathered outside, and many of the members spent the time glancing back at the door as if they might miss out on something. But they were there, at least half-listening.

I returned to the bell tower to tell Lorenzo.

"How's he doing?" I asked the security. They hid from the sweltering sun behind the cool walls of the tower.

"Not well," one of the security said. "The sun and wind sucks water from the human body. He needs to come in soon or else he might..."

I relayed the information to Lorenzo.

His eyes drooped, and his voice was scratchy. "I can't come down, Father. Not yet."

"But you succeeded. There were people in mass."

"I saw. Not enough."

"Can I get you some water at least?"

"No. Don't come near me."

As night neared, his skin blistered. He clung to his rope, refusing to let anyone near. His breath came shallow, and he nodded off. Each time his head fell, he jerked it back up with such force I feared for his life.

Below, more people gathered. They settled onto the paved walkway and stared up at Lorenzo's limp body against the dual moons. A few took out their smarts, but instead of snapping photos, they turned on the screens and set the devices beside them until a glittering blanket spread out below us.

"It's like a sea of stars above and below," Lorenzo murmured. "Do you think they believe?"

If I said yes, would he come down?

"No. But they might. You've given them that reminder. Come in now."

He remained, floating in streaks of silver light throughout the night.

As the sun peeked over the distant horizon, he bid me to conduct mass. Blood dripped from his cracked lips, and his voice barely reached my ears.

"Come with me."

"No." He coughed, sputtering and fumbling with the edge of the rope. "I want to see them go in."

They did go in—so many that they filled the sanctuary and barely left room to kneel. My voice shook as I recited the liturgy of the word. My hands trembled as I lifted the Eucharist. The silence was too thick. We were all waiting.

For a scream. A thump. A crowd gasping.

Clapping? Roaring cheers?

The doors burst open. "They've got him down."

105

I rushed out with the rest of the congregation and shouldered through the bodies to the bell tower. The steps took my breath from me, and when I burst through the door at the top, I couldn't speak.

Lorenzo lay on his back, his eyes closed. His chest didn't move.

A security officer shook her head. "I'm sorry, Father. We caught him before he fell, but he was too weak. He died."

I fell to my knees and placed my forehead to his clammy cheek.

Now, you are trying to say he was insane, that it was some desperate act for personal acknowledgment. You're saying he committed suicide and must be incinerated. I know the accusations, but the undeniable fact is that people look up. They put away their smarts. They bask in God's hope. They enter The Church of Five Saints to pray instead of document. These are things Lorenzo gave to them. You don't have to call him a martyr, but you have to know the truth.

Black Dimension
Roy Gray

"It started with an idle thought." Mark peered through the glass of the isolation unit. "What happens if you travel at the speed of light?"

"Time stops?" Susan Polder answered straight to camera.

"For travellers it seems the distance shrinks to virtually nothing." Mark faced the camera inside the unit this time.

Suse had flicked her hair back while off camera. "Einstein?"

"Yes, he showed what happens when you travel at light speed."

"The famous twin paradox."

That was for the audience Mark thought. "Yes, but that's special relativity. His general relativity was more complex. Recent theories suggest we might have ten spatial dimensions with all but three rolled up to almost nothing."

"Ten dimensions! Seven rolled up to almost nothing!" Suse smiled to camera.

"Yes, difficult to conceive, but those dimensions are too small to notice, invisible to our senses and instruments. You need a graphic." Mark said. "It's tricky to explain without."

"We'll find one," Suse paused. "Rolled up? "

"Well, Suse, imagine those extra dimensions as infinitely-long, tiny tubes with diameters smaller than an atom. Then imagine that everything we see is attached to these tubes and continuously circles around them. That movement is so tiny we can't see an effect with our best instruments. However, in the very tiny, early universe, just after the big bang, everything was moving at light speed and all the dimensions, or tubes if you like, were the same size, including our three normal dimensions; forward/backward, sideways and up/down. As the universe evolved, slow-moving matter appeared. At that point, our three dimensions expanded, or unrolled, but the others stayed miniscule or, as physicists say, compactified." Mark looked anxiously through the glass, knowing how difficult it was to understand, but carried on when Suse stayed silent. "I speculated that accelerating something to high speed collapses the dimension, or rolls it up again. Then I wondered if we could slow down so much that one or more of the seven compact dimensions would unroll or open up. That was my idle thought and my downfall."

"Slow down? This chair here is perfectly still, but it's not opened a new dimension." Suse patted the arm of her chair.

"That's just the point; nothing is still: the Earth is spinning, it orbits the sun, the sun is orbiting the galactic centre, and the galaxy is streaming towards the Great Attractor. All those motions need to be taken into account and cancelled out to try seeing a new dimension." Mark waved his arms, simulating the various directions and spins.

"But you couldn't fling anything out into space at anywhere near the speed you need to do that, and what about the direction? How was it even possible to calculate the path?" Suse asked.

Mark remembered it being a complex calculation...

*   *   *

Mark counted 15 sites and databases then saved the history file. Good old IAU. He mentally thanked the astronomers for their superb databases. The saved details would be his references when, or if, he corrected himself, he wrote the paper. Now he had a figure and it looked reasonable, so could he do the experiment? *Coffee first,* he thought, stretching. The lab was quiet, 7 pm. No one else about as he walked to the drinks machines. The cold drinks coolers' humming flooded the corridor until he set the coffee dispenser into action. He returned to the lab cursing the overfull cup of hot coffee and blew on his semi scalded fingers once it was safely down on his desk.

He found accurate longitude and latitude data for the laboratory and factored it into his calculation. *Now let's*

108

check the mass spec, he thought, saving the figures. Coffee still too hot, he picked a laser ranger from the lab bench and walked over to the clean lab. In the antechamber he put on a coat, overshoes and cap, entry keyed his ID and went through. The university's time-of-flight secondary ion mass spectrometer system, and a faint scent of ozone, filled the small sealed lab annex. He checked the display, everything normal. It was running a calibration with oxygen 18/16 ratios, meaning his last sample was finished with results filed. He unlocked the safe, ID again, donned his gloves, unwrapped some sterile tweezers, removed the test sample from the mass spec, returned it to the safe, took the next sample out, placed it in the mass spec and started the vacuum, outgas cycle. He re-locked the safe, which was full of NASA supplied Mars Lander return samples for isotope abundance measurements, and updated the log.

His drink would be ready now but instrument time was valuable. He couldn't afford to miss slots if he wanted to complete his thesis in reasonable time. He used the laser ranger to take the measurements he needed of the mass spec's location. Now he had the data to see if his unauthorised experiment was feasible.

Back in the now coffee scented main lab, the drink was cool but, despite that, he drank it all grimacing only at the last dregs. By then he had transferred the ranger data and added it to the drawings of the mass spec. Now he could relate the ion trajectories in the Mass Spec to longitude and latitude and thence to his astronomical data.

By ten pm, after two more coffees, he completed his calculation and it looked possible. Raising the north end of the ToF-SIMS, so tilting the instrument to an angle of 4°, allowed the Earth's orbit and spin to bring the mass spec into the correct orientation for a few milliseconds in about four months, at 3:23:12 am on June 14 to be precise. So, he could accelerate the primary ions up to the right velocity and, at the critical moment, in the right direction. No need to fling anything into space, no need to achieve the exact conditions. Even relativistic effects are detectable well below light speed. The overall errors seemed reasonable, direction within a 5-degree cone angle, vector within 10%. By monitoring the secondary ion spectra he could check for unexpected effects from other dimensions.

During his four month wait Mark continued his isotope measurements and thesis while he ran tests to recalibrate targets, establish good baselines, evaluate errors and ensure detection of any effects from opening new dimensions. To raise his chances of success, he made sure the real test covered a range of vectors, values for angle and velocity...

*   *   *

"So tell us about 14 June?" Suse interrupted.

"I succeeded all too well," Mark sighed, "though at the time ...

*   *   *

For four months he had set precedents for working late, excusing it with the need to get good statistics with fully vacuum-conditioned samples. So the building was silent, apart from the hum of assorted fans. Now with seconds to go, his special target was in place and the instrument's display showing everything as standard, the ions were coursing their normal paths. Suddenly the spectra began to change. *Wow! Nobel Prize here I come*, but then the lab's radiation alarms sounded, and a series of brilliant blue flashes set his head ringing. Then, recognising their colour, his heart sank. Startled, he turned to the alarm and to the sensor that triggered it. Instinctively he knew this was bad. If the flashes were Cerenkov radiation they must have happened inside his eyes, and that was far too close for comfort. He muted the alarm wondering if his experiment was the cause. Radiation levels were back near normal, slightly raised perhaps. Was the ozone smell stronger? Usually he didn't notice it after a few minutes. Puzzled he returned to the mass spec display. He tabbed through the results on the screens, yes there was an effect, the spectra had changed, something had happened, but what?

The phone rang. "Night Lodge 'ere. A radiation alarm just lit up on our board. What's 'appening?"

Mark had keyed loudspeak. "Hello, Lab 34 B, Mark Carrera here. Sorry, a fault, I think. Everything looks OK,

110

now. I'm not working with radioactive materials. I'm checking. I'll call back."

"Ah, Mark, it's Armul here. Yes, you're the only one signed in. All night job again? OK, got to check. George is on his way up."

"Right, tell George I'm in the clean lab. Tell him he can knock on the window to save him changing."

"Oh, in the 'ole, are you? I'll tell 'im."

"OK" Mark switched the phone off, returned to the mass spec and began to tab through the spectra displays. A change was obvious through the experiment. The initial constant set of four main elements had dropped to three, two and one with increasing rapidity. This was followed by a blank period, with nothing detected, then a strong seven-element spectrum and, finally, a return to the original spectrum. A spike pattern, as though the primary ion energy had reduced to zero, disappeared altogether for a millisecond and then returned at the full 50 kv. The whole event lasted less than ten milliseconds. The times, spike and radiation alarm coincided precisely. There was no reason for a gap in the secondary ion stream so what had happened? The primary ion pulse generation had continued as programmed throughout. The source had cycled correctly through the raster and voltage sweep required, when combined with the Earth's motion, to cover his planned angular and ion velocity ranges.

Mark heard a knock at the porthole, the small round window between the clean room and main laboratory. He switched the speakerphone to intercom, "That you George?"

"Too lazy to get up are you?"

"It's well past bedtime, and I don't want to block your view. You are checking an alarm," Mark answered.

"A rad alarm not a fire. You'd better turn the lights off so I can see if you glow in the dark." George laughed at his own joke.

"OK." Mark doused the lights and looked over at George's silhouette against the outer lab through the porthole. "Happy now? Can I switch on again?"

"Yeah, only joking, it's a long night." George muttered. "No wonder they call that lab the black hole. I don't know how you can stand being in there so long. I'll reset the alarm log and then leave you to it. Don't forget to sign out when you go. G'night." The light from the outer lab streamed in as he left.

'Black hole' suddenly seemed an ominous nickname for the almost windowless lab Mark thought, realising that one explanation for his strange results would be that the ions had suddenly become very small and dense. He had made and calibrated a seven-layer deep target as the source of secondary ions. These were sputtered from the target and identified at the detector by their mass and time of flight. He had started with the primary ions set to sputter material from levels 1 to 4 of the target into the secondary ion beam. Anything affecting the primary beam energy, timing or direction would change the mix of secondary ions entering the detector. Increased beam energy would show up as atoms from deeper layers, but a reduction would leave only surface layer atoms to be sputtered from the target and simplify the resulting spectrum.

He remembered a theory that the gravitational force may be a result of leakage from the compacted dimensions. In this theory only a fraction of the total gravitational force was experienced in normal space-time. Perhaps that was true. Suppose one of the compact dimensions carried the full force. If he had opened that dimension perhaps his primary ions had been collapsed to high-density, compact objects. They would shift like darts through smoke and pass through his target without causing any disturbance but, if some had not fully collapsed that would explain the deep element sputtering.

Mark turned the lights on again and looked at the mass spec. If particles could pass straight through the target they could go straight through the casing, out into the lab. Suddenly he felt sick with foreboding. He had been sitting with his head in their path. The Cerenkov radiation, if that was what he had seen, could have resulted from a pulse of high energy particles passing through his eyes, but the beam would not go anywhere near the radiation alarm. Tiny black holes evaporate via gamma radiation. A scintillation counter could test that and he knew where they were kept.

*   *   *

"Cerenkov particles?" Suse asked. "Should you explain?"

"Cerenkov radiation," Mark corrected. "In a vacuum nothing can go faster than light but light slows down when it goes through water or glass. So a fast particle can outpace light under water or in glass. When that happens you see a distinctive blue glow. This is like the shock wave, or sonic boom, heard when aircraft travel faster than sound. Eyeballs are full of water so, if a fast particle passes through, you may see a blue flash."

Mark paused, but Suse stayed silent. He carried on. "When I fetched the scintillation counter I found several sources of low level gamma radiation. One of them was my head."

"So what had happened..." Suse prompted

"Gravity seems strong because masses can be so overwhelmingly large. Physicists actually regard the gravitational force as weak compared with the electromagnetic force. One possibility is the gravitational force leaks from the compacted dimensions, and only a fraction of the total gravitational force is experienced in our familiar world. My results seem to show that this force leaks from only one of the compact dimensions, the one I opened. Gravity is very strong there, so strong I called it the black dimension."

"Black like black hole?"

Mark nodded sadly. "Somehow, within the few microseconds of my test, I must have hit the exact combination to open the black dimension. Then the ions passing through the mass spec were collapsed to the point that some were converted into tiny black holes. First the interactions between target and ions diminished as the dimension opened. Collapsed ions sped straight through the target, out of the mass spec, through my head and into the wall. Then, as the dimension closed, ions returned to normal size. Interactions between target and ions restarted at that point. Hence the spike in the mass spec and the radiation alarm.

"What about the rest of the black holes?" Suse asked.

"Micro black holes evaporate very quickly. That produces gamma radiation but they can accrete matter by absorbing neighbouring atoms, a process which also yields gamma radiation. The scintillation counter found the radiation."

"Evaporate means the black holes disappear as they radiate their energy?"

"Yes," Mark answered, "we say black holes evaporate by giving off Hawking radiation. When they are extremely small, as these are/were, it's very quick but there is a half-life. So starting with, say, a hundred mini black holes then, on average, fifty will disappear in the first half-life time period, another twenty-five in the next, then twelve and so on. However, when you are down a few, they could last a lot of half-lives before the last one finally disappears, because the chance of any particular black hole evaporating is completely random. In that time, and in a matter dense region like the Earth, some black holes could grow by accretion, which is a concern."

"Yes, but how many black holes did you make and what happened to them all?" Suse expanded her earlier question. "People are more than concerned about that, aren't they?"

"Yes, unfortunately, I probably made about a half million in those few microseconds. They carried an electric charge so they were trapped in the mass spec, in my head and in the walls of the building. The air in the lab did not stop them as it was not a dense medium," Mark noted Suse's quizzical expression and stopped.

"How do you know they didn't go right through the walls and out of the building?"

"To get out of the building they had to pass through the instrument, my head and four walls. We measured the number deposited in each by their radiation and found the numbers dropped to nothing in the third and fourth wall. I know I said they go through dense matter like darts through clouds, but the ions were charged and so were the black holes. Normal matter condensed along their track and acted as a drag on the particles. So in dense matter, like my head," Mark grimaced at this attempt at a joke, "or the walls, they lost energy, slowed and stopped."

"Dense like a solid or liquid, where the black holes could be trapped, so they either stay and grow or evaporate." Suse hurriedly explained to camera.

Mark continued, "Yes. They will stay where they were trapped until they evaporate or grow to a dangerous size. These in the wall and the equipment were all detected, and we'll be rid of them once they're blasted into space. They won't grow in the vacuum of space, so we can send them into deep space or inject them into an asteroid to try making a larger black hole for experimental cosmology."

"Is the Earth at risk?" Suse voice was slightly accusing.

"Possibly, but only if we do nothing. It will be expensive to collect and store all the black holes and blast them into space. We had to excavate chunks of lab wall and floor and hack out any bits of equipment where they might be lurking."

"'Lurking,' an apt word I think."

"Sorry," Mark grinned, "but they can't sink to the Earth's core quickly because they are not heavy, yet, though they are very dense. I turned ions, which are atoms with an electric charge, into black holes so they weren't er... heavy to start, and any that last will take a long time to accrete enough matter to put on significant mass. The building was quarantined and scintillation detectors were set around so the authorities can detect and capture the black holes they pinpoint. They had to take large chunks out of the wall. You can't just drill out a few grammes, because of the risk that some will escape in tiny particles of dust."

"But they can grow." Suse sounded accusing.

"While they are very small the process is extremely slow because their cross section, the area to interact with normal matter is very small. If they grow so does their surface, or event horizon, and the rate of growth will accelerate with time. It is risky to leave any on Earth."

"How risky?" Suse asked.

"The chances are vanishingly small that any would devour the planet, but do you risk that? It's not like climate change, floods, storms - massive losses but eventual recovery. One survivor black hole and the entire Earth could be swallowed, no recovery. Yes it would take a long time but there would be a long and devastating period before the end. It's quiet now but would not stay that way."

"We'll need more graphics when we broadcast this." Suse said, looking past the cameraman to her producer. She turned back to Mark "Will they all be found?"

"Yes and then they'll be sent them into space and I'll go with them. But that may not be the end of the story."

"You mean others can repeat your experiment?" Suse asked. "I thought you can only get the right conditions every 270 years. You were just lucky er.. unlucky in the particular circumstances." Her smile was sympathetic.

"It could happen naturally via cosmic rays. It probably happens regularly somewhere in the universe every day. My colleagues are calculating the probabilities as we speak, because the effect has cosmological implications." Mark said. "I found another way for the universe to get us. You can add cosmic ray black holes to the list along with giant meteor impacts, super volcanoes, nuclear war, and global climate change."

"Is that likely? I know giant meteors impacts are very infrequent."

"No it's not very likely." Mark answered, "but, unlike all the others, it doesn't matter when it happens, or happened." He smiled mischievously, "it may have happened a million years ago and left a little black hole steadily eating away at the Earth's core ever since. One day it might grow big enough for us to notice."

Suse looked alarmed. "How would we know?"

"I wouldn't worry. It's very unlikely. It was one of the arguments I used to try and avoid my fate, as that situation is a sort of giant version of my head. The argument was in vain." "How do you feel about that? Sorry," Suse smiled, "at last, we get to the standard reporter's cliché question."

"Well, I'm not exactly happy about it, but the alternative is worse. I was very close to the mass spec when it happened and most of the remaining black holes are in my head. I always dreamed of heading for space, but then I always expected to return."

One more question "Why the secrecy?" Suse asked.

116

"It was such a simple idea, and I couldn't find any references in the literature, so I wondered if I was being stupid. Then I found I could do it without any help and, if it didn't work, there was no need to tell so I wouldn't look an idiot."

"I thought science needed all results, even the failures. If you don't publish someone will waste effort repeating the work eventually. Surely it was your duty to publish?" The accusing voice returned.

"No," Mark answered. "It's my duty to submit or at least talk to my Professor. Publication depends on others. But you are right, my reputation might have suffered but that was no excuse." He sighed, "As it turned out I wasn't stupid but I was an idiot."

Suse smiled, "I'm glad to see you haven't lost your sense of humour."

Mark tapped a finger on the glass partition separating him from the world until take off. "No, but I've lost everything else."

A Prayer in Death
Imogean Webb

Moonlight glimmered down atop baby pink petunias as Angelica Daniels sat on her porch. The smell of tobacco and oil-fried potatoes drenched the humid air. Cicadas and toads screeched from treetops located only a few yards away near the dirt road. She tapped her fingers against the ceramic teacup and rocked herself on the front patio swing. The southern bell, with wrinkles tugging her aging face, gazed out at her yard and sighed.

"Unnerved?" Her husband, Thomas Daniels, called from inside the house. She glanced to the white door and traced over the rip in the soft netting material near the top corner.

"Should I not be?" She coughed, looking down at her distorted reflection in the liquid. Loose bits of blond hair, escaped from her once neat bun, now clung around her face. "I don't believe any wife in all of Roanoke would bear the thought of her husband in harm's way without some distress."

Footsteps drew close as Thomas ambled to the door, hands shoved away inside his trouser pockets. "Most, I assume in observance to much offensive southern tradition, would not need to. Their husbands would stand in agreeance, unopposed to such insufferable exploitations."

She stood abruptly, setting her cup down on the outdoor stand beside her, and marched over to the door. With a quick glance to the torn cheesecloth screen, she returned her gaze to him. He wore his ash-blond hair combed-back where the ends always curled around the base of his neck. His navy-blue eyes scanned over her face for some kind of understanding.

"And what of the piece of cinder thrown into our home with an inked note? Is that not enough warning for you?" She retorted.

"Angelica," he whispered as he rested his forehead against the cloth. "I cannot abandon my resolutions. What kind of man do you believe me to be?"

Her eyes danced back and forth, searching his face for some answer. "A dead one."

* * *

Powdered wigs, neatly reserved upon wooden mannequin heads, sat in a single row along an aged alder table. Thomas picked at the lining of his black, silk robe as he lingered on the sight of sun rays peeking through a slip of the window's curtain. Lost in thought, he remained unnaturally still and somber, devoid of emotion. Today, he would proceed with his verdict on the civil case between Lee Harvey and Harry Williams. It would warrant unfavorable remarks towards his family among residents, but alas, it needed to be done.

At the last session, the jury on the case was hung for ruling in favor of the defendant without sufficient evidence to dismiss the plaintiff's claim. Less than a quarter of a century ago in Virginia, it was proclaimed that individuals born of Native American blood on their father's side of the family were to be considered no longer slaves, but citizens. Harvey, the plaintiff in the current case, petitioned the court for freedom for herself and two children, afraid that her current owner had plans to bid them off down south.

A knock from the hall echoed through the spacious changing room. Thomas snapped out of his daze, stood, and brushed the silk robe. He straightened any loose pieces of black material into their proper places. Before departing, the young judge turned, looked at the powdered wigs over his shoulder, and left without taking one with him. Times were changing; Thomas knew that. Regardless of the inked warning that had been thrown through his door several nights before, that threatened dire consequences, the judge knew what needed to be done. This wasn't just about his family or the Harvey's or the Williams'. This case would pave the road for generations to come.

* * *

Thunder trembled the walls of George Daniels's city home. A violent storm unlike his family had seen all

119

hurricane season would serve Thomas's memory for years to come. It was almost as if the Earth itself knew of the horrors committed earlier that day unbeknownst to him.

Windows juddered inside their wooden frames, ready to shatter into a hundred shards. Hail drummed rhythmically upon the shingles of the roof. Lightning, brighter than their warmest candles, flashed almost in sync with his little brother's persistent cough. The youngest was recovering from a terrible case of influenza a week earlier. Phlegm was still deep within his lungs, stuck like clay.

His mother rested against the curve of the cream-colored sofa. She muffled her sobs into a handkerchief and held tightly to a knitted, cotton blanket. Young Thomas poked a wooden block towards his toddler brother, tired of playing games, tired of participating in any activities except ones that might bring him answers. Where had his father disappeared to all afternoon? They'd planned to practice his Latin and Geometry. Things were boring, and the more his mother cried, the more curious he became.

He spoke softly, "Ma Mére." She turned away from him, faced the window, and whimpered into her handkerchief. "Why are you upset? If you are so sad, you should go to bed. Send for Meriday. It's late, but I'm sure she'll be fine. She can bring Antony to play. We won't be loud."

Since she was still unresponsive, Thomas—barely old enough to court a lady—stood with his chest out and his fist balled. He stepped closer and attempted to appear mature and collected.

He lifted his chin slightly. "You could at least tell me why. I'm old enough that you should no longer hide sad news or sad events. I'm almost a man now, and I should be respected--"

"What do you know?!" She snapped. His shoulders dropped as she stood easily a foot taller than him. He'd never in his entire life heard her raise her voice, much less scream at him. "You are but a boy! *A boy*! ... Fine, you want to know? Since your ego is bloated to where you think you are grown, I'll tell you. Meriday and Antony are

120

gone—murdered for supposed *thievery* from Michael Quarter's store. Beaten and hung by the river."

A stillness came over Thomas. It crept across his shoulders, down his arms, and covered his body. Surely, she couldn't mean what she had said. Some confusion, possibly? He searched her puffy red face for an explanation other than the words she spoke. When a moment more passed, his mother returned to her seat and took up the knitted blanket which had been made by Meriday several years before.

Beaten and hung like animals? Left to die as if they were criminals? There was no doubt of their innocence in Thomas's mind, so the accusations were absurd. Unlike other slaves owned by many in town, the Daniels had bought Meriday and her son's freedom only two months prior. They'd contracted them to assist with chores around the house, and they were paid fairly. There would have been no need for them to steal.

Thomas watched his mother. She buried her face in the blanket as a heavy burden found itself a home inside his chest. Antony's mother and his own shared their childhood together. After Thomas was old enough to understand conversation, his father said that men of color should be equal to those who were born white, but only the laws of greedy men disagreed. After saving enough money and treating Meriday and her son to a good life, they purchased their ownership, and set them free.

Yet, somehow, this was not enough. Thomas crouched down, his knees pressed against the carpeted floor as he stared at the diamond pattern of brown and black. Antony, his best friend—almost closer to him than his own brother—was dead. He was gone. And during that horrible storm, Thomas had gotten what he'd ask for. A lesson made for men.

*   *   *

Unable to sit still during the preacher's sermon, in his hands, Thomas fidgeted with a wooden crucifix. He ran his thumb over the feet of the carven figure of Jesus Christ while he watched preacher, Edward Royce, stand at the pulpit and refer to the book of Jeremiah. Angelica had already tried to console her husband twice by pulling his hands to her, but alas, had failed.

On the opposite side of the church, across the way, Harry Williams sat. Large ears jutted from the sides of his head. Salt-and-pepper hair remained combed to the side and glued into place. He scratched his crooked, hooked nose as the congregation watched Reverend Edward speak goodness.

With the main aisle splitting the church into two main sections, Thomas glanced over at the slave owner again. With the oncoming court date in only a week, many townsfolk were agitated and tense. Their separation within the pews stood as an unspoken symbol of divide amongst those of the church. Those who supported Thomas sat on his side; those who supported Harry sat on the opposite. Unuttered, but nevertheless, it was there.

"Amen," Edward spoke in conclusion of the sermon.

The congregation responded, "Amen." Thomas and Harry remained in their seats, locked in a stare-down while everyone rose and headed for the exit. Angelica placed a hand on her husband's shoulder, reminding him that it was time to go. He glanced to her then back to Harry who now stood and strolled over to the two with his wife shortly behind.

"Mr. Daniels." He nodded. "Mrs. Daniels."

Thomas stood. "Mr. and Mrs. Williams."

"It's the good Lord's day. Those who worship are blessed." Harry grinned.

Thomas sighed, "That is one thing we can agree upon."

"Now." Harry shoved his thumbs into the pocket of his slacks. "...stealing a man's property and calling him a liar under oath—in front of God—is the prime example of false-heartedness. Wouldn't you also agree, *sir?*"

"You know, lying in front of the Lord *along* with hurting any of God's children, women, or men especially through slavery, I believe, Mr. Williams, is a much greater sin."

Harry's neck grew red as he stepped towards Thomas. "Watch your mouth, boy. The fact of the matter remains that the jury agreed with me. You're no God. Your judgment in this matter is blasphemous and unconstitutional."

"The jury is partial and supported a verdict on false evidence."

"The *jury* is taking a good white man's word. Might I add that I've always helped many in this town when needed. They agree with me, and you silenced them for your own personal agenda!"

Thomas remained calm and kept his voice low. "I hung them for biased decisions which proved their perspectives were swayed by outside influence, partiality to the defendant's claim. I believe that has more justice in it than this town has ever seen."

Harry searched Thomas's face for any sign of weakness or doubt. At the pulpit, Edward stood with his hands clasped around his bible. He watched the two men like a father allowing his boys to fight, ready to intervene only when necessary.

"If you choose to rule in favor of the plaintiff, I will appeal the verdict, Mr. Daniels."

Thomas shrugged. "I haven't given any ruling yet, Mr. Williams."

Harry stepped away with his nostrils flared and face on fire. "No... but we already know. And there will be *consequences*."

With nothing left to say, Harry and his wife took their leave. Thomas stood silent. He gripped the crucifix in his hand tight as he closed his eyes.

'Lord, give me the courage and strength to follow your truth and plan,' he thought.

Angelica, standing right behind him, laced her arm with his. A simple touch to remind him that she was always on his side, even though he had rejected her comfort many times already that day. She'd continue until she broke through to him. Now, it was time to go. He opened his eyes and sighed. In a brief nod of acknowledgment, he glanced to Edward and received a brief nod in return before turning for the door to leave.

*   *   *

Frogs croaked along the bank of Wolfe Creek; the sun warmed the murky waters. With a cast of his fishing line into the stream by a fallen oak, Thomas waited upon a large rock. He had enough money to buy fish from the

123

store if he wanted. Finances weren't a concern for the judge. An escape from the realities of men to focus his mind elsewhere, to him, had always been the appeal of the woods.

From down yonder, a small, tan boy stepped out from the bushes onto the bank. Dirty, holed pants, two sizes too large, hung from his hips, only attached by the snugness of a rope belt. Thomas knew the youngster. He'd seen him a handful of times in court, sitting in the aisle next to his brother. Micah Harvey was the plaintiff's youngest son.

"Micah?" Thomas called out. Startled, the boy of nine years stared at him without response. Thomas tipped the end of his straw hat and nodded for the him to join. "Come on down here with me. I'd like to ask you some things." Still hesitant, the boy glanced over his shoulder and then back to the judge.

"You ever cast a line before?" Thomas asked. With a small head shake, Micah walked over and climbed onto the rock. The not-on-duty judge smiled and handed him the pole.

"Thank you, sir," Micah whispered.

"No problem at all." Thomas held up a hand. "How's your family? Your brother and mom?"

Micah reeled the line back in and then cast it back out. "You want the truth? Wurrsome, sir."

"Wurrsome? Of the possibility of losing?"

"No. Of Mr. Williams winning, sir, and what it mean for us. Be shipped off ta' Mississippi. Man named Nathaniel Woodard's ready to make payment."

Thomas's gaze drifted to the water where wind caused the bobber of the line to bounce. "And your thoughts? How are you feeling?"

Micah sighed. "In truth?"

"In truth."

"My mother hopes you're fair. My brother believes it foolish ta' trust any of you white men. Both sides of our family—black and the native—been tricked. I... pray ta' the Lord that you're gonna' stand up for us. That you ain't no coward."

"Micah," Thomas coughed, "... my wife might call me foolish. Half the town might hate me. Believe me though when I say I stand solid and true for the law. On my word, I'm no coward." He took his straw hat off and looked to the boy. "You understand what I'm trying to say?"

Micah turned towards Thomas, unsure of whether to trust him or not. His words seemed genuine but apprehension remained.

Without pushing the matter, Micah whispered, "I believe so, sir."

And the two of them, for the rest of the afternoon, exchanged stories and listened to the toads holler while fishing on the bank of Wolfe Creek.

*   *   *

On the courtroom wall behind Thomas's chair, the insignia of two carved angels hung over a glossy, wooden cross. Thomas scanned the room of motivated men, each filled with intention, but also with curiosity. With his hands clasped together, he shifted his gaze to Harry Williams. In his seat, Harry shuffled about uncomfortably as if he had a rash on his behind.

Biting his fingernails, arms crossed in front of his chest, he looked over his shoulder at the back of the court room before he locked eyes with Thomas. The case stated against him remarked upon his disreputable action of attempting to sell humans no longer considered property.

His plea? Harry claims that Lee Harvey's a liar; she's slave born through-and-through. He states in his defense that he has every right to sell or trade as he pleases because she still qualifies as his property. Although, under Virginia law, individuals born of Native American blood inherited on the father's side of the family shouldn't be considered as such, regardless if they are also of African American descent. He must prove through sufficient evidence that she is lying about her heritage.

When asked to provide proof of his defense against her claim for freedom, he contributed a small, hand-written notebook with names and dates of all the slaves kept through generations of his family's plantation. Fortunately for the plaintiff, there were timeline discrepancies between his notebook and the records of sales kept at the bank.

The jury—despite this knowledge—gave their vote to Harry in the last session.

Before the previous court adjourned, Thomas ruled the ballots hung due to inconclusive evidence. Now, sitting in his chair, he stared out at a crowd. They all were familiar with his philosophy towards slavery. Thomas had to make this statement for freedom, regardless of the rest of the nation's ideologies. He reached for his gavel and cleared his throat.

"In ruling the jury inadequate to make a decision in the case of Harvey vs. Williams, and under the eyes of God, abiding by Virginia legislation, I will provide a single settlement," Thomas spoke.

Over a few feet from Harry's lawyer, Lee Harvey shook her foot relentlessly. She sat next to her legal representation with her eyes fixed onto him for an answer. Under her table, she fiddled with the end of her skirt, anticipating his proclamation. Behind the two, Micah and his older brother waited.

Thomas glanced around the room of anxious townsfolk again. Every seat had been filled. Regardless of differing opinions or backgrounds, each person wanted to know his verdict, his decree. It was necessary.

Deep down, Thomas knew that it wasn't just about the courtroom though. It was about changing things for the better. Justice should prevail for better or worse. He had to contribute in the best way he knew, and if his experiences in life taught him anything, it was this: Every individual should be born equal and free.

"This court will now rule in the favor of the plain—"

A single gunshot rang. The sound reverberated off the walls. People hollered and screamed as they ducked below the backs of the benches. On the last aisle, pointing a revolver still towards the front of the courtroom, a man no older than seventeen with wild dirty-brown hair, grimaced.

The corners of his mouth pinched together, and his neck turned scolding hot. He lowered his weapon before he rounded for the exit a few feet away. The room of individuals was stunned to silence. They stared, slack-jawed. As the shooter departed, the door swung behind him.

Out in the hallway, a man wearing a tight vest and suspenders shouted from down the way by the offices, "Drop it!" The boy fired again, two quick shots. The Sheriff, in retaliation, fired three back. A high-pitch scream escaped the seventeen-year-old as a hit penetrated his thigh. He dropped to the ground, and the Sheriff raced forward. "Doctor! Get me the Doctor!"

Inside the courtroom, behind the judge's stand, Thomas's gavel lay on the ground. His hand dangled limp and defunct. His eyes, blank and lifeless, stared up at the ceiling. And above his brow, masked in blood, he bled the bullet hole.

*   *   *

Thomas's brother, Phillip Daniels, crouched outside on the porch and worked on patching up Angelica's broken door. He layered new cheese cloth tightly between the two pieces of framework and nailed the boards shut. With a hammer in his lanky arm's grasp, he struck each nail hard. From the open doorway, Angelica carried a water glass over to him.

"Thank you. Much appreciated," he said.

She waved dismissively. "It's no trouble. You're the one mending my door together. It's the least I can do."

He nodded and gulped down half the glass with sweat gleaming from his forehead. "Well, I'm sure Thomas would cut my hands off from the grave if I didn't."

She smiled softly, walked over to the porch post, and leaned against it. "You might be right. He has a funny way of handling business, you know, even in death."

"You speakin' about the chancellor ruling in favor of Thomas's initial verdict?"

She glanced to the side. The edges of her mouth quivered for a moment. "The Lord works in mysterious ways, we all know. The appeal remained true to the first hearing which is unheard of in these parts. Something—something in my bones, Phillip—tells me that God heard his prayer in life and granted it in death."

He hammered down the final nail and stood rubbing his sweaty face against his pima-cotton shirt.

He hacked phlegm into his mouth then spat it into the grass. "I may not be well-versed in likeness of my brother, but we both understood things others might not. Seldom do the motives of man and our Lord's intention flourish together. The world's changing though. Maybe for once, they aligned, if only for a moment."

Angelica, eyes locked and heavy, stared at Phillip. The sadness was obvious to anyone who might hold conversation with her longer than a minute or so. Something was missing from her voice as she spoke. Maybe it was the way she took her time, never in a hurry to attend church or finish errands? Although most didn't agree with her late husband, they pitied the widow for her loss.

"The night before the hearing, you know what he asked?" She laughed, her voice light, almost helpless. "He asked me, *'What kind of man would I be to abandon my resolutions?'*" Shaking her head, she folded her hands together. "I should've told him he was the best I had ever known."

Martyr's Courage
Jessi L. Roberts

Martyr, for most, the name of our sect of Christianity was synonymous with cowardice, because we refused to fight in the Ordained's unjust wars.

As the salivating saboar stalked toward me, my beastly executioner, I glanced at the cheering crowds above and then at the knife in my hand. War would've been easy. I'd have had a chance in battle, even on an alien planet, but here, a knife was no chance, not against a ton of predatory boar.

It felt like years ago when my family came in after a hard day of farming. We had just sat for our evening meal when a knock sounded.

We all stood. Dad opened the door.

A Chix soldier with two golden studs piercing the flap of gliding skin that ran from his wrist to ankle rode his huge warhound into our house like he owned the place. Dad stepped back, knowing better than to get in the way of the predator that was double the weight of a Human. The Chix stared upward at Dad. If the furry Chix hadn't been on the warhound, he wouldn't have come past Dad's waist. Chix were small, but no one dared mess with the diminutive creatures when they rode predators big enough to kill but small enough to easily go through a Human-sized doorway.

"What do you want?" Dad's voice had a tinge of cold to it that I'd never heard before.

The Chix's deep blue eyes landed on me. "Your daughter, Rekkela Arkan is of military age."

I stood stiff, my whole body icy. "But-but, we're pacifists."

"Not my problem," the Chix said. He pulled a roll of paper from his saddle pack. "Here are the papers. You get them filled out and show up at the nearest training grounds, or it's the red tattoo."

"A death sentence for refusing to fight?" Dad demanded. "She's just a girl."

The Chix turned his glare on Dad. "Our rulers are ordained by God. If you refuse to serve them, you spit in God's face, and you deserve what you get for being a coward who won't fight for those ordained by Him." He yanked the warhound's mane and rode the creature out of our house.

Mom pulled me into an embrace. I returned the hug as she sobbed. I wanted to cry too. I couldn't fight the Ordained's war on another planet, not when the war was unjust. I wouldn't let myself kill the innocent to save my own life. Doing that would cost my soul.

It was fight or die, lose my soul, or lose my life.

"You should run," Dad said. "Head for the swamp. Maybe you can hide there until the war's over."

I gazed outside. "I'd die there. Maybe if I get a red tattoo and go to the auctions, someone will buy me for something besides the pits."

Mom sniffled, but Dad nodded. "It's up to you."

I looked around our house. I wasn't going to be part of the war. *God, please, protect me.*

The next morning, we said our prayers, then I packed a change of clothes and headed for the nearest training grounds. Maybe things would go better for me if I turned myself in, rather than running.

The trees did little to protect me from the hot sun and nothing to stop the humidity from sticking my clothes to my skin. Finally, I came to the open field where there was a breath of breeze, but little more than that.

Humans and Chix trained in the field. Many of the Chix rode their warhounds, while the Humans had no mounts.

A silver-furred Chix rode to me on a black warhound. He'd been scarred by the war, but still sat tall. "You here to enlist?" he asked. He bore three piercings, telling me he was probably the leader.

I steeled myself and straightened to stand tall. "No. I'm here to surrender. I won't fight in this war."

"You're part of the Martyr sect?" he asked. His bushy

130

tail wilted.

"Yes," I said. "I'll take the red tattoo. I won't go to war."

"Coward!" a young Chix shouted.

"Go to the pits!" a Human my age jeered.

"Maybe instead of calling them Martyrs, we should call them pitbait. It's all they're good for."

More jeers reached my ears. One Human girl threw a stick at me, but it bounced harmlessly off a tree.

I stood tall. I was doing the right thing. It didn't matter what the world thought of me as long as I followed God's will.

The leader spun his warhound and glared at his troops. "Cowards run from death, not toward it. How many of you were drafted? How many are here, because you were afraid of getting a red tattoo?"

The soldiers quieted, many looking at their feet.

The leader gazed back at me. "Are you sure you won't reconsider?" His voice was gentle. "Maybe you could get a job as a medic. It's not guaranteed, but it would be a chance to survive without killing."

Maybe I could. I imagined learning to treat the injured, but the medics were forced to treat injured pit fighters as practice. I'd be stuck at the pits, treating people who got ripped to shreds in those horrible fights. Could I do that?

God said to help prisoners. I wouldn't be contributing to the violence, I'd be bringing healing to the injured. "I'll do it," I said softly. My gut clenched. Part of doing this felt like I was taking the coward's way, but maybe it was just logical and right.

The leader pulled some papers from his warhound's saddlebag. "Get these filled out. I'll have you talk to the medics. You'll be sent to the pits for practice."

A wave of dizziness washed over me. I'd be at the pits, maybe not killed in them, but still at them, still dealing with wounds that should never have happened.

"I'm Takaski Yashu. Follow me."

"Rekkela Arkan," I said.

"If you're enlisting under me, you'll call me Ochan." Takaski looked around. We'd wandered a short distance from the soldiers, out of earshot at least. "I'm sorry. You shouldn't be forced into this. None of them should. All I can do is try to keep you alive," he said. "My advice, when they do the combat training, go along with it, even if you disagree. If you don't, it will go badly for you."

"I won't fight," I said.

"Training isn't fighting. Keep your head down and hope you get to be a medic, then you can avoid fighting. You refuse to train now, and they'll still toss you in the pits for insubordination. Survive training, and you might be able to do some good as a medic."

I looked away. I'd be lying, pretending to do something I wouldn't do. That couldn't be right, but if I didn't do that, I'd die.

Why was I afraid of death? I'd go to paradise. There was nothing about death that I had reason to fear, but the thought still chilled me. Maybe it was the pain that came before death.

"Pray the war ends before you're deployed," Takaski said. "I won't help you disobey the Ordained even if I respect your courage. My advice, don't get killed for refusing military training only for the war to end before you'd be deployed. Pick your hill to die on. Don't die over something pointless."

A little hope burned in my chest. Even if Takaski didn't hold my beliefs, he respected them. God had given me a leader, not an abuser.

After only a week of training, I stood at an operating table and waited next to my mentor, an old gray Chix medic. A crowd of Chix perched on tree limbs above a pit, which had been dug into the ground to imprison the fighters. A few Humans stood around the edges.

A kark's roar erupted from the pit, and the crowd cheered. I looked away and tried not to hate them for cheering at a blood sport. Even knowing that Jesus cared about their souls, I couldn't help but imagine them cheering for my death.

The fight ended with a screech of pain and more cheers.

A couple of minutes later, a pair of Chix riding warhounds pulled an injured Elba from the pits, his side badly torn. They dragged him roughly onto my table.

People always said the Elbas were beasts, monsters from a lawless planet, but the real monsters were the Chix, even if the Elba was over twice their height and could kill a Human in a single blow. The Chix were the ones who wanted blood, not the Elba.

The gray Chix doctor glared down at the Elba, then strapped him to the table. The Elba only groaned. He was too weak to fight.

"Clean the wounds," the doctor ordered with a flick of his tail.

I searched for the salve which numbed and disinfected wounds. All I found was the harsh disinfectant fluid that burned when applied to un-numbed wounds. "We need painkiller," I said. "I don't see the numbing stuff."

"That's too expensive for pitbait," the Chix doctor spat. "He's strapped down. Just disinfect the wounds."

I shuddered. The Elba was in so much pain already, and I'd only be adding to his suffering. I grabbed the disinfectant and walked to the Elba. "I'm sorry," I said. "There's no painkiller." I quickly trimmed his fur away from the wound on his side. Not only did he have a new bite wound with a lot of punctures and tearing, but under that, he bore the scars of numerous old wounds. I started squirting the disinfectant into the wounds, wincing as I did so.

The Elba tensed and pulled against his restraints on reflex.

"I'm sorry." I blinked away tears. He likely hadn't done anything evil, just gotten on the wrong side of the war when the Ordained invaded his home.

Finally, I finished with the disinfecting. He lay on the table, breathing hard from the pain.

The Chix doctor only watched. "Stitches now," he ordered.

I winced. This never should have been done without a painkiller.

The Elba looked at me then gave a nod. "Not your fault, kid," he said softly, his voice strained. "Do your best."

I nodded in return and did what I could to stitch the injuries. I felt the Elba flinch as I drove the needle through his skin, but I kept working until I was done, while the real doctor supervised and sometimes offered criticism. Finally, I tied off the last stitch. By then, the Elba slave's owner, a tall Human with blond hair, had arrived.

I glared up at the man, a person who threw people into the pits to fight to their deaths, the one who had led to the Elba's torture. As I glared, I unstrapped the Elba, who stumbled to his feet. He was too weak to fight.

"Thanks," the Elba whispered as he stood.

I looked away. I hadn't done anything for him, just put him back together so he could fight for his life again. I watched as his sadistic master herded him away, then it hit me. That Elba had been stitched up before. I was probably the only person who felt bad about his pain.

That night, I couldn't stop thinking about the Elba and the other slaves who he'd be forced to kill in the pits. If I stepped out of line, if the military realized I wouldn't kill, I'd be in the pits with them.

I slid out of my cot and crept from the barracks which were within walking distance of the pits. The other soldiers kept sleeping, but a guard stood at the door.

She watched me. "You're supposed to be asleep."

I shrugged. "I can't. Figured some fresh air would help."

She nodded. Going outside at night wasn't exactly against the rules, and we were supposed to exercise.

I wandered through the long grass and dense trees until I came to the pit. It was little more than a hole in the ground with walls too steep to escape from. Huge branches hung over it, all of them intertwined so the arboreal Chix could get a good view of the fights that went on. In the moonlight, the black shadows of those trees stretched long, like claws and bars on the ground.

I stared down into the pit. Sand covered the floor, but the claw marks of creatures who had tried in vain to escape were visible on the walls. A few patches of darkness stained the sand, places people or animals had been gutted while the crowds cheered for more blood.

I walked around the pit. A row of slave cages stood under the trees. Dark shapes slumbered within. Without thinking, I headed toward them.

134

"Halt!" a guard shouted.

I froze as he approached. He was Human, a big man with red hair. "What are you doing?" He shined a light in my face.

"I'm from the base," I said. "I was just getting some fresh air." This guy was private security, not military like the guard outside our barracks.

"You're not allowed around the slaves. Get out of here."

"Okay, I'm going," I said. I hurried back to the barracks, nodded to our guard, and flopped down in my bed. Even then, I couldn't sleep. It had looked like only one guard was watching the slaves. What if I could free them somehow? On this planet, their odds of survival in the wild were low, but the odds were still better than having to survive in the pits.

I lay in bed, plotting for the entire night. The next morning was the Sabbath, so we got the day off. I didn't go to any of the local churches. They'd all be spewing propaganda about how we should serve the Ordained as they sent soldiers to be butchered or butcher others. Instead, I searched for the shops. Trees full of Chix shops hung above me, along with a few Human shops that were on the ground. Though many of the shops closed for the Sabbath, maybe a few would be open.

I walked into a clinic selling drugs, one that specialized in animals. Guilt pulsed within me. I'd have to lie about this. Lies were wrong, weren't they? I needed to lie to free the slaves, not save myself. It was like the midwives in Egypt who lied to protect the babies. A lie to help the innocent wasn't wrong, was it?

"I've got a kark," I told the Chix at the counter. "He's shy, and I need to drug his food so I can get a look at his teeth. Do you have anything for a small kark that could knock him out?"

"The safest stuff's the paralysis serum," he said. "It'll paralyze them, but it won't knock it out, so you need to get some sort of numbing if you're doing anything painful."

I nodded, struck by the irony that this guy cared more about the pain of an animal than others cared about the suffering of people in the pits. "I just want to get look at his teeth. If there's something bad there, I'll be getting someone else to pull them."

He handed me a bottle. "There's enough in there for a couple doses. Just read the instructions. It says the dosage for a targan, but everything besides Chix end up taking the same dosage."

"Thanks," I said. I paid him and hurried to another shop where I bought two bottles of the local wine. Hopefully, the guard liked it. I did a little more shopping, including getting survival gear, snacks, a laser knife, and some rope.

When night came, I left again, this time with the wine and a raincoat. Rain poured down on me, but I managed to sneak past the guard by the barracks. Hopefully, she wouldn't be blamed for letting me sneak past her, but if she was, she sort of had it coming. Guards were supposed to be observant, after all.

Rain streamed off me, wetting everything not covered by my coat. The slaves' guard huddled under an umbrella. The slaves' only cover was the towering trees, which weren't much, not when they were caged.

I hurried under the umbrella. Only then did I see the guard's face. She wasn't the man from last night.

"What are you doing out here?" she asked, her voice soft, not aggressive like the man's had been.

"I have trouble sleeping." I grabbed a second wine bottle from under my jacket and took a few swigs. It was pretty mild wine. It would take a lot to actually get drunk. I stuffed it back under my jacket.

She watched the bottle.

"You want some?" I asked.

"Sure."

As I reached for the drugged bottle, Takaski's words came back to me. *Pick your hill to die on. Don't die over something pointless.* These slaves would be my hill.

I handed it to her, leaving the good one under my jacket. "Take it all. I don't want to get in trouble for drinking. The military's pretty strict about that."

"Thanks." She took a long draw on the wine. I prayed she'd drink enough of it. It was a tasty flavor, meant to be drunk in one sitting.

She drank more. She'd probably been thirsty. I stayed beside her, sheltering under the umbrella.

"You should get some sleep, kid," she said, her voice still gentle, though a bit slurred.

I shrugged. "I'm not tired."

The woman stumbled a bit, then shook herself. I tried not to watch her obviously. The trouble with this particular drug was it did nothing to the mind. I'd have to make sure she didn't yell before the paralysis fully took hold. As I waited, the rain ended.

She stumbled again. This time, her legs tangled, and she fell. I pounced on her and covered her mouth. She struggled weakly, but the drug had kicked in, making her no match for me. Her eyes were wide, and I felt her breaths coming in frightened gasps. "I'm sorry. It's okay," I whispered. "I'm just letting the slaves go. I won't hurt you."

Finally, she went limp, though she still breathed fast. I left her under the umbrella and headed for the slave cages. The Elba I'd stitched up stood first, his ears perked.

I pulled a laser knife from my jacket and sliced the lock on his cage. "I'm getting all of you out," I said.

He shoved the door open. "A lot of people feel bad, but not many actually do something. I didn't know you had it in you."

"I didn't know either." I hurried to the next cage. There were dozens of slaves. A couple of them were my age. Were they like me, people who had refused to fight and been sentenced to death for it, or were they guilty of some other crime?

The second I released them, most bolted into the trees, some with a mumbled thanks, others not even taking the time to do that.

Now that I released them, I'd be branded a terrorist. My odds of surviving that would be even worse than my odds as a Martyr. I stood, staring at the vanishing slaves.

The Elba touched my shoulder. "You need to go too," he said softly.

Just then, someone shouted. We were out of time.

The Elba took off, limping as he went. He wouldn't be fast enough to escape, even if they didn't send tracking warhounds after him.

I took off, not toward the swamps where the other slaves had run but headed toward the barracks. If I could lead them on a chase, it might give the others time to escape.

I ran, my feet quiet on the spongy ground. Shouting erupted, and a light blazed in my direction. I swerved and bolted into the denser trees, but not in the direction the slaves had run. I wouldn't lead my pursuers to them. Trees whipped at my face, tearing at my clothes and slowing me, but I kept running.

The little training I'd had gave me strength I never had before, the strength to run from my enemies.

A warhound's yowling howl tore through the trees, a predatory cry that turned my skin to ice. If they'd come for me, I'd never escape.

As the howls and yowls of hunting warhounds closed in, I kept going, my breaths coming fast, the humid air choking me. Now, I ignored all but the biggest branches. It didn't matter if I lost an eye to the trees, I'd lose my life if I got captured.

Foliage crashed behind me. I turned just in time to be bowled over by a warhound.

I hit the ground, driving the breath from my lungs.

"Got her!" a Chix soldier shouted. She jerked her warhound back, not letting it bite me.

More warhounds crashed through the trees. I was surrounded. I sat up, my hands on my head. Moonlight shown through the clouds, illuminating Takaski.

He stared down at me, his bushy tail drooping. "Get up," he said. His voice was soft.

"What about the others?" one of the young soldiers asked.

"Those are escaped slaves. We don't do volunteer work. They want the slaves back, they can pay us." He sighed as his eyes landed on me again. "She's a deserter, so she's our responsibility."

I stood, my body aching. "I did the right thing."

"You'll die in the pits for this." There was no anger in Takaski's voice. Did I even detect a note of kindness?

I lifted my chin. "I'm not sorry."

He gave a tiny nod. It would probably be the last note of respect I'd get in my quickly dwindling time in this life.

Two days later, I stood in the pit I'd freed the slaves from, the crowds above cheering for my blood. I gripped a knife, not much of a defense for a Human girl. It was intended to give me enough hope I'd try to fight whatever beast they unleashed on me, just enough hope that those watching would get a show.

A saboar stalked down the ramp and into the pit, feline grace combined with hooves, spikes, and jaws big enough to kill in one snap.

At least with a saboar, my death would he fast. *God, please give me courage.*

The crowds cheered, some calling me a terrorist and even a coward. They were wrong. War was the coward's way out, a way I had rejected. I'd picked my hill to die on, and I had no regrets.

I glanced at the knife in my hand. It wasn't going to save me, not from my monstrous executioner.

I threw the knife into the sand, then gazed upward. "Today, I go to paradise." I stared at the crowds, meeting their gazes. "Where will you go?"

The crowd jeered at me, but a couple looked away. Had I struck a nerve? Would some of them repent? *God, let my death be an example,* I prayed.

The saboar chose that moment to charge. I stood firm and stared at it as it bore down on me. Its massive jaws opened, consuming my vision.

The End
Michael Krog

I

The village of Quan-lo lay alongside the river Tan, not a hundred miles from the Sea of Japan. Ten years earlier, the village had been home to nearly two thousand men, women, and children living happily, growing rice, raising pigs and chicken. Everyone within a three days walk knew pigs in Quan-lo were the fattest and best tasting pigs in the region. Legend told of a pig a hundred or so years before whose meat was eaten by the Emperor on a journey to the sea to tame the ocean. He had tasted the pork of the pigs of Quan-lo and been so enchanted he had stayed in the village for three more days before his advisors had at last prevailed upon him to continue his journey. Every year thereafter, a solitary pig had made the weeklong journey to the emperor's table.

The village remained for almost another hundred years just the idyllic place the tale told of. Children played in the streets. Young mothers walked together to the market, men fed the pigs, and both worked the rice paddies. Old ladies gossiped about the younger ones, and old men drank their tea in the tea shops. Life went on as it always had.

Cho was the blacksmith for the village of Quan-lo. If your hoe broke, Cho was the man to repair it or make you a new one. If the Tin family's horse lost a shoe, they handed their silver to Cho, as they had to his dad, and his dad before him, and his dad before him, and so on into the depths of history. Cho, like his dad before him, was a large man, all muscles and sweat. The girls of the little town would find themselves walking by his shop daily. They would cover their mouths, full of whispers and giggles, as they walked by. His wife would sit with her sewing and smile to herself. Her mom would stand up and

140

yell at the poor girls and off they would run, full of giggles and fear. Momma Han's family was of a Mongol line, and her threats would make Cho himself fear for his safety, and the muscular blacksmith was the largest man in Quan-lo.

Rice was grown. Cho made horseshoes and hoes. Cho's wife made babies. Cho's mother-in-law made threats. The Tin family ran the town and made lots of money. Young girls walked by the blacksmith shop and giggled. Cho's wife smiled and sewed. Cho's mother-in-law yelled and chased the girls away, and life went on as it had.

Then came the communists and, shortly thereafter, war. Cho put on a uniform and said goodbye to his wife and little ones and went off to fight in the war. He did his duty, as every so often his ancestors had. He came home and did not talk of the war. He made horseshoes and still made an effort to work harder when the girls walked by.

Life went on. War came and went for years. The blacksmith had done his duty. He was older, and his children were not old enough yet to carry a rifle. Life went on.

II

Then it changed. The old ways fell away to new ones, and communism replaced the empire. Government men came and took charge. Everything would be better they promised. And as so often it does, government made things worse, so much worse. Away from the village, they built a smaller village of huts. The rice paddies were gone, replaced with dry, dead fields of grain. The pigs, once the pride of Quan-lo, were long ago eaten. The chickens too, were gone. So many of the people, too, were gone. The little village off to the side of the old village slowly filled up with men who committed what were called crimes against the people.

Hung reached for his empty bowl and ran his finger around the inside.

"Nothing."

No one responded. Hung did the same thing every day. The guards dispensed the bowls. One bowl for several men, once a day, a handful of bites some days, others one or two. Cho was sure Hung had complained back when he had been Hung Tin and ridden around town on his horse, proud and rich. Hung was the only surviving Tin. Most of the Tins had died in the early days of Mao's reign. Hung had led celebrations after the Japanese had been driven from China and had proudly declared himself a Communist, a common man. Cho had laughed while he hammered out his plows and scythes. Hung was no more common than any other rich man, but the Tins were rich, and they lived different lives. He had given it no thought.

Then all Hung's family, mother, father, brothers, sisters, aunts, uncles, cousins, all were slaughtered over the course of a week as enemies of the state. Hung had somehow survived, and Cho realized that this time things were different. How correct he had been he did not appreciate until his wife fell ill.

Watching Hung, all skin and bones, like himself, wipe the sides of the empty bowl for a scrap of food, Cho was past scorn. It took to much energy. The camp. The camp killed everyone, rich or poor, young or old. They all died equally in the camp. The only ones, as far as Cho saw, who were safe were the young men with the guns and that squirrelly man from the government. Women quickly found their way to the beds of the Red Guards, and just as often they found themselves in a camp. Town leaders spouted the lines they heard and felt safe. One accusation, one switch in the winds, and they too were in the camp. The poor delighted in the fall of the rich. They rose and felt the power. Just as quickly, they turned on one another as the chaos only fed on chaos. No one was safe, and the camp was never too full.

Cho, who had perhaps taken too much pride in his physique, maybe smiled a little too much as the young girls had sauntered by giggling and looking, now had little to be proud of. Months in the camp had seen to that. Months in that little thatch hut, months of little more than a handful of bites every day to eat had stolen his muscles

142

and his frame. Once, he had felt pride as he had pounded steel, bending it to his power. When he retired at the end of the day, laying next to his wife, he knew he had done something, he had made his own little difference. Metal, hard, unyielding metal had bent before him and done his bidding. The Tin's horses wore his shoes. The rice paddies, now long gone, were tilled with his hoes. The pigs, the pride of Qhan-lo—they too, long gone—were slaughtered with his knives. Now, he was a giant walking skeleton who hoed dirt and was told he was growing wheat.

Cho, as his father before him, and his father before him, was the biggest man in the region. Even now, he dwarfed the four men who sat around him. Now, though, he was a grotesque parody of a giant. If bone and skin could walk and talk, it was him. He was six and a half feet of walking, talking skin and bone. All too often, he sat, back against his hut, his feet before him and his arms resting on his once strong legs, leg muscles that once lifted plowshares on their own and looked at the mockery that was left. Skin draped over bone. He had watched in wonder as his muscular frame wasted away. Would his skin droop and hang down as muscle disappeared? It turned out no. At least, not for very long. Now it clung to the bone, almost as if the bone would pop through the skin, making a very delayed appearance. He walked around the camp, a giant walking skeleton with skin tightly bound over bone. He marveled that he was alive. He came to think that his bones possessed some life of their own. He often, looking down at his wasted frame, imagined that long after he was gone, his flesh all gone, his bones would still be walking around this camp, just going through the motions: standing in line, carrying a practically empty bowl to their spot by the hut and pretending the bowl had enough food in it. He laughed too much. It was not that funny he knew. Still, he laughed. The others looked and him and smiled. They knew Cho was strange at times, and it felt good to smile again.

Min sat in the dirt next to him. He had taken one bite, as he did every day. He was too weak to walk and would die soon. Cho helped him him when the group had to move, an arm around him as Min leaned on him. The smaller man could barely stand anymore, but still he refused to eat more than his one bite. The others refused to eat until he had eaten it. Somewhere, Cho was sure, the gods were laughing. He ate his bite, and then they ate. Someone, Cho thought it was Hung, had refused to eat until Min had taken a bite, and the others had followed his lead. Min took one bite and looked at Hung. "Happy now?" his look had said. Hung had said nothing, simply wiped his dirty hands on his clothes and then reached in and taken his little share. Then the others had taken their couple of bites.

Min would die tonight or tomorrow. Did it make a difference? He had changed everything. They would all die, that was true, but now they died with hope. How was that possible? Cho was not sure, but he had watched it so often over the weeks since Min had come out of the pit that he knew it to be true. Min was still a mystery to the group. He said little about himself, only singing his song to the dying; but that was not all. Min, wasted away and dying, yet still living on for weeks after he should have died, lived with a smile on his face. Weeks before, a wagon had appeared at the gates with a single guard in the driver's seat and lying in the back, skin and bones was Min. The guard yelled at him to get up, and, to the amazement of everyone watching, Min had risen up and walked to the gate. He was already skin and bones as he walked through. Then he had endured the pit, which killed many a man. Yet, he persisted.

Even today, as Cho sat and watched the dying man, he knew little of Min. He had known him as a man from a nearby village, before, when China was not communist, before all the death. Since crawling off the back of the wagon, he talked little. Before the pit, he cried dry, silent tears and talked to his dead children at times. He talked to no one at first, but slowly Hung, who from his first meeting with Min had taken a strange fascination with the man, had drawn some little pieces of his story out of him.

His village was well known to the people of Quan-lo, Cho knew him to be a merchant of the town, having stopped in his shop on occasion. Then, Min had worked in his tea shop, an almost-bald, short, scrawny man approaching middle age whom Cho had thought would never stopped moving. He was always cleaning pots, rolling out dough for noodles, cooking, cleaning, and so on, quietly. His village was gone now, most of its citizens dead or forced into the cities. Min was the final survivor of the camp there. The guards had wanted to shoot him and get it over with. Fate had laughed at that plan as the government inspector had forbidden the shooting of prisoners. It was bad press. He ordered the transfer of the prisoner to Quan-lo. A week later, the guard had fallen ill. He died days later. Min, ready to die, as he said daily, lived on, to what purpose he did not know.

III

"Bowls, bowls." The shout came from the guards. The guards showed signs of hunger, and the hungrier the guards looked, the smaller the meals for the prisoners were. The government had signs up by the serving tables proudly proclaiming each meal was ten ounces per volunteer(they were not called prisoners or inmates. They were volunteers.) Over time, Cho had marveled as the size of an ounce grew smaller and smaller as the scales were adjusted to reflect an accurate measure. Once a month, the government inspector came in from town and inspected everything, proudly telling the volunteers how great a job they were doing as he made sure the scales were accurate. Once, months before, a man had spoken up and protested. He had gone into the pit for a week and come out much for the worse and never spoken again, dying less than a month later.

When Cho first came to the camp, the guards had walked around to collect the bowls. Now, they sat at the gates, lounging around the cart and calling for them, only moving to beat those who fell on the way to return the bowls. More and more, those who fell stayed where they fell. The guards were careful not beat them to death on the spot. When they died hours or a day later, they were marked in the books as being sick. No one was murdered in the camp.

145

The guards beat their truncheons on the gate post and continued calling out for the bowls. Min tried to rise from the ground and fell, his face in the dirt. Cho moved to help him and Hung slowly rose, weak as ever, gathering the bowls.

In weeks past, Hung would complain, "They feed us nothing, they could at least gather the bowls." Now, almost too weak to stand after the long day, he gathered the bowls and moved towards the gate. Min protested Cho's assistance and moved his arms to raise himself. His strength failed him, and he collapsed again. The third member of their group, Han, helped Cho, and together they lifted Min and walked into their hut. Cho kept an eye on Hung, making sure he delivered the bowl. Bowls that were not returned were not filled the next day. Their bowls were all red, with the symbol for pride on it. Pride for Communist China, they had been told. No one else could use them. If they all died, the camp lost the bowls. There was that much more food for the guards.

The other two members of the group waited at the hut, backs against the wall. They simply sat, their eyes facing out seeing little, knowing even less. They sat that way night after night. No one spoke unless Hung or Min spoke first. Cho rarely spoke. He, like the others, waited to die.

Somehow, after walking through the gate, Min had made his way to their hut. He made their group five and Hung had protested. Cho had told him to shut up. Min had looked at him and offered to leave. "Does it matter where I die?" he had asked. Hung had told the man to sit down. After that, Hung was always ready to do what Min asked. The man complained about everything. Cho was sure that Hung had suckled at his mother's breast and told her the milk was not sweet enough. Yet after their initial meeting, he never said a negative word to Min.

It took a moment for the pair to walk Min to the hut, and Hung reached the hut as they did. Cho gently propped Min against the wall. Hung offered his shoulder for Min to lay his head against. Min, almost unconscious, accepted it. Cho sat down and stared into the sky, saying nothing. Hung absently stroked Min's head, staring into the distance.

"I think Min will not make it till tomorrow," Hung said to no one in particular.

For the longest time no one said a thing. The other two, who had long since died inside, said nothing. Cho finally, responded.

"He has earned it."

"Who will sing to him?"

"We know the song."

Hung continued to stroke the dying man's head. Cho watched. He remembered stroking the heads of his little ones in much the same manner. Unbidden, the names of all seven children rushed upon him. He smiled. All the little things that had made him laugh as a father briefly swept over him. Sadly, the memories, bittersweet though they were, lasted but a moment.

The moment at hand came to the fore.

"Who do you think will be waiting for him?" Cho asked.

"Lee."

In the evening, the men always moved into their huts. The guards made sure. Each guard had a book, and, in it, it said room checks were to be made at seven, and so by seven everyone had to be in bed. The inspector had come by one evening shortly after Cho had moved into the camp, and the prisoners of one hut remained outside. The guard chief on duty was in volunteer clothing that same night.

Inside, they laid Min on his bed and Hung covered him with a single threadbare sheet. Min raised up and looked into Cho's eyes.

"Do you think they forgive us?" he asked.

Cho assured the man they did, with a confused look to Hung.

From the outside, they heard the sound of the guards approaching. The skeletal men hustled to their beds. Seconds later, the door opened, and in walked a figure none of them had seen before. He was tall for a China man, standing not quite as tall as Cho. He had the healthy pallor of a well fed individual, and he was in shape. While even the guards showed signs of malnutrition, the man in the doorway was obviously from the capital. He was muscled and healthy. As did many men of importance, he wore the Mao suit sharply, with not a wrinkle in it, and it seemed to Cho dirt would not have the courage to stick to it. He walked into the middle of the room, a single guard standing in the doorway.

"Get up," came the bark from guard. Cho started to rise as the guard barked out again and started to move towards the closest pallet, which was Min's. Min did not move or respond, and the man moved a leg back to kick him.

A surprisingly strong "No" came from the next pallet over, from Hung. The guard stopped and moved towards Hung. The man in the suit quietly stopped him and told him to leave. His voice was just above a whisper, but it stopped the guard at the first syllable. The man was quiet and turned to Hung as the guard left. That was when Cho realized they were in trouble, something was wrong. This was not an ordinary inspection. This man was at the camp for some other reason. Cho was not sure how he knew. The man was not remarkable in any way other than his self-composure. He gave away nothing, and his face betrayed nothing that resembled passion or even life. He could have been a piece of furniture if not for the obviousness of him being a man. Cho was sure, however, that the man could eat or order all their deaths with the same lack of enthusiasm. He scared him, and this surprised him. Some part of him, deep down, could still be scared, still cared enough.

IV

The man stood still over the near dead Min for what seemed like an eternity.

Cho looked over to Hung and saw what he thought might actually be fear on the man's face. If he'd had the energy to laugh, he might have done so. Despite his own fear, he still asked himself: afraid? Of what could any of them be afraid? The five of them in this little hut, what was left for them to fear? They were skin and bone, walking skeletons, mere phantoms of men who were just waiting to die. More than once over the past months, Cho had witnessed a man try to charge the guards, in a welcomed suicide rush. The guards could not shoot the charging men, but the resulting beatings still ended in the release of death. He looked over at the two pallets in the corner, where there other two hut mates lay, not even bothering to move. Others checked out long before the death came. Who knew what they had done, or what they had seen before they arrived in the camp. They ate, they breathed, they obeyed, but that was all. They were as alive as the pallets they slept on.

Then there was Min.

He looked back at the man from the government. The man remained standing over Min then spoke to the room.

"The men in the huts before I came in here, the ones still bothering to live, some of them are crying," he said. Cho was sure he meant the sentence as a question, but he did not answer. The man looked over Min's form a moment longer then turned around.

"Men who have not shed a tear, men who have been waiting to die for months. Men who do not even feel hunger any longer, men who do not even feel sorrow as their comrades die every day around them. These men are weeping."

Once again Cho was silent. He looked to Hung, sure that he had the sense to remain silent.

"Now why are these men crying?" He said this no one and yet to everyone present. Still there was no answer, and he continued.

"I asked them, and one man spoke up, all he told me is 'Min is dying tonight'. I asked myself, 'Min is dying?' One man is dying, who cares, but these men do. Why should they care that one man is dying? But they do. And if they care, I have to care. After all, you are all my responsibility."

The man called out to the guards for a seat, and one of them hurriedly sat up a stool for him to sit on. He sat down and faced Cho. His next words were unexpected.

"Tell me about Lee."

There was so much to say. Cho was sure he was right about the man. This man went right to the important question. Not tell me about Min, what was there to say? So much to say. But better to ask what did he mean to others and the story of Lee told that story.

Cho told the story. Trying to say little, he started at the end and hoped against hope that it would satisfy the man, somehow knowing that it would not.

Cho told his story:

"Lee died three weeks ago. He wanted to live and fought harder than anyone, he refused to believe we all are going to die. But he was a big guy," Cho looked down at his flesh and bones, "Almost as big as me. And he used that to stay alive. I guess you can't blame him, he was like a drowning man and flailed around to grab on to something, but all he could grab onto was his size, so he used that. When the guards were not looking, he would take other men's food. I am sure he killed at least a dozen men, not by hitting them or such, but by taking that last little bit of nourishment that would have kept them alive.

"So one morning, we are at the roll call and Min looks around and Min who does not say much actually asks me where Lee is. He is worried because Lee was coughing the night before. I ask him, "Why do you care, Min? You of all people, why do you care?" All he says is, "He was coughing," and then the idiot leaves roll call and heads over to Lee's hut. Somehow the guards are not looking, and he makes it. But the one bad thing: the chief guard was there that day.

"The chief guard is this little guy, shorter than all the others, and he is a mean, little bastard. He is, better fed than all the others. He lords over the lesser guards, carrying around a little pouch with bread and cheese in it, and he munches on the food in plain view of everyone. He is not always at the roll call. If he is in a good mood he will just watch. That day, he was in a bad mood, and I knew Min was in trouble the minute I spotted him. The guards move to start calling the roll, and when they get to Min's name, no one is in his spot. The chief goes crazy immediately. He looked around, and then, from Lee's hut, we all heard it. There was singing from the hut. We had heard it from the pit days before. We'd heard throughout the day from Min, every day since he had come out of the pit, humming it or softly singing it.

"The little guy, he was almost foaming at the mouth, he was so worked up. He took a club from one of the guards and rushed to the hut.. No one moved. Then I sighed inside and moved to help. I was sure that he would beat Min so badly he would die, and he'd already been through so much. I went through the lines and got in the hut right after the little guy with his club.

"There Min was, cradling Lee in his lap, and he had Lee's head in his hands, and he was singing to him. The chief guard paused a moment and then just started beating them both. He was so mad, I thought he would kill them. I am sure that would have landed him right in here with us. I do not know why—we die here every day—but you cannot kill us."

Cho laughed. The statement was so absurd it merited little else, but that was all he had.

"So much death. Men die here every day, but you...." He trailed off for a moment, thinking the man would say something; but the man sat on his stool and patiently waited.

"I will never know why I did it, not for the rest of my short life, but I threw myself on top of them, and that little guy just got madder and started screaming and just kept on swinging that club." Cho pulled off his shirt and turned around for the man too see. His back was a mass of sores and bruises, still discolored after three weeks. The skin, which was just laying over bone, had been torn away, and, in some spots, still shown through. He started to cry, not for sympathy but just from tiredness. No tears would come out, there was not enough in him."

He waited for something from the man, but the man sat on the stool and waited.

Hung started to talk.

"He would have killed them all, all three of them. His guards waited outside getting all excited. They did not

151

care, one even said he hoped he killed them, he joked about taking his little pouch and eating it in front of him after the chief was tossed in with the prisoners. Then one guard came over and rushed in and dragged him out..."

"He picked up the little bastard and carried him out," interrupted Cho, "just like he was a little kid. I think he swung the chief over his shoulder, it was all hazy, after the beating."

"He got a beating, he should have died that night, but he is still here. Cho is still here," Hung said weakly, but defiantly. "He will live through this; you cannot kill Cho." He was proud of Cho.

At last the man displayed some emotion as he simply smiled and said, "Hmmm. Really?"

Hung mumbled a yes as he looked down. Cho took over the story.

"The guard carried the chief out and calmed him down, assuring him the prisoners would surely die that night, but they would just log it as a normal death. The chief left, surely storming off to vent his anger on the bottle in his office. Inside the hut, I struggled to sit upright and helped Min up, but the smaller man refused to leave Lee, continuing to cradle the dying man in his lap. Outside, the guards went through the morning inspection and sent us volunteers out into the fields to work the barren soil. It was the first time they had ever broken their protocol.

"Lee lay with his head in Min's lap, rarely moving, occasionally mumbling.

'What is he saying,' I asked.

'He is telling little Li Ling to go back to bed, there is no food, and he is tired.' Min smiled. 'I told my own little Bai that many times.' Min rocked the larger man's head in his lap and stroked his head, telling him Li Ling was fine. He was weeping quietly as he did so, telling Li Ling she was going to be fine. He sat that way for a long time, stroking Lee's head and telling Li Ling it was going to be fine, 'go with Mr. Chen. He will get you some food.' At one point, he looked up at me and said, 'I lied, there was no food, no food anywhere.'

152

"Lee died right before the noon bell rang out for lunch. Only, as most days, there was no lunch. I went to tell the guards Lee had died and then got Min up to go get in line to get our empty bowls and head to our assigned eating areas. Twenty minutes later, we would line up again and return our bowls.

"Lee was the first Min sang for. I still am not sure why it mattered, but it was so beautiful, the song. We do not know what the words mean, he just sings to the dying. But it gives them—everyone—peace. After Min came out of the pit, he was still quiet, but he was full of peace. You could see it in him with everything he did. It is hard to describe. He had some sort of quiet joy. Is that crazy?"

Cho looked at the man, but the man gave no answer.

"I do not think he realized what he had really done until that afternoon after the guards passed out bowls. We were sitting in front of our hut eating our couple of bites, although then we got three bites. Min took his one bite and then everyone took theirs. I asked him, still aching from the beating, 'Why did you do that?' There was only one "that" that day, it needed no explanation.

"'He was dying,' Min answered.

"'Chang died yesterday,' Hung said.

"'I know.'

"I pressed him, my bruises and aches told me I had the right.

"'No one should die alone, alone and scared. Even Lee was worth more than that,' was all he said.

"It did not matter what any of us thought. The camp took care of everything. The camp cried out for hope, knowing there was none. Min's actions had changed everything. He had given it a spark, and the camp nurtured it.

"We ate our dinner that night and sat there, quite unsatisfied. We were standing up as it was getting dark, and it was almost time for everyone to be on their bedroll. Two men from a hut down the row walked up. The first one said to Min, 'Lao is dying.' The second one said with him, 'he calls for Min. Everyone knows what you did for Lee.'

"The first man took him by the hand and started to drag him away. Hung and I just watched for a moment, too surprised to do anything. Hung and I looked at each other and then followed.

"There was such singing from the hut that night, the guards came. They busted into the hut and came upon all the hut mates and Min around Lao, singing. They put down their clubs and walked back to the guard shack. The singing went quieter, though, just a sweet whisper."

Cho watched the face of the man, but the man just sat and listened, so he added his own thoughts.

"That was the start. After that no one died alone, no one died without hope."

Cho sat quietly, and the man sat still. He was in one of his long, silent pauses, and Cho thought the interview was over. The man simply sat there, thinking silently. In the end, instead of getting up, the man asked another question, only he phrased it as an order.

"Tell me about Min and Lee."

VI

"When Min arrived at the camp, he was inconsolable. He would do nothing. He sat down and we thought he had given up, like those two." Cho moved his head towards the other men in the hut. "We were wrong, of course. Hung saw it first, noticing that he cried, softly. It is hard to cry with nothing, nothing at all in your belly. Where will the tears come from? But you could still hear him at times. He would say nothing, nothing at all to anyone, just go through the motions every day. He ended up in the pit for a while until the Westerner died. After that, he was alive, more alive than any of us. And Lee, well you have to understand, he did not hate anyone. He just wanted to stay alive. He really thought some of us would make it, and he was determined to be one of those people, even it meant he killed others to do that. Something though, something about Min just set him off, he hated him, and he hated Min's,"—Cho paused--"He hated Min's forgiveness."

"After the pit, Min was so different. Oh, he was still quiet, rarely talking, but he was," Cho stopped, unsure what to say, and Hung offered the word, "Joyful." Cho nodded his head in agreement. "He was at peace, nothing could shake him from what he had found. He hummed that song as he went throughout his day. At first Lee would was fine with Min and just ignored him when he came out of the pit. Lee did not hate anyone here but the guards, those he was powerless against, and he hated them for that. Min, though, he refused to hate anyone, and that would have been okay for Lee, I think, but Min treated everyone with the same joy that he went throughout the day with, and that pushed Lee over the edge.

"Then the lunch line happened. We would all line up every day and go through the motions, even though they stopped serving lunch two weeks before. The guards still handed out the bowls and still kept their record books.

"Min, though, he made his way up there with that calm he always had, you could just see it in him—it was like the very air around him possessed this calmness and, like Hung said, joy. When the guard handed him the empty bowl, he thanked him. The guard was so surprised he was speechless for a second, not just because Min spoke, but because he meant it. He was so calm, and he was even happy. Then, of course, the guard next to the one handing out our bowls beat him with his stick and told him not to talk in line. He beat Min to the ground—it did not take much—we were all so weak. But Min just slowly got up and went to his spot with his empty bowl, humming that song. Lee, the whole time he was watching Min with hate on his face, his hands clenching. I do not know where he got the energy to hate so much.

"After that Lee terrorized the little guy.

"After lunch that day, we were sent back out to the fields, and Lee wasted no time in taking his anger out on him. Min walked ahead of Lee, trudging along in our little, ragtag formation to go hoe the dirt. Lee was behind me, and he slowly made his way up the formation. He pulled men back into his spot and took theirs. He was careful. The guards were tired and hungry, too, but they made the effort to keep us in order. He finally got up behind Min, who as always was singing his song just under his breath. Then Lee looked around to be sure the guards were not looking and pushed Min to the ground making a big show of tripping over him. He fell on him, hard. The funny thing was I think Lee hurt himself just as much as he hurt Min. The guards were on the two right away and yelling at them to get up, holding up their sticks. Min actually got up first, and he smiled at Lee and apologized for tripping him. Lee spit at him. 'You clumsy ass,' he said. Lee rushed up and told the guards what happened, and Min bowed over and over, apologizing loudly. Then the guards yell at everyone, we moved on.

"And that was how it went for a little while. Any time Lee could—and he made sure he found himself around Min every chance he got—he would terrorize Min. In line, he would push him. Out in the fields, he would work next to him and trip him or push him whenever the guards were not looking. He tried to make Min's life terrible."

Cho paused for a moment.

The man waited.

"It was almost comical, watching it. Lee was so determined to live, but he spent all of what little energy he had on punishing Min. I really think that is why he got sick in the end. He put everything into his hate. When the sickness came, he had nothing left to fight it with. Min, though, was just Min. He went on throughout his days the same. It drove Lee even crazier. He would bump into Min in a line, maybe push him down, and Min would smile at him from the ground and apologize. He would say, 'It was an accident. My fault, Lee.' Lee would just get angrier and angrier.

"Eventually, Lee got his chance, though. He had been waiting for Min, to catch him alone, and he did. I was nearby and heard them. Min was on the ground, and Lee was standing to one side, kicking him. He was already exhausted from his efforts, and they were weak kicks. It was almost comical, one man bleeding on the ground, and

156

another skeletal figure of skin and bones, out of breath from ten seconds of fighting, kicking him weakly. If he saw me at first, I am not sure, he just kept on kicking him, pure hate on his face. I came up to him, and then I saw he had started crying. All he said to me was, 'He thanked them. We are all going to die, and he thanked them.' Then, he walked away.

"Min was on the ground. He had a bloody nose and was a little bruised up, but that was all. For all his hate, Lee did not have the strength to beat Min to death. Something happened to him after that. I think it was his hate that drove him. He faded away. That happened six weeks ago. Three weeks ago, he died. Min, he should have died long before Lee. He poured everything he had into the dying, but it seems to have kept him alive longer than any other man in his condition."

VII

The man nodded and thought for a long time. No one talked. Cho, who was sure he was going to kill them all, was actually happy when all he did was ask another question.

"Tell me about Min and the pit."

Cho thought for moment, and Hung started talking, fear in his voice.

"It was the Westerner. He is the one who started it. It was him and all his singing in the pit." He stammered through his words. The man's silent moments scared him more than a host of guards standing by with their sticks. The man sat quietly on his stool, his eyes on Cho. He ignored Hung entirely.

So Cho took up the story again.

"Hung's right. It all started with the westerner. He arrived three days before Min, and the guards tossed him right into the pit. It was early morning, and during formation, a car pulled up, and four guards and a government official stepped out. Everyone was watching. It was the first government man to come here and the last, until now.

157

"Then a white man stepped out. He was nearly naked, all he had on were some tight clothes around his waist, and he had on shoes and socks. You could barely call them shoes. They were ragged things with holes in them and his toes showing. That was it. He looked like they had roughed him up. He had bruises all over his back. His fingertips were bruised and swollen, and blood stains ran from his fingers down his arms. He was holding papers in his hands. That was really all we saw of him. They walked the white man over to the Commander and the government man talked to him and pointed to the pit after a bit, repeatedly. They were arguing. The government man pointing at the pit, and the Commander shaking his head. Then the government man did something we had never seen before, but it was the scariest thing any of us could see. He walked over to the white man and snatched the papers out of his hands. He walked back to the commander and tore the papers into pieces. He said something to the commander and pointed at the pit. Everyone in the formation gasped. The Commander went pale for a minute, and then he started screaming at his guards, and they went to grab the Westerner. He did the oddest thing. He fought them off and quickly ducked into the car. Then, before they could even grab him back out, he emerged holding something. He had the biggest smile in his face. As they took him to the pit, I tried to see what it was. It looked like a long string with beads on it, like prayer beads but much longer.

"That was it. Five minutes, and he was gone into the pit. After that, no one saw him again, except for Min, three days later. We heard him though, every day. He would sing, a lot, one song in particular, over and over. The guards would yell at him and pour buckets from the latrine on him, but he just kept on singing. Not too loudly, but he sounded so peaceful.

"Then Min showed up.

"He was dead inside, or at least we thought he was. So many of us have seen so much, it kills us inside. We are all the last ones left. All of our families are gone." He spoke with no emotion, and the man listened with none, merely taking it in.

158

"My wife went first, she was so hungry, and she got sick just as winter came, then each of children, one by one, in one winter, all gone and the ground so cold you cannot even dig them graves. The Maoists came around, and we had to stack them. I stacked my own little ones out in the town square, a hundred feet from my blacksmith shop, and then they burned them while they made jokes.

"The very next day I was at a meeting, another meeting about how to plant wheat, winter wheat. They promised, and it was a dry day and windy, the ground so dry dust was blowing, and I had dust all in my eyes as I went inside and in my mouth. I cleared my throat. I could not see, and I spit. When I cleared my eyes, I looked around and realized I had spit right in the direction of Mao's picture." He almost laughed, bitterly, "Next thing I knew, I was here."

Cho looked up, and the man was sitting there, listening. Hung spoke up, "Cho, tell him about Min and the pit."

"I know, it is just important to know. Everyone here, everyone was this close to giving up, inside, before. We are all going to die. We know that, but after Min and the pit, we are able to die like men again."

Cho looked at the man. Nothing had changed in him, but he knew the man was listening more than he had been. Maybe it was the eyes. They saw. But did he understand? Cho was not sure.

"I told you he was a ghost when he arrived, going through the motions. I thought he would be dead in a week or so. But then, one night, the night before they tossed him in the pit, he came and sat down with us at dinner, before bed, when we actually had some little bit of food in our bowls. I noticed he ate his little portion, but he hated it. And he cried the whole time, just a tear or two, and the littlest sobs. He was in so much pain. And we all knew pain, but his was hurting him more than the hunger. That night, he talked to his girls the whole night, telling them it was going to be alright, then on occasion he would say he was sorry. He said it over and over, 'It's going to be alright,' then tell them he was sorry.

"The next day, he snapped.

"We were walking to the fields to plant our winter wheat. Four, five seeds in hole, we were ordered. Mao says wheat, like men, must stick together to be strong. Min fell to his knees, crying and begging his girls to forgive him, and telling them, 'It will be alright.' He was not right in his head. The guards were yelling at him and ordering him up. For a while, he knelt there, starting to get louder, asking for forgiveness, saying, 'It will be alright.' Nothing could move him, and then one of the guards hit him, and he laughed and started to get up, yelling at the guard to hit him, saying, 'Kill me! Kill me, please,' begging them to hit him. They did not know what to do, and the next thing, we knew he was in the pit. He was there a week, and they let him out the day after the westerner died."

Cho stopped talking. He was done. But this time the man did not hesitate. He looked hard at Cho, "What happened in the pit?"

"No one knows. He was in there with the Westerner, the white man, and at first, they were quiet, but by that evening, they were both singing. Different songs, but mostly the one he sang to the dying. Over and over, it was peaceful and beautiful. Even some of the guards started to sing it until the Commander threatened to put them in volunteer clothes.

The man thought for a minute. Then he said, "A song, just a song?"

"You said you knew him before. Tell me."

IX

"I had seen him a little here and there, but we did not really know each other. Before I was put in here, I spent two days in his town up the road. We got there, and I spent the day loading seed bags onto wagons. I did not mind because they gave us triple rations for being on the work detail We were going to save our town they told us.

160

We worked all day and were dog tired, but we thought about all day our next meal. We got three meals, good meals. That was the best food we'd had in months. My mouth watered all day just thinking about it. My muscles ached from moving so many bags of seed. And we loved it, working again for food. We all hid some in our pants to take back with us.

"That evening, we slept on the wagons, the best sleep we'd had in forever. I laid my head down on those seed bags, and—maybe it was because I had a full stomach for the first time in ages—I fell asleep and slept like a baby. Then, in the middle of the night, I woke up. It took me a minute to realize why, but then it hit me. I smelled meat. Meat, can you believe it? I jumped up and ran towards the smell. It was coming from the far end of the street, and I rushed into the house, I didn't even stop. There they were, an entire family, yesterday starving to death now eating meat. Meat, I haven't seen meat since then. We had already eaten the horses a month ago. There were grandparents and parents and aunts and uncles seated and eating in silence. Some of them were crying, but no one was not eating. Min was there, eating, sitting there and eating, staring into nothing."

The man sat on his stool. Cho had stopped talking again. He could have sworn the man almost smiled. Then he asked Cho what was almost his last question.

"Had you seen Min earlier on that trip?

Cho looked confused and thought for a bit.

"Yes, I had seen him that afternoon in the street near the market where we were working. He had his children with him, and he was with another man and his children. Both men were telling them it was going to be okay. It was odd. Each took the other's children and left.

The man asked, "Were the children at the dinner?"

Then it hit Cho. "Oh my, oh my, Min." He said it. The man stood up and started to walk out. He stopped at the door to ask his last question. "What was the song? How did it go?"

Outside, the man walked towards the gate. Outside sat his men, waiting for their orders, half a dozen jeeps, full of solders. The Commander and an aide rushed to meet the man.

"Well, well what did you find?" he asked with a quick bow.

The man was still thinking about the song, and the Commander asked again.

After a moment, the man answered. "I think that you let someone give them hope, Commander."

The commander went pale, but the aide answered. "Hope," he said. "What is hope? Let them have hope, who cares?"

"Indeed. Who cares?" the man answered quietly.

He walked out the gates and gave a short order to his troops. As they obeyed, he continued walking and walking. Behind him, shots started to ring out, as his troops did their work. The man walked on until the shots started to fade. Slowly, the man started to hum. Then the humming turned into singing. Then he started to cry. It was beautiful. He sang and sang. Would they ever forgive him?

He sang: "Aaave aaave AAAVE Maria."

The Moles of Vienna:
A Story in the World
of the Last Brigade
William Alan Webb

Vienna, Austria
3:51 am, September 7, 1683

The distant boom of Turkish cannon achieved its purpose of keeping the Viennese and their defenders sleepless. In his family's room near the bakery he owned, Heinrich Güsse stared at the top of his box bed while his infant daughter Gerda gurgled at her mother's breast beside him. His wife's body heat made his left side wet with sweat and, even with the window shutters and the door of the ornate bed opened to let in the night air, inside the stout piece of furniture, it remained hot.

Sleep was elusive. Hunger twisted his stomach, as it did all Viennese after two months of the Turkish siege. The headache that started at the crown of his head and ran down his neck into his shoulder blades never abated, even for a moment. Even if he were not in constant pain, however, the clatter of horse's hooves along the street outside would have awakened him. It was that time of day when shopkeepers reloaded their shelves with whatever goods had been smuggled into the besieged city.

Sweating in the darkness, he lay atop the blanket and prayed for sleep to return, but as the minutes ticked by, and his bed linen grew wetter, he gave up. The lighting of a lantern across the street sent dim lighting into his bedroom. It belonged to Walcher the metal smith, who always lit it around four. Rolling on one side, he lifted the pocket watch off the night stand and squinted to read the time. Three minutes until four o'clock; Walcher was right on time, as usual. It was time to get up.

Dressing in the dark was tedious. After slipping on his close-fitting, brown breeches he pulled hose on over them and pushed his feet into a pair of worn-out, square-toed,

163

black shoes. His long shirt, white but smeared with food stains and smelling of bread, hung over his belt. Despite the heat, he slipped on a long coat of the same material as his breeches, followed by his Tyrolean hat. As the siege continued, many people quit bothering with societal conventions of dress, but Güsse felt it was more important now than ever to stick to Austrian customs. Leaving as quietly as he could, he kissed the Crucifix standing on a wooden pole beside the door and crossed himself, asking for God's protection as he went about his work.

Aside from merchants and their wagons, silence hugged the city under a blanket of air so still that the scuff of his shoes on the paving stones sounded preternaturally loud. The bakery was three blocks west of his home and abutted the city's main wall west of the Danube River, not far north of the Carinthian Gate. As he approached it, he once again thought of the wall as God's shield against the ravaging hordes of Satan.

The Emperor's Food Minister had told the bakeries that were still open to experiment with recipes using sawdust mixed with some of the few available flours, such as rye and barley. Güsse's recipe had impressed even the famous monk, Marco d'Aviano, who was coming by after dawn with the minister and other officials to discuss what would be needed to bake large quantities of the bread. He needed to have everything prepared for their visit, so getting up early was actually a benefit. Once again, God knew what he needed before Güsse did.

All three of the bakery's windows appeared as black squares in the darkness of the night. One of the panes had cracked during a Turkish cannonade two weeks before. Once he fired the ovens, the scent of bread would snake through the perpetual reek of horse dung and sewage hanging over Vienna like a fog. With the new recipe using sawdust, the scent had a woody smell, mixed into that of bread. Stopping before the front door, he closed his eyes and tilted his head back for a last look at the stars.

Tink.

He didn't move at the noise, even though it sounded odd. It was so faint that, any other time of day, he wouldn't have heard it. He mentally shrugged.

Tink.

He looked around. It sounded metallic. Had the keys on the big ring in his pocket clinked together? It didn't sound like that.

Tink, tink, tink.

What *was* that? It seemed to be coming from...the wall? How could that be? He took a few steps in that direction, then some more, until he could touch the rough, cool stone towering far over his head into the night. He put his right ear against the cool stone.

Tink, tink, tink.

He heard that through his left ear, not the one pressed against the wall...what was going on? His mind worked through what it could mean, and then his eyes widened. He dropped to his knees. The flagstones so close to the wall were dirty but not caked with horse manure, so he brushed away straw and dust to fit his ear against them.

Tink, tink.

The sound was coming from underground! And that could only mean one thing.

*   *   *

Charles Angriff knew it was a dream, because the man's beautiful face smiled down at him from an impossibly great height. The long fingers of the man's right hand beckoned Angriff to rise, but his limbs wouldn't move. He was paralyzed with fear, an emotion he rarely knew in waking life, yet which now overwhelmed him. Tears ran down his cheeks, although he knew not why he cried.

"Do not fear me, Charles."

He could move again, but hugged his knees while hiding his face. The power emanating from the angel, for what else could it be, left him quavering as he never did in waking life.

"Do not fear me, for your time has come. The Lord has need of you this day."

He answered in a voice that shook with fear. "Why me? I am no great man."

"All men who stand against evil in the Lord's name are great. Will you accept your burden?"

"Let God command me, and I will obey."

* * *

September 7, 1863
6:44 a.m.
"Lieutenant."

Despite the heat Angriff shivered under a thin blanket without waking up, but his unconscious mind registered that something kept pushing his left shoulder. A glimmer of consciousness returned, enough to feel the wet hosiery inside his boots and remember how it got that way.

"Lieutenant."

"Mmm...Keppler? Was ist los?" *What is happening?*

"Der oberst will dich." *The Colonel wants you.*

"Sag ihm, ich komme gleich." *Tell him I'm coming straight away.*

As much as it hurt his aching back just to sit up, Angriff stretched and then managed to get to his feet. Snoring men lay all around him on the floor, and he picked his way through them to the piss pot. Once finished there, he took a handful of water from the wash bowl and rubbed his face to liquefy some of the caked mud that had dried there after they'd dug the last tunnel. Using a filthy rag hanging by the bowl, he wiped his face and went outside.

Dawn lightened the shadows enough that he could read the pocket watch his grandfather had given him. He'd slept for fewer than four hours. It was a long walk from his quarters near the Carinthian Bastion to the center of town. Shafts of sunlight cast wan shadows over the narrow side streets running north and south, while nearly blinding him on the eastern avenues. He felt his toes squish in his boots with every step he took toward the regimental headquarters in the direction of Stephensplatz, near St. Stephens Cathedral. Ground water so close to the Danube had made the last tunnel they'd dug a nightmare, sometimes forcing them to wade through knee-high water. Soft, saturated skin sloughed off in painful sores that made Angriff limp on the unforgiving stone pavement.

Colonel Werfel looked even worse than Angriff. In the wake of the devastating Thirty Years War, dozens of new duchies, kingdoms, and states had risen from the ashes of the Holy Roman Empire. Thirty-five years after the Treaty of Westphalia, the veteran officers who fought in that horrific conflict were mostly gone, to be replaced by sycophants, royal relatives, and politically influential officials whose chief qualifications were they could afford the finest and most ornate uniforms. Werfel was the exception to that rule. As a lieutenant, he'd fought through the last five years of the war and, because so many men died in the fighting, rose rapidly afterward in service first to the Elector of Bavaria, Maximilian I, then to Ferdinard Maria and most recently to Maximilian II Emanuel.

Two Bavarian sentries holding pikes flanked the heavy oaken door of an inn that still had its windows. Angriff knew them both in passing and nodded as he entered the front room. He found Colonel Werfel standing beside a table with several other men. Steam rose from cups of something dark pushed well away from the maps cluttering the surface.

Werfel's haggard face looked up at Angriff, who had stopped ten feet from the table. Stringy, gray hair surrounded a bald crown but in private he doffed his peruke, which lay over a chair so that the powdered, white curls hung like tree branches heavy with snow. A man stood on either side of the Bavarian regimental commander, one well-dressed in the Austrian fashion, his peruke scented with lavender, while the other wore the robe of a monk.

"Gröss Gott, Lieutenant." *Greet God, lieutenant.* "Thank you for coming so quickly, I know that you and your men only closed the latest tunnel late last night and so you must be very tired."

"Service in the name of the Lord refreshes me, Colonel."

Werfel waved him forward. Usually the Colonel jested with his officers for a moment, often jibing Angriff for his overt religious enthusiasm, but not that time. Now his expression remained grim.

167

"Allow me to introduce Herr Doctor Johannes Schiller, the representative of Vienna's garrison commander General Count Ernst Rüdiger von Starhemberg. And this is Friar Marco d'Aviano, advisor to the Emperor. They have come on a matter of great urgency."

Neither of the visitors did more than nod to acknowledge him, which was fine with Angriff. His hands ached from the past week's round-the-clock digging and his right shoulder burned from the exertion. Furthermore, dirt caked the back of his hands and under his nails. He also stank to the point where he could smell his own reek, even over the mouth-watering scent of bread coming from the kitchen.

"That is an unusual family name Lieutenant," said d'Aviano. "I've known several Kriegers, but never anyone named Angriff before."

"Nor have I, domnus. It was bestowed on my distant grandfather by King Karlmann, son of Ludwig the German, for service in war. Family lore says that he was fearless in battle, and the king named him Nicholas the Angreifer to honor him, and gave permission for his family to take the name Angriff."

"His blood obviously runs in your veins."

"Do you drink coffee, Lieutenant?" Doctor Schiller said, as if Angriff was a member of the aristocracy with ready access to that exotic delicacy.

"I have never tasted it, my lord."

"Well then, you must certainly try some. God's spirit certainly refreshes us, as you have said, but I have never heard that He objects to a little help. Coffee delights the senses and keeps our eyes from closing. Perhaps you should think of it as the method by which God refreshes your soul."

Schiller waved to a beefy man preparing food in the kitchen, and, seconds later, he stepped forward holding a chipped ceramic cup with curls of steam rising from within. Clearly unused to having such important people in his dining room, when the man nodded in what he must have thought was the proper fashion, his lank hair flopped around his head and dripped sweat on one of the maps.

Schiller wiped away the sweat and bade the man hand the cup to Angriff.

"Thank you, Herr Güsse," d'Aviano said before Schiller or Werfel could speak.

"Yes, my lords." The man disappeared back into his kitchen.

"Please, enjoy," Schiller said, indicating the coffee with a wave.

Angriff stared at the dark brown liquid, then sniffed it and touched it with the tip of his tongue. It burned, and he leaned back, spilling a little.

"Blow on it so that it cools."

Glancing at the doctor, he noticed Colonel Werfel behind him, looking annoyed. When Werfel saw Angriff looking their way, he made a sign with his finger to hurry up, to which the lieutenant nodded. Blowing on the coffee for ten seconds, Angriff sipped just enough to get the flavor. To his surprise, he liked it. The bitterness reminded him of the strong chocolate he'd tasted during the visit of some Spanish dignitaries to Munich, when he and his men had stood for inspection. After the ceremonies had ended, the Spanish delegation served a hot chocolate beverage that Angriff would never forget. And here, he'd found something a little bit like it, but different, too.

"It is very good, my lord. Thank you for your generosity."

"Nonsense, Lieutenant, it is but a token of the gratitude that we Austrians owe to those who left their homeland and came to the defense of Christendom." But Schiller's demeanor changed then, from almost jovial to something grimmer. It wasn't simply the twisting of his smile into a frown, but also the sudden sag of his shoulders and bend of his knees, as though a blacksmith's anvil had been affixed to his back. "I must now ask something very difficult of you and your men, Lieutenant."

Angriff had known that was coming. Men like Schiller no doubt saw themselves as being beneficent to the lower ranks, but Colonels didn't share luxuries with mere lieutenants unless they wanted something extraordinary.

"If by our labors we might bring honor to God and Bavaria, Herr Doctor Schiller, you need only command, and we shall obey."

"Fair words, Lieutenant, and I'm sure you mean them, but you and your men just finished a counter-tunnel yesterday, did you not?"

"I lit the fuse just before midnight, Colonel. Perhaps you heard the explosion?"

Schiller seemed embarrassed. "I did not. My labors sent me to my rest early last night. I am told it was a very difficult tunnel to dig. May I presume the explosion was large?"

"Not so large, but very hard to put in place. As they always do, the Turks fought like devils as we loaded our powder. We had to fight until the last possible moment before evacuating the tunnel to keep from being buried, and I'm sure some of them worked until the last to stop our fuse from igniting the powder. They had gotten with twenty feet of the wall right of the Carinthian Gate but hadn't yet placed their own charges. The Lord brought us to battle in time to stop them."

At that moment, the Turkish siege guns opened fire and began their daily bombardment. The dull thunder echoed through the room.

"They're early today," said Colonel Werfel.

"They remember what happened last time," Schiller said in response. "Do you know the story, Lieutenant?"

"Didn't the siege last into winter?"

"Yes, quite so." The crash of a large caliber Turkish round shot hit the wall of a house somewhere close by, followed by the sound of walls crashing and timbers cracking. As the conversation continued, Angriff listened for the sound of flames that might indicate if the Turks were using heated shot. "And as you can tell, Satan's helpers do not intend to make the same mistake again. What you may not know is that at this moment three armies are converging on Vienna from the west, the northwest, and the north."

Angriff's fatigue vanished. "Aber Das ist Wunderbar!" *But that is wonderful!*

"Yes, if the Turks do not in get here first."

"My lord?"

"There is a new tunnel that is dangerously close to the walls, Lieutenant . The man who brought you your coffee heard noises this very morning, digging noises. Heeding his warning, we sent men into a cellar near the Carinthian Gate, and they heard digging noises, but they were not skilled enough to determine from exactly where they came. That is why you are here. The reputation of the Bavarian miners is well known throughout the city, and when I asked Colonel Werfel who his best tunnel men were, he said you and your company. I know you spent the last week digging and fighting underground..." Schiller pointed at a small shovel hanging from Angriff's belt, the dish of which had been ground to a sharp point. "I can see by the blood staining your weapon that you fought beside your men. I expected nothing less. And now I have to ask you, in the name of the city, the Emperor, and of Almighty Christ, to do it one more time."

"Of course, Colonel. I consider it my holy privilege."

"Excellent, Lieutenant, on behalf of the Emperor and the people of Vienna, I am grateful. But I will not lie to you about the state of the city's defenses. If you cannot stop this tunnel before a mine is set off under the wall, then I fear Vienna is doomed. I do not have to tell you how short we are of food..."

"Is it true my lord, that General Count von Starhemberg has decreed fainting on sentry duty a capital offense?"

"Yes, Lieutenant." Angriff started to say more, but stopped himself. D'Aviano glanced at Schiller with a disapproving expression of narrowed eyebrows. Schiller continued. "Beyond needing food, we have also taken heavy casualties during the siege. We are running out of men, ammunition, and yes, even hope. If the enemy breaches the walls, Vienna will surely fall. Your burden is heavy."

"I will bear it, my lord."

*　　　*　　　*

171

September 7, 1683
8:05 a.m.

The coffee made Angriff more alert for a short period, but as he trudged back to his quarters, his eyes kept closing of their own accord. The Turkish bombardment was in full progress , and the sounds of breaking glass and stone should have been enough to keep him alert, but they were not. After two months, they had simply become the normal backdrop to life in the Austrian capital, and his exhaustion overwhelmed his senses.

Vienna reeked of animal droppings, burnt wood, powdered brick, and death. As he walked down a narrow street, a woman staggered by going the other way. Dried blood covered her face and shirt. When she saw him, she held out a lifeless infant wrapped in a blanket.

"Bitte hilf meinem kinder." *Please help my child.*

A month before he might have told the woman in gentle tones that her infant had passed into God's hands, and gone with her to find her priest and arrange for burial. But now he stared back at her with slack face and lidded eyes and kept on walking.

Colonel Werfel promised they would receive all the help he could give to speed completion of the new tunnel. Men to carry dirt, as much planed wood as could be found, whatever extra food could be turned up, and all the powder and balls they might need. As he rounded the last corner before coming to the house where his men slept, he smelled smoke and had to detour around the flaming ruins of a large house, where a man with his clothes on fire ran down the street waving his arms and screaming.

The calfs of his legs burned by the time he got back to his company's quarters. Pushing through the heavy double front doors, he entered a short, dark hallway that led to a large room that had once been a music hall. Heavy drapes blocked floor to ceiling windows, which not only keep out the morning sunlight but also deadened the sound of the Turkish cannonade. Scattered on every flat surface and in every chair sprawled his men, all of them sound asleep and snoring. The room stank of sweat and mud.

Angriff picked up a dented metal pot and pulled the sharpened shovel out of his belt. Holding it by the haft, he beat the wooden handle against the interior of the pot to create a loud, dull clanging.

"Wach auf, Jungs, es ist Zeit zur Arbeit zu gehen!" *Wake up, lads, it's time to go to work!*

His men woke up with groans and curses. Most officers would not accept such grumblings, but such officers rarely matched their men's hard labor, either. Angriff was the exception and refused to allow any man under his command to outwork him.

"Wake up. The Turks are digging again, and we've been ordered to stop them again."

The first man to his feet was the man Angriff relied upon more than any other, Sergeant Heiligbrunn. Several inches shorter than Angriff's six feet, Heiligbrunn bore the stoop and the scars from decades of mining salt. Arms, legs and chest were all thickly muscled, but it was in his face you could see the years of heavy, underground labor. A long scar interrupted his black beard from the left jawline halfway up the cheek, while his nose bent to the right from having been broken too many times. Like most of the men, though, his eyes matched the mid-color blue of his uniform pants and coat. And like all of them, he was filthy.

"I'm sorry, Lieutenant," he said, sleep still slurring his words. "I didn't hear you come in."

Angriff smiled down at the huge man. "I didn't make much noise. Tell the men to assemble out front in five minutes."

In fact, it was nearly ten minutes before the remnants of his company stood at attention in the street outside. Angriff could already feel the day heating up as the sun rose higher.

Lack of sleep sapped his ability to think so he stood waiting like a man in a trance, staring as a pack of rats feasted on one of their number who'd been run over in the middle of the street. An old woman emerged from an alley and shooed them away, picking up the mangled carcass by its tail. Holding it close to her eyes, she sniffed it before putting it in a cloth bag hanging over her shoulder. Angriff thought the other rats must be well-fed to let one small human steal their meal without a fight.

Thirty-seven men lined up in two rows outside the house where they were quartered, all that remained of the ninety men he'd led into Vienna less than two months earlier. Only two non-commissioned officers could still fight. Lance-Corporal Keppler stood on the far left and Sergeant Heiligbrunn stood next to Angriff.

Angriff knew most of his men from their jobs in the mines around Berchtesgaden, but even as sunlight lit their faces, he didn't recognize many of them. It wasn't just the fatigue that left black circles around their eyes and slackened their features. None of them had bathed in a month, and a thick layer of sweat, skin oil and dirt covered them like a gray-brown paste. Even their uniforms looked more of a dark gray color than blue.

"You've earned a long rest, men, but the Turkish sappers have been digging again, and this time we may be too late to stop them." When a large round shot screamed overhead and landed a block away in an explosion of broken masonry, none of the Bavarians even flinched. For his part, Angriff barely paused. "But it's our mission before God to try, and that's what we're going to do.

"Colonel Werfel promised to send us extra rations and more hands to help with the dirt. He's also sending us more pistols, powder, balls, and anything else he's got that we can use. Are there any questions?"

Most officers would never have asked such a question, but these men were his neighbors. One was kin to Angriff's wife. But it was more than that, he didn't think the arrogance and imperiousness of most officers was the best way to lead men.

A short man with gnarled fingers held up his left hand. "Isaac?" he said.

"Do you think we might eat today, Lieutenant?"

Angriff smiled his most reassuring smile. "I do, Isaac, but I can't guarantee what it will be."

A few of the men laughed, and Angriff laughed with them, even though he was not joking.

*   *   *

174

September 7, 1683
9:23 a.m.

Colonel Werfel was as good as his word. In the deepest part of the cellar of a leather-maker's shop near the western wall, between the Carinthian and Burg Bastions, Angriff's men gathered around a pot of steaming broth that had bits of meat and barley floating near the top. A heavy set civilian with a long beard ladled out generous portions into the men's bowls, along with a chunk of *kommissbrot*, dark bread made from whatever flour was available. There was even a small block of hard white cheese and a barrel of watery beer to wash it down.

Once he had let his men eat, Angriff strode into their midst, which signaled them it was time to work. About the only candles left in the city were those made with tallow, and they tainted the already foul air with an acrid overlay. Worse were the lanterns which only had fish oil left for fuel. When combined with the rancid-meat smell of the candles, the combination was hard to breathe without retching.

"Sergeant, can nothing be done about the smell?" cried a man named Schmidt.

"The rest of us thank God for it, Schmidt, because it smells better than you do!"

Two of the men brought in a wooden drum with a skin stretched tight over it and placed it near the cellar's western side. At the sight of them, everyone else went silent. Lance-Corporal Keppler dug a handful of beads out of a small bag and poured them onto the skin. All eyes in the room focused on him.

Vibrations from the Turkish spades, voices and the hammering of nails all caused the beads to jump and bounce, but so did the muted thunder of cannon fire which filtered through the layers of stone and dirt over their heads. It was known that the Turks often fired a cannonade to mask the sounds of their tunneling, and this is where the expertise of Angriff's men became critical. There was the slightest difference in the effect the two sounds had on the beads, a very subtle variance that only a master miner could discern. In Angriff's company, that man was Lance-Corporal Keppler.

Never a tall man, years underground left Keppler with the rounded back that was so common among salt and coal miners it was called Bergmannshöhle, or Miner's Hunch. Like a gnome from legend, he huddled over the drum skin, his nose only a few inches from its surface, holding a flaring candle so that it threw a puddle of light over the beads. Several times he glanced to one side or another, or twisted his head to see the beads at a different angle. Angriff never failed to marvel at Keppler's talent for reading the beads, but sometimes wondered at his theatricality. Still, during their two months in Vienna this would be the ninth tunnel they'd dug, and so far, Keppler had been dead accurate with his predictions of where the Turkish sappers were digging.

After ten minutes, he rose and retrieved something from his rucksack. Hinged along the center and made of thinly beaten tin, it folded out into a funnel with a narrow spout. Keppler had found the strange device in a burning shop not long after they had come to Vienna and immediately recognized its value. He had offered to pay the shopkeeper, who stood in the street weeping as his life's work burned to the ground, but the man said that if it would help him against the Turks Keppler was welcome to it. The shopkeeper called it an ear trumpet.

Holding it against the stone of the cellar's western wall, Keppler closed his eyes and listened. Nobody spoke as he moved down the wall and disappeared into the shadows. One of the men took up an oil lamp and followed, but the rest held back. They were all used to the near dark conditions and glanced at each other as the minutes wore on. For his part, Angriff's fatigue began to catch up with him, and he found it hard to keep his eyes open.

"Here! Down here, he's found it!"

Exhaustion vanished, and Angriff followed his men seventy feet down the wall. They went so far as to pass into the cellar of the adjoining building through a hole knocked in the wall that separted them, probably by the owners at the start of the siege. Many residents fled to their cellars as shelter against Turkish cannon shot, but if their house was hit and set on fire there was no way to get out. The holes prevented that. So many cellars had been connected by holes that it was possible to travel long distances entirely without having to ascend to street level.

Keppler marked the spot to begin digging with a large circle drawn by using the charred end of a piece of wood. As his men gathered at the spot and began organizing their picks, shovels, baskets, and other tools, more lantern light gave Angriff a better look at the charcoal circle.

As it came into focus, the circle began to shimmer with swirling colors of white and gold. Angriff stared at it, transfixed, and after a few seconds, it seemed to sink back into the Earth like a tunnel stretching away into infinity. Rays of light so bright that he blinked shone like the sun had come into the cellar. Then a man came into focus, the same young man he'd seen in his earlier dream, smiling in a way that made him know, know with absolute certainty, that once he entered that tunnel, he would never come out alive again, but instead would go to be with God. He couldn't say how he knew it, he just did.

*   *   *

"Lieutenant? Are you well sir?"

Angriff blinked, and the light disappeared. Sergeant Heiligbrunn stood beside him, frowning in worry. He smiled and patted the larger man on the shoulder.

"Danke, feldwebel, Ich bin nur sehr müde." *Thank you, Sergeant, I am just very tired.*

"You scared me, sir."

"Send a runner to Colonel Werfel, and let him know we're ready but can't begin until we get wood to shore up the tunnel and the men he promised to haul away the dirt."

Wood had become scarcer than food as the siege had worn on. The Turks had gangs of men dedicated to nothing more than cutting and hauling trees out of the Vienna Woods south of the city, and then planing them into planks to shore up their tunnels. Dozens of smithies had been set up to forge nails, hammers, picks, shovels, and iron sconces for the tunnel walls. Within Vienna, however, stocks of wood had long since been depleted, most of the trees being long since felled. The only source now was salvaging unburned wood from destroyed buildings. Likewise with nails, which had to be dug out of the ruins, straightened, and re-used.

Once the miners removed the heavy square-cut stone slabs that made up the cellar's western wall, the noise brought the home's owner down to discover the source of the noise. Extending a candle-holder with a lit candle, he waved it until he could make out details of the uniformed men holding picks and shovels. Angriff watched him and could tell that, for just an instant, the man thought about protesting the damage to his cellar, but changed his mind and turned to retreat upstairs.

"Sir!" Angriff called. "You on the stairs, halt!" The man took two more steps before stopping.

"Wh-what can I do for you...captain?"

Angriff didn't correct him for using the wrong rank. "We require you to leave the candle."

"But sir, if–"

"If you wish, I will write you a receipt so the city may recompense you after siege is broken. But for now, you *will* leave the candle."

"Of course." With obvious reluctance the man laid it on a step and went upstairs.

As his men got ready to begin the tunnel, Angriff walked into their midst to inspire their efforts and also give them some bad news.

"We all know the stakes, lads. If the Turks undermine the wall, they will take the city and then, not only will *we* die, but so will every good Christian man, woman, and child. So we've got to work hard and fast, and not stop until either we are all dead, or we destroy the Turkish tunnel...or both. We are fighting the Anti-Christ, but take heart, for God is with us."

His men did not cheer, and Angriff knew they were saving their energy for digging.

"May the Lord Jesus Christ bless our efforts, give strength to our limbs and lightness to our hearts."

When it appeared he was finished, the men nodded, a few crossed themselves, and they all got ready to work.

"One more thing," Angriff added. "Make this a four foot tunnel."

*   *   *

September 9, 1683
11:18 pm

Once the building stones were out of the way, the miners had dug into Vienna's underground footing, but the going was slow. They a hit patch of densely-packed clay mixed with rocks, mostly sandstone, which had to be laboriously dug out and then rolled or carried into a growing pile at the far corner of the cellar. And even when there were no rocks, clay was far heavier than looser packed dirts.

Twice the first day, they had to detour around a boulder too large to move. Normally, they could have tried blasting it with gunpowder, but aside from the time that would take, the Turks would have heard the explosion. Surely they already knew the Bavarians were digging a counter-tunnel. The hard part was figuring out the exact location of such a counter-tunnel, so care was taken to be as quiet as possible.

By the middle of day two, every man could clearly hear the *ch, ch, ch* of Turkish shovels, interspersed with an occasional *tink* as metal struck metal or stone. Turkish tunnels tended to be taller, because plentiful wood allowed for stronger, higher walls. Most of the time, all but the tallest man could stand up straight in a Turkish tunnel. Angriff's order to dig a four foot tunnel forced the miners to bend forward but also required less digging and wood.

Lance-Corporal Keppler guided their path by taking regular soundings. At his direction, the Bavarian tunnel had veered sharply right, to the north, after starting on a northwesterly course. At the ninety foot marked, it angled downward for ten feet before leveling off again. But as Angriff sat beside the tunnel's entrance that night, the blue of his uniform obscured by thick layers of ground-in clay, he heard Keppler pushing through the line of men passing baskets of dirt out of the tunnel.

"Step aside! Out of my way! Move!"

Since noise was the sapper's biggest enemy, the fact that Keppler raised his voice meant something urgent and dangerous. All eyes in the cellar focused on the tunnel mouth. Angriff pushed to his knees and then to his feet.

He jerked the filthy uniform coat to straighten it and ran a hand through his oily hair.

Not one inch of Keppler's face was without dirt. He bled from a dozen tiny nicks, but none of that was reflected in his eyes as he sought sight of his commander.

"I fear that we're too late, Lieutenant. There are no more sounds of digging, only curses and grunts."

"They're loading in the powder," Angriff said. Rubbing his eyes, he spoke in the most animated voice he could muster. "How much further do we have?"

"Ich weiss es nicht." *I don't know.* "Not far. Ten feet, perhaps less. But that will only intersect their tunnel, they are perhaps forty feet beyond us to the northeast."

"So they are already under the wall..."

"Yes."

Angriff only hesitated for a few seconds. "I want fresh men rotated to dig every five minutes. When it's your turn, dig like Satan himself is chasing you, because he is. Diggers move into the basket line after their turn at the front, moving down to the next station every five minutes. When you're last in the tunnel passing baskets, then you go back to dig again. You men there." He pointed to a group of men wearing the white and red uniform of the Habsburg troops who had been detailed to help the Bavarians as musketeers. "Ready your weapons, but leave your muskets. Bring pistols and knives only, there is no room for anything larger. When we break through to the Turkish tunnel, you will follow me. In the meantime, say a prayer that Almighty God grants us His blessing."

"I don't think there's enough time," Keppler said.

"There is surely no time to waste, Corporal. Go now, and dig!"

He stepped to one side as the cellar erupted in activity, making his way to the stairs which led to the house above.

"God *is* with you, Lieutenant," said a voice from the deep shadows under the stairs. "He is very proud of you."

Angriff picked up a candle from a nearby table and held it out to see the speaker's face.

"Domnus d'Aviano," he said, bowing his head. "I didn't know you were here."

The monk smiled. Angriff could almost feel the man's strength pouring from his body like a physical force, which was made all the more powerful because of his humble robe and kindly eyes.

"Wherever men glorify God by fighting the machinations of Satan, there I will be. Your hour is come, Lieutenant. All Vienna prays for you."

"Thank you." Angriff turned away to hide the expression he could not prevent from overcoming his face.

"What troubles you, my son?"

"I'm afraid, Domnus."

"Is it death you fear?"

"Not for me, no. But I have four sons, and if I die, what will become of them? We are not rich folk, and I fear for their sake, and that of my beloved wife, their mother. And also, if I am being honest, I fear that I will prove unworthy in the eyes of the Lord."

D'Aviano reached out and touched his shoulder. The skin of the monk's hands was rough, like that of a laborer.

"God does not task us to exceed our capabilities. He knows your heart, and if He has put you in this position, then it's because He knows you will succeed. As for your family, your sons, and the sons of your sons, and their sons beyond them, will thrive whether you are with them in physical form or not. And one day, they will face their own challenges and, like you, they will succeed."

He couldn't explain why, but d'Aviano's words filled Angriff's heart with hope. His fatigue vanished as the monk's words had been a tonic. Without realizing it, he gripped the handle of the sharpened shovel at his side.

"Thank you, Domnus. Your words are like manna from Heaven to this starving man."

D'Aviano chuckled. "I wish you were right, Lieutenant. A nice loaf would taste good about now."

*   *   *

September 10, 1683
12:31 am

"Lieutenant! We've struck their wood!"

Angriff nodded and turned back to the monk. "Pardon me, Domnus, my hour is upon me."

"Go with God, my son."

Motioning to the ten Habsburg soldiers to follow him Angriff set off down the tunnel. A rough plan had come to his mind. It was crowded with the basket line still there, but he told them to stay in place and to be ready to pass dirt the other way, that is, back toward the tunnel's end.

Once at the tunnel's terminus, he knelt beside Keppler. In the dim lantern-light, he saw the Lance-Corporal put a finger to his lips. They clearly heard voices speaking Turkish. The only barrier separating the Bavarian tunnel and the Turks was that of the boards lining the Turkish one, where light shone through the gaps. Keppler put his mouth within an inch of Angriff's ear so that his whisper couldn't carry to alert the enemy.

"Their powder barrels are somewhere off to the right."

Angriff nodded and put his mouth up to Keppler's ear, and they continued switching off throughout the brief conversation. "Do you know how far to the right?"

"I would guess about fifty feet."

Motioning to the Sergeant in charge of the Habsburg soldiers to join them, Angriff pitched his voice as quiet as he could. "Here's what we're going to do–"

*   *   *

Five minutes passed before everyone was in place, and they all clearly heard the Turkish word everyone dreaded, sigorta. *Fuse.* It meant the powder was in place and ready for the fuses to be lit. Time had run out.

The boards used to hold up tunnels did not need to be thick, only the supports did. Nor were they usually nailed tightly in place, because that was not necessary for them to hold dirt out of the tunnel. In other words, the integrity of the tunnel depended on the supports and the ceiling, not the side boards. All sappers knew this.

Sergeant Heiligbrunn was the Bavarians' strongest man. He stood next to the wooden wall and, swiveling his hips to put all of his strength behind the blow, he swung a large hammer at the boards, while everyone else backed up to give him room. Instead of holding the hammer so that only the face struck the wood, he held it so the entire lengthwise head smashed into the adjoining tunnel. Wood cracked and splintered under the blow. Two seconds later,

Heiligbrunn launched his shoulder at the jagged gap and crashed through, ripping a man-sized hole in the wood.

A startled Turk took the brunt of Heiligbrunn's charge in his chest. He was driven backward and had no chance to block a jab to the nose by the head of the sledgehammer. He fell, holding his nose, until a second swing of the hammer crushed his skull.

Angriff entered right behind the Sergeant, a pistol in each hand. Glancing to the right, he saw two shadows moving in the darkness at least fifty feet down the tunnel. He dared not shoot that direction, lest the ball miss his target and touch off the barrels of black powder that surely must be down there. Instead he turned left, where another Turk raised a pick to bring down on his head. The explosion of his pistol startled everyone within hearing range, echoing as it did off of the tunnel's wooden sides. The ball hit the Turk in the sternum, and he staggered backward before crumpling.

"Hurry, Keppler, hurry!" Angriff yelled. Facing west toward the Turkish tunnel's exit, he couldn't see more than fifteen feet in the darkness. Apparently, they had surprised the Turks in the process of lighting their fuses, since all of the lanterns, candles, and torches were gone. The only light came from small oil lanterns held by the men who were responsible for lighting the fuses.

Angriff waited for the Imperial troops to join him, but none did. At the other end of the tunnel, he heard the ring of metal on metal, followed by grunts and a voice crying in Turkish "anne, anne." *Mother, mother.* Then Heiligbrunn came up behind him.

"We were just in time, Lieutenant, they'd already lit the fuses. Another minute would have been too late."

"Where are the Habsburgs?"

This time it was Keppler who spoke. "They fled in panic, Lieutenant. Horst tried to stop them, but they threatened to run him through."

"Damn their coward's souls!" Angriff rarely swore, but this time his anger couldn't be contained. How could they flee knowing what was at stake? "I'll bring them up on charges...but first we have to secure this tunnel. Lance-Corporal Keppler!" He waited for Keppler to come close

183

before continuing. "Build a wall behind me using the dirt from our tunnel. If we can finish that it will give us a point to defend while we haul their out their barrels of powder, but make sure you leave me a space to get out. Sergeant, you begin unloading their powder into the cellar."

"We could leave it in place and pour water over it, Lieutenant, that would be faster."

"No, the garrison is almost out of powder, so we will use the Turk's own powder against them. But hurry. And bring me one small keg. If all else fails, I'll bring the tunnel down here and buy us time."

"Lieutenant—"

"Hurry, Sergeant, we have no time to debate!"

Fumbling in the semi-darkness of the single oil lamp, Angriff reloaded the pistol he had fired. Kneeling as close to the flame as he dared, he first measured powder from the horn hanging around his neck, eyeballing the amount based on long experience. He followed that by laying a thin strip of cloth over the barrel mouth and inserting a ball, both of which he then pushed down the barrel with the gun's ramrod. It took six hard slams to get the ball all the way down and in place. He then primed the pan with more powder and flipped down the frizzen. The pistol was ready to fire again.

Man after man piled up dirt behind him. He glanced behind to see the wall already at knee height, as Lance-Corporal Keppler dumped basket after basket of dirt on the pile before handing it back to the man behind him. Meanwhile, Sergeant Heiligbrunn and his men wrestled with the heavy barrels of powder. Seconds later Heiligbrunn ran up to him, puffing.

"There are at least thirty barrels, Lieutenant. It will take an hour to move them all."

"We do not have an hour! The Turks could be here any minute to find out what went wrong. You *must* get them out of here."

But Heiligbrunn pointed down the tunnel toward its entrance. "I think we are out of time, Lieutenant."

Lights appeared from the direction of the Turkish front lines, coming their way. Angriff noted four distinct lights, and he assumed there would be at least that many more men holding weapons instead of lamps. That meant no fewer than eight men, possibly many more.

"Damn," said Keppler.

"I'm fetching the boys, Lieutenant," said Heiligbrunn.

"Wait."

Angriff stood, thinking of his options and doing the calculations in his mind. Between his company and the men sent by Colonel Werfel to help with the heavy lifting and basket work, he had perhaps fifty men, all of whom were exhausted. If he had them fight, they could not unload the Turkish powder barrels. Nor could they finish the dirt wall in time. They might outfight the Turks, but they might not, too. And if they did not, the Turks could still set off their powder and bring down the wall. As Angriff saw it there was only one real option.

"Bring me a keg of powder and a fuse."

"But, Lieutenant–"

"Hurry, Lance-Corporal."

"How long should I cut the fuse?"

"Ten seconds."

"That won't give you enough time."

"Stop arguing! Forget the dirt wall, put all of the men to getting that powder into the cellar."

Heiligbrunn nodded and ran to the end of the tunnel. Keppler returned within forty-five seconds with the powder keg and fuse. The lights had grown much closer now, no more than two hundred feet away and moving fast. He handed Angriff the keg, which weighed thirty pounds, and tucked the fuse under the lieutenant's arm.

"Lieutenant, I...I–"

Angriff used his free arm to grasp Keppler's forearm.

"Tell my wife I love her, Franz, will you do that for me?"

"You're coming back, sir."

"But if I don't?"

Keppler nodded.

"When you hear shooting, get everybody back into our tunnel and into the cellar. Do you understand?"

The lance-corporal nodded again. Angriff thought he saw tears, but the blur could been caused by the water in his own eyes. Then he turned toward the Turks. He began to walk, slowly, although his heart pounded as if he'd just

185

run for miles. Chill sweat rolled down his forehead. He stopped and glanced back toward the tunnel his men had dug. It would be so easy to light the keg, turn and run...but he was too close. The explosion might set off the Turkish powder, the wall would collapse, and a final enemy attack would break the depleted Viennese defenders, leaving the Muslims to sack and murder at will.

"Lieutenant?"

He whirled to find the young man from his dream standing beside him.

"Where did you come from?"

At his smile, Angriff's fear evaporated. Whatever happened now, he knew it would be alright.

"I am always with you. For now, I think we had better make haste, do you agree?"

"I...yes, of course. Are you coming too?"

Once again, the beatific smile crossed the man's face "Of course."

Angriff picked up the candle and hurried as much as he could without dropping the keg. Once he stumbled, but the young man held him up. He'd gone more than one hundred feet when one of the Turks fired a musket. The ball ricocheted off a wooden wall with a muted *kunk* and disappeared down the tunnel. He had to hope he was far enough away from the Turkish powder. Kneeling, he put the keg next to one wall. Running steps could be heard on the hard-packed dirt floor.

The candle gave little illumination so he searched for the fuse hole by touch. The Turks were less than fifty feet down the tunnel when he found it and inserted the fuse. With the candle barely flickering, it took two precious seconds for the fuse to light. Angriff stood then and saw a horde of men no more than twenty feet away.

He drew the two flintlock pistols and fired without aiming. Both balls hit their targets, as they always did when Angriff used a firearm. The two men fell, and others tripped over them. He drew the sharpened shovel and swung it one-handed at a Turk who dove for the fuse. The blade struck the man's arm and knocked it away. Another man took advantage of his open stance and rammed a short spear into Angriff's stomach above his belt.

186

Pain lanced through his body, but Angriff grabbed the shaft of the spear and, using it for leverage, swung the shovel backhanded into the Turkish spearman's neck. More Turks crowded over him, some clawing for the fuse and others stabbing or kicking him.

Then the fuse reached the powder.

*   *   *

September 10, 1863
1:27 a.m.

The explosion woke Heinrich Güsse as it did most of the Viennese who lived in that quarter of the city. As usual, he'd left the doors of the box bed open to cool off, but even so, he didn't hear the blast so much as feel its vibration. And although not an expert on military matters, like most of Vienna's citizens, he had come to know the difference between a big explosion and a small one. This one sounded small, so for that he was grateful.

Also like his fellow Viennese, Güsse knew about the men they all had come to call the Maulwürfe von Wien, the *moles of Vienna*, who fought the enemy far underground, out of sight, in what must have been the nastiest fights to the death. Like that lieutenant he had served coffee to the other morning. He thought of the man then and said a quick Lord's Prayer that Christ should bless him and all of the other Maulwürfe with His grace. Then he lay down and tried to go back to sleep. In less than three hours, he'd have to rise again and see if there was any flour for baking bread that day.

The Queer
Graham J. Darling

It all came out in gym class.

Mister Poynter, in his ratty tracksuit, was dishing out one of his "serious talks." While he ran on and on, we and the rest sat around pretending to listen: we trading looks and nods on who to beat up in the shower today, and the rest trying hard to f-a-a-ade out, natch.

When just like that, the guy's goat voice cuts out in mid-bleat, his mole eyes go wide, and he makes like he's reaching for the next word in a place it usually was but isn't now and'll never be again. Then this weirdo kid jumps up and catches him before he hits the floor, and starts hilariously humping his chest and yelling "Call 911! Oh God, call 911!"

This looked like a good time to step out behind the school for a smoke. But we checked back in when the fire engine showed up—Brad the Rad got to hook a helmet that later made us a cool ashtray.

While those dudes were jump-starting old Poynter—and asking each other who'd taken the call, or had they really all just piled into the truck without knowing why?--911 Kid flops against the wall bars like a spaz. Even after the ambulance came and left, he was still all sweaty and shaky, like he'd just run a mile away and two miles back. The whole damn class was gawking at him.

Then he looked up and around. "I saw... saw his heart stop," he said. "Suddenly I could see inside him, inside every one of you..." And he touched the shoulder of Mitch the Twitch, who went all still, straightened up, and never copped crank from us again.

He'd never given us grief, this kid, about forking over his milk money; or he'd take his licks when we found him broke, usually from paying some other chump's tab. Scrawnier than most, otherwise everyone-in-a-blender average; no homies, spent his spare time mumbling on his knees in a corner—the quiet type, and we like 'em quiet.

But now he'd pulled some Respect his way, and so away from us. And then we started to get some lip from the sheep, especially those who'd begun following him around, listening to his stupid stories. Time to cut him down to size.

But when we hid his lunchbox, a crow brought him a sandwich through an open window. When we dinged him with dirt clods on the way home, bears came out an alley and chased us away. When we stuffed him into a locker, someone let him out behind our backs without the key. When we dunked his head in the can, the toilet water turned into *eau de toilette*. When we tried to give him a wedgie, the waistband kept reeling out till it made a pile on the floor. When we dog-piled him on the playing field, he got up from under and walked away like we weren't there.

His hat, tossed back and forth with him in the middle, would fall short and land back on his head. Tacks on his chair turned to rubber, gum in his hair melted away, tied shoelaces came undone, spitballs missed, towel snaps backfired painfully, "Kick Me" signs wouldn't stick, hate mail got lost, whisper campaigns went nowhere. And even though we could corner him anytime and bring him to tears, we got no satisfaction from it, because you could tell they were for something about us and not for himself at all. And the pics turned out blank.

We couldn't use any of this. Though he never did either, from what we could see. When he wasn't wasting our time, he was wasting his own, with kid stuff. Every morning, he'd walk in through that homeroom door, take his seat and write down the teacher's ramblings like the rest (we don't have to, since we already know the only thing worth knowing). Math gave him trouble, though he helped other suckers with their history homework—except he wouldn't do our essays. And he paid no mind to the pecking order, but would talk to every doofus who'd talk to him. He'd listen to their prawwwblems, and in their own home jabbers, tell 'em what he told us, that someday they'd get away to a world we didn't rulez—as if.

Day by day, we smelled the rising stink of hope, heard more mutterings behind our backs, saw more eyes meeting ours. It got so bad we even offered to cut him in, if he'd just shut up and get with the program. No deal.

The last straw came when we tried to mess up his act by siccing the school slut on him. Instead, the day after they "accidentally" got locked in together in the supply room, she started a No Nookie club and got all her friends to join. That made us madder than ever.

So after the last bell, we carried him over to the old quarry, stripped him down and pitched him in. When we fished him out, he still had this goofy face on, so we dragged him back up and did it again—only this time, he somehow managed to miss the water.

Swimming accident. Kids fooling around. Happens every day. We got time off class for grief counseling.

Funny thing though, when we let go of him then—it was like everything turned upside-down and bass-ackwards. All at once, it was him who was hanging still, up in mid-air, looking sadly down on us. And it was us along the edge who were falling headfirst, with the whole world, away from him, into a dark sky crawling with twisty clouds glowing red in the sunset. It seemed to welcome us like a wide-open mouth filled with flames.

But finally, it was him who went splat, and we're still here.

The stream that sprang up from the rock where he hit, we stuffed with dirt till it stopped flowing. The flowers that people left, we threw away till they stopped coming.

Things soon got back to normal, pretty much.

Life is good again.

In Vino Veritas
J. B. Toner

Long ago, when Vaticon Prime was simply known as Earth, an architect submitted plans to Pope St. John XXIII for a new building on the Vatican grounds. The Pontiff returned them with a single handwritten comment in the margin: *Non sumus angeli*, "We are not angels." The good architect, it seems, had neglected to include restrooms.

Happily, one need not share the blood of the Seraphim to inhabit the Heavens. My name is Friar Clump, and I live and work in the asteroid town of Lindisfarne, deep in the gas cloud of Sagittarius B2. This blessed cloud is a mighty, 150-light-year-long testament to Our Fair Lord's desire for our happiness—for it is composed of billions upon billions of liters of Space Alcohol. My brother monks and I harvest this bounty in its raw form and prayerfully refine it into beers and wines that gladden hearts across the Milky Way.

That morning, when the visitors arrived, their timing was wonderful. Fr. Damascus, his hands raised in benediction, was just uttering the words of dismissal: "The Mass is ended, go in peace to love and serve the Lord." We all felt the subliminal shudder underfoot as a ship coupled with the airlock, and young Brother Juniper smiled.

"Guests!" he said. "Perhaps they'll break their fast with us, and we can test our morning lager on fresh palates."

I slapped him on the shoulder. "Come, let's go serve the Lord some beer in these least of His people."

The two of us headed for the airlock. Through the portholes, we could see that she was quite a large vessel— and outfitted with photon cannons, at that. A breath of foreboding stirred my cassock.

"Greetings in Christ!" Brother Juniper called, as the airlock door cycled open. "What brings you to Lindisfarne, friends?"

A man walked in. His stature was medium, his features average. He wore the epauletted indigo uniform of

The Peace, and four men with plasma rifles paced behind him.

"Conduct me, please, to your abbot," he said. His voice was mild, his eyes tranquil. My foreboding was a winter wind.

Abbot Trenneth met us in the great hall. Like Brother Juniper, he was a tall man; like me, a fat one. But there was that in his face that was not troubled by the sight of military-grade ordnance. "Gentlemen, you are welcome to our abbey. Your weapons, less so."

"Father, be so good as to assemble all of your people."

A pause. "And who shall I say is calling?"

"I prefer to introduce myself only once."

Abbot Trenneth gave Brother Juniper a nod, barely perceptible. The quick, birdlike young man trotted over to the old, knotted rope hanging from the archway and gave it three tugs. The bong of the bells felt somber this morning.

As our brothers filed into the hall, more soldiers came marching in from the ship. Armed as they were, any one of them could have incinerated every one of us. When we were all gathered, the medium man stepped forward.

"I am Janissary Adamson of Kenoma. As you see, I represent The Peace; and as you know, religious observance of any denomination is illegal in our territories."

"Mr. Adamson," I ventured, "Sagittarius B2 lies comfortably within the borders of Grey Space. Very comfortably indeed, you might say."

"Depending on what time of day you typically retire, that may have been true last night when you went to sleep. You awaken, however, under the terms of a new treaty. This entire megaparsec is now a domain of The Peace."

A rustle of murmurs.

"Silence, please. Unlike our enemies, we do not resort to barbarism to enforce our mandates. And as you must know—surely—one of the greatest foes to all peace is organized religion." He held up his hand to forestall reply. "Our time, however, is too limited for debate. As I say, you will not be coerced. But I assure you that, like all of our citizens, you will very soon choose to put an end to your observances. And your lives will be so much the richer for it."

Brother Juniper burst out, "But we'd rather—"

A sudden volley of hisses cut him off, the hisses of compressed air. The front row of soldiers had fired on us, but not with deadly intent. I felt a prick in my breastbone, like the trespass of a mosquito, as something broke the skin. With a rapid glance, I saw that all of us had been likewise pricked.

The abbot's voice made the hall's air ring. "What is the meaning of this, Adamson?"

"It's easier to demonstrate than explain. But perhaps before we begin, you should take a moment to lead your people in prayer."

Glowering like an event horizon, Abbot Trenneth raised his right hand. "In the Name of the Father—"

I couldn't bear to listen. Fifty atmospheres of sorrow and despair weighed down on me. All joy, all hope, perished utterly and forever. I sagged with the misery of it, then slumped to the floor, feeling cold tears on my face. It was a long moment before I could register the fact that every one of my brothers had done likewise.

"Friends, you have been implanted with the Liberty Module: the first step toward freeing you from your self-imposed prison. The Module regulates the production of serotonin in your brains, and is coded to activate whenever it detects the audio or visual intake of religious terminology. If you read or speak the names of any saint, deity, or doctrine, you will experience instant, overwhelming depression."

We sat and wept.

"However!" Adamson continued. "You need only speak or read the phrase, 'Hail to The Peace.'"

Sudden vigor flooded my limbs, and I felt myself smiling for sheer, pure merriment. Bounding to my feet, I threw my arms around my nearest brother, and he laughed in delight. We were all standing again, and many of us dancing.

Then, gradually, we began to understand. The smiles faded.

"In a few months, the conditioning will be irreversible. Till that time, I shall leave a contingent here on Lindisfarne to ensure that no attempts are made to flee into Grey Space. Congratulations! You are all citizens of The Peace."

He turned on his heel and strode from the hall.

*　　*　　*

Incense hung in the air of the chapel. Candles flickered on the altar. But there were no hymns, no prayers, no Eucharist; we sat in the pews, silent.

Weeks had passed. Every few days, one of us would try again to persevere by will of man and grace of God, and breathe just one Hail Mary. Every time, we failed. If only they would torture us, I thought! I felt I could die cheerfully in a heathen oven, singing Glorias while the eyeballs boiled in my sockets. But this—

I sat there for a time, then rose. We spoke little these days. There was still the work, the Seraph's vocation of brewing our once-blessed brews. But labors not offered to the Lord became toil.

Heavily, I trod the hall to the wine vat. I was bottling today. One of the soldiers lounged in the corner, his rifle leaning heedless on the wall. I filled a bottle, corked it, began to melt the wax.

But I felt so heavy. The shackles on my immortality grew ever grimmer. Glancing over at the guard, I surreptitiously tucked the bottle into my cassock. Then I headed for the restroom, sat on a toilet, locked the stall door, and started to drink.

Strong stuff, this vintage. Inside ten minutes, I was mumbling an old Tuscan drinking song. Five minutes later, I was weaving stratagems: smash the bottle, slash the soldiers' throats! Five minutes after that, I was curled up on the bathroom floor.

"Oh my God, my God," I whispered, as the room bobbed and wheeled around me. "Oh my God, please help me. Please help us." A grown man, fetal on the ground with his forehead pressed to the cool porcelain, I prayed in wretchedness: "Our Father, Who art in Heaven, hallowed by Thy Name; Thy Kingdom come, Thy will be—"

I stopped.

194

"Wait. Wait, wait, wait!" Clawing madly at the toilet paper dispenser, I flailed and reeled my way to my sandalled feet. "I just ah—just said the ah—thingummybob—Our Father!" Turning swiftly, I bashed my nose on the stall door hard enough to pour blood down my cassock. It probably hurt, but we'll never know.

Fumbling frantically at the lock—sprawling through the door to the tiles beyond— I crawled like a fevered penitent to the hall. Providence, you know, is not always subtle: it so happened that exactly as I emerged, Brother Juniper was passing by. I clutched at his robe as if it could heal my afflictions.

"June," I spluttered. "Juniper. Juniper!"

"Brother, I'm here. I'm right here. My friend, what have you done to yourself?" He knelt and got my arms around his neck. "Come on, let's get you to bed. Can you stand?"

"Nonono, listenlisten. Uh... what was I... Oh! Listen: Our Father, Who art in Heaven, hallowed by Thy Name!"

He crumpled. "Why?" he sobbed. My friend, my brother, our little saint; It hurt to see him thus—but the hurt was dim and distant. "Why would you?"

"Juniper, look at me! Look! Hail Mary, full of grace, the Lord is with thee. Blessed art thou amongst women, and blessed is the fruit of thy womb, Jesus!"

Hugging his knees, rocking back and forth, he nonetheless began to nod. "I see. The chapel."

It's sacrilege, of course, to drink Communion wine as if it were just wine. But there were bottles in the sacristy that had never been consecrated—hence, they were in fact just wine. Shaking with despair, Juniper gulped down a whole bottle in a matter of minutes. And slowly, glacially, a smile crept across his face. The first genuine smile I'd seen in aeons.

"Hail... Mary." His smile broadened, and he clapped his hands like a child. "Yay!"

"C'mon June, we gotta tell th'others."

Leaning blindly on each other, we staggered our way to the great hall and yanked the bell-cord again and again. The brothers and the soldiers came running. "Look!" crowed Juniper. "Look what we can do! Glory be to the Father, and to the Son, and to the Holy Spirit."

The monks of Lindisfarne cried bitterly, but they understood. And then one of the soldiers did a silly thing: called out defiantly, "Hail to The Peace!"

Now buoyed by serotonin, the holy men (carrying Juniper and me like sacks of grain) stampeded for the wine vats. Like dying farers from a desert land, they hurled themselves at the elixir. Splashing, spraying, gulping, they drank themselves beyond the reach of the Liberty Module. The soldiers stood outside in the hallway, glancing back and forth at one another, baffled. And I began to sing:

"Faith of our fathers, living still, in spite of dungeon, fire and sword..."

And my brothers all sang with me. We flubbed the words, we cracked the tune, we slipped and fell all over one another. But we raised our voices and praised our God.

The captain of the guard entered the chamber. At his side was a hologram of Janissary Adamson. "You see the situation, sir," the captain said. "I'm requesting instructions."

"Monks!" barked the hologram. "You will stop that sedition immediately."

We sang all the louder.

"Soldiers! Stand by to fire on the traitors."

A dozen rifles.

"I warn you one last time to cease this activity!"

Abbot Trenneth fell to his knees in the pool of wine, his arms spread wide. "Into Thy hands, O Lord, I commend my spirit!"

We joined him on our knees, still singing. "Faith of our fathers, living faith, we will be true to thee till death!"

Adamson roared, "Fire!"

...And here we are.

About the Authors

H. David Blalock has been writing Speculative Fiction for nearly 40 years. His work has appeared in novels, novellas, short stories, articles, reviews, and commentary both in print and online. Since 1996, his fiction has appeared in over two dozen magazines including *Pro Se Presents, Aphelion Webzine, Quantum Muse, Shelter of Daylight Magazine, The Harrow, The Three-Lobed Burning Eye, The Martian Wave,* and many more. His current novel series is the three book Angelkiller Triad from Seventh Star Press. He serves as editor for parABnormal Magazine from Alban Lake Publishing. For more information, visit his website at www.thrankeep.com

Ian DiFabio is a writer from Michigan. His favorite authors are M. R. James, Algernon Blackwood, G. K. Chesterton, and fellow Michigander, Russell Kirk. He only wishes he could one day be one quarter as good as they were.

L. A. Story is a professional daydreamer and a naturalized Mississippian. She lives in an enchanted forest with her husband, a druid poet, and several small dogs who believe they are vicious wolves. She lives near her four brilliant children whom she believes are scary smart with world domination potential. Among said children, two have managed to produce four grandchildren who are possessed of equally frightening intellect. Check out more about L. A. by visiting her website at lastorywriter.com

Teel James Gleen was born in Brooklyn but has traveled the world for forty plus years as a stuntman, fight choreographer, sword master, jouster, illustrator, storyteller, haunted house barker, bodyguard, and actor. One of the things he's proudest of is having studied under Errol Flynn's last stunt double. He continues to teach sword work in New York.

He has worked regularly as an actor on *Guiding Light* and *New York* soaps alternately doing stunts and acting in over 300 episodes. He's worked as an actor and stuntman (in a fight scene with Hawk) on the *Spenser for Hire* TV series and in episodes of *The Equalizer.*

His most famous small screen appearance was as Vega (and fight choreographer) in the worldwide web series "Street Fighter: The Later Years."

As a writer, his stories have been in print in scores of magazines from *Weird Tales* to *Mad.*

He is also the winner of the 2012 Pulp Ark Award for Best Author.

Www.theurbanswashbuckler.com

Teel James Gleen on amazon for author page.

Tyree Campbell is a man of many hats: writer, editor, and publisher. He is the author of numerous short stories and novels including the *Nyx* series and *A Wolf to Guard the Door.* He helps run Alban Lake Publishing.

https://albanlakepublishing.com/

t. santitoro is an author, poet and editor, currently living in NEPA. She is editor of a minimal poetry magazine, Scifaikuest (Alban Lake Publishing), and has written a sf novel (The Saint and the Demon, with Ron Sparks—Sam's Dot Publishing) and a novelette, (The Legend of Trey Valentine--Alban Lake Publishing).

The Legend of Trey Valentine by t.santitoro | infiniterealms

http://store.albanlake.com/product/the-saint-and-the-demon

Robert J. Krog is a writer and Editor residing in Memphis, TN with his wife and children. He is the author of *The Stone Maiden and Other Tales* and *A Bag Full of Eyes*. He edited *A Tall Ship, a Star and Plunder*, two editons of *Potter's Field*, and *End of the World Potluck*. He has short fiction in anthologies from various publishers including "The Beauty of Being" in *Tomato Slices* by Amoeba Ink. Www.krogfiction.wordpress.com
https://www.amazon.com/Robert-J-Krog/

Koji A. Dae is an American writer living in Bulgaria. When not writing, she raises strange creatures known as children and shops for second-hand bargains around town. She has work published in *Short Editon, Luna Station Quarterly* and forthcoming with *Frostfire Worlds*.
https://kojiadae.ink/

Roy Gray's short fiction, nonfiction and even 'poetry' have appeared in magazines (eg Interzone and Sci Phi Journal), anthologies, journals, trade press, and online. He is not the Roy Gray who writes erotic poetry which also can be found online.
Roy's chapbook "The Joy of Technology," Pendragon Press 2011 – now a self-published e-book, could persuade some he is that other Roy Gray, but there are a least two of them, and this Roy's poetic efforts remain decidedly chaste.
Roy won two Science in Print (Physics in Print) awards and, in collaboration with Phil Emery, a UK 'Public Awareness of Science' grant in 2003.
He has a degree in Physics and worked for a major pharmaceutical company. His specialty was

packaging for new products. He lives in East Cheshire England.
https://roy444.wordpress.com/about/
https://www.facebook.com/roy.gray.589

At the age of twenty-five, **Imogean Webb** loves to spend time with her four-year-old along with another baby on the way. Books and storytelling have always been her passion. She intends on finishing college in the next two years at Southwest TN Community College with the hopes that her writing career will have jump-started.

Jessi Roberts lives and works on her family's cattle ranch in eastern Montana. She has a flock of chickens, a golden retriever, some cows, and a few horses. She enjoys Fantasy and Science Fiction. Her head is full of wild Sci-Fi story ideas, some involving apocalypses and others involving aliens. She often like interspersing real-world politics into fictional universes.
https://jessilroberts.wordpress.com/
https://www.amazon.com/Jessi-L-Roberts/

Michael Krog was born in Memphis and, after a misspent youth and a stint in the army, returned home there to run a small business and write in his spare time. He has previously been published in anthologies published by Dark Oak Press and Media, Pros Se Productions, and Alban Lake Publishing. He currently resides in Arizona with his wife and son, teaches grade school, and writes in his spare time.

William Alan Webb grew up in Memphis with a lifelong obsession for History, and a deep belief in the greatness of America. A lifetime of reading and writing has left him with the belief that's a great way to live. Together with his wife of 41 years and seven

dogs, he lives now in West Tennessee doing what he loves most, reading and writing.
www.thelastbrigade.com

Graham J. Darling (www.grahamjdarling.com) of Vancouver Canada breeds singular hybrids of diamond-hard Science Fiction, mythopoeic Fantasy and unearthly Horror. His stories have peered out from *Sword and Mythos* and *Pulp Literature*, and snarfed Second Prize in the National Fantasy Fan Federation (N3F) Short Story Contest. As Graham D. Darling PhD, he's a consulting Chemist who designs molecules such as the universe has never seen; as Doctor Carus, he's an alchemist of the year 1300 who demonstrates medieval science and technology to school kids and passers-by.

J. B. Toner studied Literature at Thomas More College and holds a black belt in Ohana Kilohana Kenpo-Jujistu. He's published poetry with *First Things* and *Dappled Things* magazines, and his first novel, *Whisper Music*, was recently published with Sunbury Press. Toner lives in Massachusetts with his beautify wife and daughter.
https://jbtonerz.wixsite.com/website/

CPSIA information can be obtained
at www.ICGtesting.com
Printed in the USA
BVHW041656270220
573547BV00008B/100